In the Blasted Lands, hills were split by gaping fissures. Fumaroles bubbled and steamed, and the air was heavy with the stench of a sorcerous decay. Foul vapors drifted in noxious clouds along the ground; they left a feel of dampness and filth on the skin.

A slavering roar spun Conan around, an involuntary "Crom!" wrenched from his lips.

Facing him was a creature twice the height of a man, its gangrenous flesh dripping phosphorescent slime. A single rubiate eye set in the middle of its head watched him with a horrifying glimmer of intelligence. Its fanged maw gaped; its curving needle claws were raised.

Fangs bared in a snarl, the foul creature dashed to meet him.

"Robert Jordan (is) one of the few writers to successfully capture much of the spirit of Howard's original character."

—Science Fiction Chronicle

Look for all these Conan books

CONAN
THE UNCONQUERED

BY
ROBERT
JORDAN

A TOM DOHERTY ASSOCIATES BOOK

CONAN THE UNCONQUERED

Copyright © 1983 by Conan Properties, Inc.

First printing: April 1983
Fifth printing: June 1986

A TOR Book

Published by Tom Doherty Associates
49 West 24 Street
New York, N.Y. 10010

Cover art by Kirk Reinert

ISBN: 0-812-54231-2
CAN. ED.: 0-812-54232-0

Printed in the United States

0 9 8 7 6 5

CONAN

THE

UNCONQUERED

WESTERN SEA

VANAHEIM

ASGARD

CIMMERIA

PICTISH WILDERNESS

BOSSONIAN MARCHES

BORDER KINGDO

Velitrium

SCHOHAN

GUNDERLAND

TAURAN

Galparan

Black R.

Shirki R.

Tanasul

NEMEDIA

Numali

AQUILONIA

Tarantia

Belverus

Thunder R.

Shamar

Alimane R.

Kordava

ZINGARA

Tyborg R.

Ianthe

OPHIR

Red R.

Khorshemish

KO

ARGOS

RABIRIAN MTS

Khoratas R.

SHEM

Eruk

BARACHA ISLES

Messantia

Asgalun

River Styx

Khemi

Luxu

SIPTAH'S ISLE

STYGIA

Sukhmet

KUSH

DARFAR

Xuthal

BLACK

Zarkheba R.

Xuchot

CHAZAUD

Prologue

Storm winds howling off the midnight-shrouded Vilayet Sea clawed at the granite-walled compound of the Cult of Doom. The compound gave the appearance of a small city, though there were no people on its streets at that hour. More than the storm and the lateness kept them fast in their beds, praying for sleep, though but a bare handful of them could have put a finger to the real reason, and those that could did not allow themselves to think on it. The gods uplift, and the gods destroy. But no one ever believes the gods will touch them.

The man who was now called Jhandar did not know if gods involved themselves in the affairs of mortals, or indeed if gods existed, but he did know there were Powers beneath the sky. There were indeed Powers, and one of those he had learned to use, even to control after a fashion. Gods he would leave to those asleep in the compound, those who called him their Great Lord.

Now he sat cross-legged in saffron robes before such a Power. The chamber was plain, its pearly marble walls smooth, its two arched entrances unadorned. Simple round columns held the dome that rose above the shallow pool, but ten paces across, that was the room's central feature. There was no ornamentation, for friezes or sculptures or ornate working of stone could not compete with that pool, and the Power within.

Water, it might seem at first glance, but it was not. It was sharply azure and flecked with argent phosphorescence. Jhandar meditated, basking in the radiance of Power, and the pool glowed silver-blue, brighter and brighter until the chamber seemed lit with a thousand lamps. The surface of the pool bubbled and roiled, and mists rose, solidifying. But only so far. The mists formed a dome, as if a mirror image of the pool below, delineating the limits that contained the Power, both above and below. Within ultimate disorder was bound, Chaos itself confined. Once Jhandar had seen such a pool loosed from its bonds, and fervently did he wish never to see such again. But that would not happen here. Not now. Not ever.

Now he could feel the Power seeping into his very bones. It was time. Smoothly he rose and made his way through one of the archways, down a narrow passage lit by bronze lamps, bare feet padding on cool marble. He prided himself on his lack of ostentation, even to so small a thing as not wearing sandals. He, like the pool, needed no adornment.

The passage let into a circular sanctorum, its albescent walls worked in intricate arabesques, its high vaulted ceiling held aloft by fluted alabaster columns. Light came from golden cressets suspended aloft on silver chains. Massive bronze doors barred the chamber's main entrance, their surfaces within and without worked in a pattern of Chaos itself, by an artist under the influence of the Power, before madness and death had taken him. The Power was not for all.

The forty men gathered there, a fifth part of his Chosen, *did* need this show of splendor to reflect the glory of their cause. Yet the most important single item in that chamber, an altar set in the exact center of the circle formed by the room, was of unornamented black marble.

Two-score men turned silently as Jhandar entered, saffron robed and shaven of head as the laws of the cult demanded, just as it forbade its women to cut their tresses. Eager eyes watched him; ears strained to hear his words.

"I am come from the Pool of the Ultimate," he intoned, and a massive sigh arose, as if he had come from the presence of a god. Indeed, he suspected they considered it much the same, for though they believed they knew the purposes and meanings of the Cult, in truth they knew nothing.

Slowly Jhandar made his way to the black altar, and all eyes followed him, glowing with the honor of gazing on one they considered but a step removed from godhead himself. He did not think of himself so, for all his ambitions. Not quite.

Jhandar was a tall man, cleanly muscled but slender. Bland, smooth features combined with his shaven head to make his age indeterminate, though something in his dark brown eyes spoke of years beyond knowing. His ears were square, but set on his head in such a fashion that they seemed slightly pointed, giving him an other-worldly appearance. But it was the eyes that oft convinced others he was a sage ere he even opened his mouth. In fact he was not yet thirty.

He raised his arms above his head, letting the folds of his robes fall back. "Attend me!"

"We attend, Great Lord!" forty throats spoke as one.

"In the beginning was nothingness. All came

from nothingness."

"And to nothingness must all return."

Jhandar allowed a slight smile to touch his thin mouth. That phrase, watchword of his followers, always amused him. To nothingness, indeed, all must return. Eventually. But not soon. At least, not him.

While he was yet a boy, known by the first of many names he would bear, fate had carried him beyond the Vilayet Sea, beyond even far Vendhya, to Khitai of near fable. There, at the feet of a learned thaumaturge, an aged man with long, wispy mustaches and a skin the color of luteous ivory, he had learned much. But a lifetime spent in the search for knowledge was not for him. In the end he had been forced to slay the old man to gain what he wanted, the mage's grimoire, his book of incantations and spells. Then, before he had mastered more than a handful, the murder was discovered, and he imprisoned. Yet he had known enough to free himself of that bare stone cell, though he had of necessity to flee Khitai. There had been other flights in his life, but those were long past. His errors had taught him. Now his way was forward, and upward, to heights without end.

"In the beginning all of totality was inchoate. Chaos ruled."

"Blessed be Holy Chaos," came the reply.

"The natural state of the universe was, and is, Chaos. But the gods appeared, themselves but children of Chaos, and forced order—unnatural, unholy order—upon the very Chaos from which they sprang." His voice caressed them, raised their fears, then soothed those fears, lifted their hopes and fanned their fervor. "And in that forcing they gave a foul gift to man, the impurity that forever bars the vast majority of humankind from attaining a higher order of consciousness, from becoming as gods. For it is from Chaos, from ultimate disorder, that gods come, and man has within him the taint of enforced order."

He paused then, spreading his arms as if to embrace them. Ecstacy lit their eyes as they waited for him to give the benediction they expected, and needed.

"Diligently," he said, "have you labored to rid yourselves of the impurities of this world. Your worldly goods you have cast aside. Pleasures of the flesh you have denied yourselves. Now," his voice rose to a thunder, "now you are the Chosen!"

"Blessed be Holy Chaos! We are the Chosen of Holy Chaos!"

"Let the woman Natryn be brought forth," Jhandar commanded.

From a cubicle where she had been kept waiting the Lady Natryn, wife of Lord Tariman, was led into the columned chamber. She did not look now the wife of one of the Seventeen Attendants, the advisors to King Yildiz of Turan. Naked, she stumbled in the hobble that confined her ankles, and would have fallen had not two of the Chosen roughly held her erect. Her wrists, fastened behind her with tight cords, lay on the swell of her buttocks. Her large brown eyes bulged in terror, and her lips worked frantically around a leather gag. Slender, yet full-breasted and well-rounded of hip, her body shone with the sweat of fear. No eyes there but Jhandar's looked on her as a woman, though, for the Chosen had forsaken such things.

"You have attempted to betray me, Natryn."

The naked woman shook at Jhandar's words as if pierced with needles. She had dabbled in the teachings of the cult as did many bored women of the nobility, but her husband made her different, and necessary to Jhandar's great plan. With his necromancies he had learned every dark and shameful corner of her life. Most noblewomen of Turan had secrets they would kill to hide, and she, with lovers and vices almost beyond listing, was no different. Natryn had wept at his revelations, and rebelled at his commands, but seemingly at the last she had accepted her duty to place certain pressures on her husband. Instead, the sorcerous watch he kept on her revealed that she intended to go to her husband, to reveal all and throw herself on his mercy. Jhandar had not slain her where she lay in the supposed safety of her chambers in her husband's palace, but had had her brought hither to serve her purpose in his grand design. It was death she feared, but he intended worse for her.

"Prepare her," the necromancer commanded.

The woman flung herself about futilely in the grasp of the men who fastened her by wrists and ankles to the black altar stone. The gag was removed; she licked fear-dried lips. "Mercy, Great Lord!" she pleaded. "Let me serve you!"

"You do," Jhandar replied.

From a tray of beaten gold proffered by one of the Chosen, the mage took a silver-bladed knife and lifted it high above the woman's body. His follower hastily set the tray on the floor by the altar and backed away. Natryn's screams blended with Jhandar's chant as he invoked the Power of Chaos. His words rang from the walls, though he did not shout; he had no wish to drown her wails. He could feel the Power flowing in him, flowing through him. Silvery-azure, a dome appeared, enveloping altar, sacrifice and necromancer. The Chosen fell to their knees, pressed their faces to the marble floor in awe. Jhandar's knife plunged down. Natryn convulsed and shrieked one last time as the blade stabbed to the hilt beneath her left breast.

Quickly Jhandar bent to take a large golden bowl from the tray. Blade and one quillon of that knife were hollow, so that a vivid scarlet stream of heart's blood spurted into the bowl. Swiftly the level rose. Then the flow slowed, stopped, and only a few drops fell to make carmine ripples.

Withdrawing the blade, Jhandar held knife and bowl aloft, calling on the Power in words of ice, calling on life that was not life, death that was not death. Still holding the bowl on high, he tilted it, pouring out Natryn's heart blood. That sanguinary stream fell, and faded into nothingness, and with it faded the glowing dome.

A smile of satisfaction on his face, Jhandar let the implements of his sorcery clatter to the floor. No longer did a wound mar Natryn's beauty. "Awake, Natryn," he commanded, undoing her bonds.

The eyes of the woman who had just been stabbed to the heart fluttered open, and she stared at Jhandar, her gazed filled with horror and emptiness. "I . . . I was dead," she whispered. "I stood before Erlik's Throne." Shivering, she huddled into a ball on the altar. "I am cold."

"Certainly you are cold," Jhandar told her cruelly. "No blood courses in your veins, for you are no longer alive. Neither are you dead. Rather you stand between, and are bound to utter obedience until true death finds you."

"No," she wept. "I will not—"

"Be silent," he said. Her protests died on the instant.

Jhandar turned back to his followers. The Chosen had dared now to raise their faces, and they watched him expectantly. "For what do you strike?" he demanded.

From beneath their robes the Chosen produced needle-sharp daggers, thrusting them into the air. "For disorder, confusion and anarchy, we strike!" they roared. "For Holy Chaos, we strike! To the death!"

"Then strike!" he commanded.

The daggers disappeared, and the Chosen filed from the chamber to seek those whose names Jhandar had earlier given them.

It was truly a pity, the necromancer thought, that the old mage no longer lived. How far his pupil had outstripped him, and how much greater yet that pupil was destined to become!

He snapped his fingers, and she who was now only partly Lady Natryn of Turan followed him meekly from the sacrificial chamber.

I

Many cities bore appellations, 'the Mighty' or 'the Wicked,' but Aghrapur, that great city of ivory towers and golden domes, seat of the throne of Turan and center of her citizens' world, had no need of such. The city's wickedness and might were so well known that an appellation would have been gilt laid upon gold.

One thousand and three goldsmiths were listed in the Guild Halls, twice so many smiths in silver, half again that number dealers in jewelry and rare gems. They, with a vast profusion of merchants in silks and perfumes, catered to hot-blooded, sloe-eyed noblewomen and sleek, sensuous courtesans who oft seemed more ennobled than their sisters of proper blood. Every vice could be had within Aghrapur's lofty alabaster walls, from the dream-powders and passion-mists peddled by oily men from Iranistan to the specialized brothels of the Street of Doves.

Turanian triremes ruled the cerulean expanse of the Vilayet Sea, and into Aghrapur's broad harbor dromonds brought the wealth of a dozen nations. The riches of another score found its way to the markets by caravan. Emeralds and apes, ivory and peacocks, whatever people wanted could be found, no matter whence it came. The stench of slavers from Khawarism was drowned in the wafted scent of oranges from Ophir, of myrrh and

17

cloves from Vendhya, of attar of roses from
Khauran and subtle perfumes from Zingara. Tall
merchants from Argos strode the flagstones of her
broad streets, and dark men from Shem. Fierce
Ibars mountain tribesmen rubbed shoulders with
Corinthian scholars, and Kothian mercenaries
with traders from Keshan. It was said that no day
passed in Aghrapur without the meeting of men,
each of whom believed the other's land to be a
fable.

The tall youth who strode those teeming streets
with the grace of a hunting cat had no mind for the
wonders of the city, however. Fingers curled
lightly on the well-worn leather hilt of his broadsword, he passed marble palaces and fruit
peddlers' carts with equal unconcern, a black-
maned lion unimpressed by piles of stone. Yet if
his agate-blue eyes were alert, there was yet travel
weariness on his sun-bronzed face, and his scarlet-
edged cloak was stained with sweat and dust. It
had been a hard ride from Sultanapur, with little
time before leaving for saying goodbye to friends
or gathering possessions, if he was to avoid the
headsman's axe. A small matter of smuggling, and
some other assorted offenses against the King's
peace.

He had come far since leaving the rugged
northern crags of his native Cimmerian mountains, and not only in distance. Some few years
he had spent as a thief, in Nemedia and Zamora and the Corinthian city-states, yet though
his years still numbered fewer than twenty the
desire had come on him to better himself. He had
seen many beggars who had been thieves in their
youth, but never had he seen a rich thief. The gold

that came from stealing seemed to drip away like water through a sieve. He would find better for himself. The failure of his smuggling effort had not dimmed his ardor in the least. All things could be found in Aghrapur, or so it was said. At the moment he sought a tavern, the Blue Bull. Its name had been given him in haste as he left Sultanapur as a place where information could be gotten. Good information was always the key to success.

The sound of off-key music penetrated his thoughts, and he became aware of a strange procession approaching him down the thronging street. A wiry, dark-skinned sergeant of the Turanian army, in wide breeches and turban-wrapped spiral helmet, curved tulwar at his hip, was trailed by another soldier beating a drum and two others raggedly blowing flutes. Behind them came half a score more, bearing halberds and escorting, or guarding, a dozen young men in motley garb who seemed to be trying to march to the drum. The sergeant caught the big youth's glance and quickly stepped in front of him.

"The gods be with you. Now I can see that you are a man seeking—" The sergeant broke off with a grunt. "Mitra! Your eyes!"

"What's wrong with my eyes?" the muscular youth growled.

"Not a thing, friend," the sergeant replied, raising a hand apologetically. "But never did I see eyes the color of the sea before."

"Where I come from there are few with dark eyes."

"Ah. A far traveler come to seek adventure. And what better place to find it than in the army of

King Yildiz of Turan? I am Alshaam. And how are you called?"

"Conan," the muscular youth replied. "But I've no interest in joining your army."

"But think you, Conan," the sergeant continued with oily persuasiveness, "how it will be to return from campaign with as much booty as you can carry, a hero and conqueror in the women's eyes. How they'll fall over you. Why, man, from the look of you, you were born for it."

"Why not try them?" Conan said, jerking his head toward a knot of Hyrkanian nomads in sheepskin coats and baggy trousers of coarse wool. They wore fur caps pulled tightly over grease-laced hair, and eyed everyone about them suspiciously. "They look as if they might want to be heroes," he laughed.

The sergeant spat sourly. "Not a half-weight of discipline in the lot of them. Odd to see them here. They generally don't like this side of the Vilayet Sea. But you, now. Think on it. Adventure, glory, loot, women. Why—"

Conan shook his head. "I've no desire to be a soldier."

"Mayhap if we had a drink together? No?" The sergeant sighed. "Well, I've a quota to fill. King Yildiz means to build his army larger, and when an army's big enough, it's used. You mark my words, there will be loot to throw away." He motioned to the other soldiers. "Let us be on our way."

"A moment," Conan said. "Can you tell me where to find the tavern called the Blue Bull?"

The soldier grimaced. "A dive on the Street of the Lotus Dreamers, near the harbor. They'll cut

your throat for your boots as like as not. Try the
Sign of the Impatient Virgin, on the Street of
Coins. The wine is cheap and the girls are clean.
And if you change your mind, seek me out.
Alshaam, sergeant in the regiment of General
Mundara Khan."

Conan stepped aside to let the procession pass,
the recruits once more attempting unsuccessfully
to march to the drum. As he turned from watching
the soldiers go he found himself about to trample
into another cortege, this a score in saffron robes,
the men with shaven heads, the women with
braids swinging below their buttocks, their leader
beating a tambourine. Chanting softly, they
walked as if they saw neither him nor anyone else.
Caught off balance, he stumbled awkwardly aside,
straight into the midst of the Hyrkanian nomads.

Muttered imprecations rose as thick as the rank
smell of their greased hair, and black eyes glared
at him as dark leathery hands were laid to the hilts
of curved sword-knives. Conan grasped his own
sword hilt, certain that he was in for a fight. The
Hyrkanians' eyes swung from him to follow the
saffron-robed procession continuing down the
crowded street. Conan stared in amazement as the
nomads ignored him and hurried after the yellow-
robed marchers.

Shaking his head, Conan went on his way. No
one had ever said that Aghrapur was not a city of
strangenesses, he thought.

Yet, as he approached the harbor, it was in his
mind that for all its oddities the city was not so
very different from the others he had seen. Behind
him were the palaces of the wealthy, the shops of
merchants, and the bustle of prosperous citizens.

Here dried mud stucco cracked from the brick of decaying buildings, occupied for all their decay. The peddlers offered fruits too bruised or spoiled to be sold elsewhere, and the hawkers' shiny wares were gilded brass, if indeed there was even any gilding. Beggars here were omnipresent, whining in their rags to the sailors swaggering by. The strumpets numbered almost as many as the beggars, in transparent silks that emphasized rather than concealed swelling breasts and rounded buttocks, wearing peridot masquerading as emeralds and carbuncle passing for ruby. Salt, tar, spices, and rotting offal gave off a thick miasma that permeated everything. The pleadings of beggars, the solicitations of harlots, and the cries of hawkers hung in the air like a solid sheet.

Above the cacophony Conan heard a girl's voice shout, "If you will but be patient, there will be enough to go around."

Curious, he looked toward the sound, but could see only a milling crowd of beggars in front of a rotting building, all seeming to press toward the same goal. Whatever, or whoever, that goal was, it was against the stone wall of the building. More beggars ran to join the seething crowd, and a few of the doxies joined in, elbowing their way to the front. Suddenly, above the very forefront of the throng, a girl appeared, as if she had stepped up onto a bench.

"Be patient," she cried. "I will give you what I have." In her arms she carried an engraved and florentined casket, almost as large as she could manage. Its top was open, revealing a tangled mass of jewelry. One by one she removed pieces and passed them down to eagerly reaching hands.

Greedy cries were raised for more.

Conan shook his head. This girl was no denizen of the harbor. Her robes of cream-colored silk were expensively embroidered with thread-of-gold, and cut neither to reveal nor emphasize her voluptuous curves, though they could not conceal them from the Cimmerian's discerning eye. She wore no kohl or rouge, as the strumpets did, yet she was lovely. Waist-length raven hair framed an oval face with skin the color of dark ivory and melting brown eyes. He wondered what madness had brought her here.

"Mine," a voice shouted from the shoving mass of mendicants and doxies, and another voice cried, "I want mine!"

The girl's face showed consternation. "Be patient. Please."

"More!"

"Now!"

Three men with the forked queues of sailors, attracted by the shouting, began to push their way through the growing knot of people toward the girl. Beggars, their greed vanquishing their usual ingratiating manner, pushed back. Muttered curses were exchanged, then loud obscenities, and the mood of the crowd darkened and turned angry. A sailor's horny fist sent a ragged, gap-toothed beggar sprawling. Screams went up from the strumpets, and wrathful cries from the beggars.

Conan knew he should go on. This was none of his affair, and he had yet to find the Blue Bull. This matter would resolve itself very well without him. Then why, he asked himself, was he not moving?

At that instant a pair of bony, sore-covered hands reached up and jerked the casket from the girl's arms. She stared helplessly as a swirling fight broke out, the casket jerked from one set of hands to another, its contents spilling to the paving stones to be squabbled over by men and women with clawed fingers. Filth-caked beggars snarled with avaricious rage; silk-clad harlots, their faces twisted with hideous rapacity, raked each other with long, painted nails and rolled on the street, legs flashing nakedly.

Suddenly one of the sailors, a scar across his broad nose disappearing beneath the patch that covered his right eye, leaped up onto the bench beside the girl. "This is what I want," he roared. And sweeping her into his arms, he tossed her to his waiting comrades.

"Erlik take all fool women," Conan muttered.

The roil of beggars and harlots, lost in their greed, ignored the massive young Cimmerian as he moved through them like a hunting beast. Scarface and his companions, a lanky Kothian with a gimlet eye and a sharp-nosed Iranistani, whose dirty red-striped head cloth hid all but the tips of his queues, were too busy with the girl to notice his approach. She yelped and wriggled futilely at their pawings. Her flailing hands made no impression on shoulders and chests hardened by the rigors of stormy, violent Vilayet Sea. The sailors' cheap striped tunics were filthy with fish oils and tar, and an odor hung about them of sour, over-spiced ship's cooking.

Conan's big hand seized the scruff of the Kothian's neck and half hurled him into the scuffle near the casket. The Iranistani's nose crunched and spurted blood beneath his fist, and a back-hand blow sent Scarface to join his friends on the filthy stones of the street.

"Find another woman," the Cimmerian growled. "There are doxies enough about."

The girl stared at him wide-eyed, as if she was not sure if he was a rescuer or not.

"I'll carve your liver and lights," Scarface spat, "and feed what's left to the fish." He scrambled to his feet, a curved Khawarismi dagger in his fist.

The other two closed in beside him, likewise clutching curved daggers. The man in the head-cloth was content to glare threateningly, ruining it somewhat by scrubbing with his free hand at the blood that ran from his broken nose down over his mouth. The Kothian, however, wanted to taunt his intended victim. He tossed his dagger from hand to hand, a menacing grin on his thin mouth.

"We'll peel your hide, barbar," he sneered, "and hang it in the rigging. You'll scream a long time before we let you—"

Among the lessons Conan had learned in his life was that when it was time to fight, it was well to fight, not talk. His broadsword left its worn shagreen scabbard in a draw that continued into an upward swing. The Kothian's eyes bulged, and he fumbled for the blade that was at that moment in mid-toss. Then the first fingerlength of the broadsword clove through his jaw, and up between his eyes. The dagger clattered to the paving stones, and its owner's body fell atop.

The other two were not men to waste time over a dead companion. Such did not long survive on the sea. Even as the lanky man was falling, they rushed at the big youth. The Iranistani's blade

gashed along Conan's forearm, but he slammed a
kick into the dark man's midsection that sent him
sprawling. Scarface dropped to a crouch, his
dagger streaking up toward Conan's ribs. Conan
sucked in his stomach, felt the dagger slice
through his tunic and draw a thin, burning line
across his midriff. Then his own blade was descending. Scarface screamed as steel cut into the
joining of his neck and shoulder and continued
two handspans deeper. He dropped his dagger to
paw weakly at the broadsword, though life was
already draining from him. Conan kicked the body
free—for it was a corpse before it struck the pave-
ment—and spun to face the third sailor.

The Iranistani had gotten to his feet yet again,
but instead of attacking he stood staring at the
bodies of his friends. Suddenly he turned and ran
up the street. "Murder!" he howled as he ran,
heedless of the bloody dagger he was waving.
"Murder!" The harlots and mendicants who had
so recently been lost in their fighting scattered
like leaves before a high wind.

Hastily Conan wiped his blade on Scarface's
tunic and sheathed it. There were few things
worse than to be caught by the City Guard
standing over a corpse. Most especially in Turan,
where the Guard had a habit of following arrest
with torture until the prisoner confessed. Conan
grabbed the girl's arm and joined the exodus,
dragging her behind him.

"You killed them," she said incredulously. She
ran as if unsure whether to drag her heels or not.
"They'd have run away, an you threatened them."

"Mayhap I should have let them have you," he
replied. "They would have ridden you like a post

horse. Now be silent and run!"

Down side streets he pulled her, startling
drunks staggering from seafarers' taverns, down
cross-alleys smelling of stale urine and rotting
offal. As soon as they had put some distance
between themselves and the bodies, he slowed to a
walk—running people were too well noticed—but
yet kept moving. He wanted a *very* goodly distance
between himself and the Guardsmen who would
be drawn to the corpses like flies. He dodged
between high-wheeled pushcarts, carrying goods
from harbor warehouses deeper into the city. The
girl trailed reluctantly at his heels, following only
because his big hand engulfed her slender wrist as
securely as an iron manacle.

Finally he turned into a narrow alley, pushing
the girl in ahead of him, and stopped to watch his
back-path. There was no way that the Guard could
have followed him, but his height and his eyes
made him stand out, even in a city the size of
Aghrapur.

"I thank you for your assistance," the girl said
suddenly in a tone at once haughty and cool. She
moved toward the entrance of the alley. "I must be
going now."

He put out an arm to bar her way. Her breasts
pressed pleasurably against the hardness of his
forearm, and she backed hastily away, blushing in
confusion.

"Not just yet," he told her.

"Please," she said without meeting his eye.
There was a quaver in her voice. "I ... I am a
maiden. My father will reward you well if you return me to him in the same ... condition." The
redness in her cheeks deepened.

Conan chuckled deep in his throat. "It's not your virtue I want, girl. Just the answers to a question or three."

To his surprise her eyes dropped. "I suppose I should be glad," she said bitterly, "that even killers prefer slender, willowy women. I know I am a cow. My father has often told me I was made to bear many sons and . . . and to nurse all of them," she finished weakly, coloring yet again.

Her father was a fool, Conan thought, eyeing her curves. She was a woman made for more than bearing sons, though he did not doubt that whoever she was wed to would find the task of giving them to her a pleasurable one.

"Don't be silly," he told her gruffly. "You'd give joy to any man."

"I would?" she breathed wonderingly. Her liquid eyes caressed his face, innocently, he was certain. "How," she asked falteringly, "is a post horse ridden?"

He had to think to remember why she asked, and then he could barely suppress a smile. "Long and hard," he said, "with little time for rest, if any."

She went scarlet to the neck of her silken robe, and he chuckled. The girl blushed easily, and prettily.

"What is your name, little one?"

"Yasbet. My father calls me Yasbet." She looked past him to the street beyond, where pushcarts rumbled by. "Do you think the casket, at least, would be there if we went back? It belonged to my mother, and Fatima will be furious at its loss. More furious than for the jewels, though she'll be mad enough at those."

He shook his head. "That casket has changed hands at least twice by now, for money or blood. And the jewels as well. Who is Fatima?"

"My amah," she replied, then gasped and glared at him as if he had tricked her into revealing the fact.

"Your amah!" Conan brayed with laughter. "Are you not a little old to have a nursemaid?"

"My father does not think so," Yasbet replied in a sullen voice. "He thinks I must have an amah until I am given to my husband. It is none of my liking. Fatima thinks I am still five years of age, and father sides with her decisions always." Her eyes closed and her voice sank to a weary whisper. She spoke as if no longer realizing she spoke aloud. "I shall be locked in my room for this, at the least. I shall be lucky if Fatima does not. . . ." Her words drifted off with a wince, and her hands stole back to cover her buttocks protectively.

"You deserve it," Conan said harshly.

Yasbet started, eyes wide and flushing furiously. "Deserve what? What do you mean? Did I say something?"

"You deserve to have an amah, girl. After this I shouldn't be surprised if your father takes two or three of them in service." He smiled inwardly at the relief on her face now. In truth, he thought she deserved a spanking as well, but saying so would be no way to gain satisfaction for his curiosity. "Now tell me, Yasbet. What were you doing alone on a street like that, giving your jewels to beggars? It was madness, girl."

"It was not madness," she protested. "I wanted to do something significant, something on my own. You have no idea what my life is like. Every moment waking or sleeping is ruled and watched by Fatima. I am allowed to make not the smallest decision governing my own life. I had to climb over the garden wall to leave without Fatima's permission."

"But giving jewels to beggars and strumpets?"

"The . . . the women were not part of my plan. I wanted to help the poor, and who can be poorer than beggars?" Her face firmed angrily. "My father will know I am no longer a child. I do not regret giving up the pretties he believes mean so much to me. It is noble to help the poor."

"Perhaps he'll hire six amahs," Conan muttered. "Girl, did it never occur to you that you might be hurt? If you had to help someone, why not ask among your own servants? Surely they know of people in need? Then you could have sold a few of your jewels for money to help."

Yasbet snorted. "Even if all of the servants were not in league with Fatima, where would I find a dealer in gems who would give me true value? More likely he would simply pretend to deal with me while he sent for my father! And *he* would no doubt send Fatima to bring me home. That humiliation I can do without, thank you."

"Gem dealers would recognize you," he said incredulously, "and know who your father is? Who is he? King Yildiz?"

Suddenly wary, she eyed him like a fawn on the edge of flight. "You will not take me back to him, will you?"

"And why should I not? You are not fit to walk the streets without a keeper, girl."

"But then I'll never keep him from discovering what happened today." She shuddered. "Or Fatima."

Wetting her lips with the tip of her tongue, she moved closer. "Just listen to me for a moment. Please? I—"

Abruptly she darted past him into the street.

"Come back here, you fool girl," he roared, racing after her.

She dashed almost under the wheels of a heavy, crate-filled cart, and was immediately hidden from view. Two more carts pressed close behind. There was no room to squeeze between them. He ran to get ahead of the carts and to the other side of the street. When he got there, Yasbet was no-where in sight. A potter's apprentice was setting out his master's crockery before their shop. A rug dealer unrolled his wares before his. Sailors and harlots strolled in and out of a tavern. But of the girl there was no sign.

"Fool girl," he muttered.

Just then the tavern sign, painted crudely, creaked in the breeze and caught his eye. The Blue Bull. All that had happened, and he had come right to it. Aghrapur was going to be a lucky city. Giving his swordbelt a hitch and settling his cloak about his broad shoulders, he sauntered into the stone-fronted inn.

II

The interior of the Blue Bull was poorly lit by
guttering rush torches stuck in crude black iron
sconces on the stone walls. A dozen men, hunched
over their mugs, sat scattered among the tables
that dotted the slate floor, which was swept surprisingly clean for a tavern of that class. Three
sailors took turns flinging their daggers at a heart
crudely painted on a slab of wood and hung on a
wall. The rough stones around the slab were
pocked from ten thousand near misses. A pair of
strumpets, one with multi-hued beads braided in
her hair, the other wearing a tall wig in a bright
shade of red, circulated among the patrons quietly
hawking the wares they displayed in diaphanous
silk. Serving girls, their muslin covering little
more than the harlots' garb, scurried about with
pitchers and mugs. An odor of sour wine and stale
ale, common to all such places, competed with the
stench of the street.

When he saw the innkeeper, a stout, bald man
scrubbing the bar with a bit of rag, Conan understood the cleanliness of the floors. He knew the
man, Ferian by name. This Ferian had a passion
for cleanliness uncommon among men of his pro-
fession. It was said he had fled from Belverus, in
Nemedia, after killing a man who vomited on the
floor of his tavern. But as a source of information
he had always been unsurpassed. Unless he had

changed his ways he would know all the news in Aghrapur, not only the gossip of the streets.

Ferian smiled as Conan leaned an elbow on the bar, though his small black eyes remained watchful, and he did not cease his wiping. "Hannuman's Stones, Cimmerian," he said quietly. "They say all roads lead to Aghrapur—at least, they say it in Aghrapur—and seeing you walk in here, I believe it. A year more, and all of Shadizar will be here."

"Who else from Shadizar is in the city?" Conan asked.

"Rufo, the Kothian coiner. Old Sharak, the astrologer. And Emilio, too."

"Emilio!" Conan exclaimed. Emilio the Corinthian had been the best thief in Zamora, next to Conan. "He always swore he'd never leave Shadizar."

Ferian chuckled, a dry sound to come from one so plump. "And before that he swore he would never leave Corinthia, but he left both for the same reason—he was found in the wrong woman's bed. Her husband was after him, but her mother wanted him even more. Seems he'd been bedding her as well, and lifting bits of her jewelry. The older wench hired a bevy of knifemen to see that Emilio would have nothing to offer another woman. I hear he left the city disguised as an old woman and did not stop sweating for half a year. Ask him about it, an you want to see a man turn seven colors at once, the while swallowing his tongue. He's upstairs with one of the girls now, though likely too drunk to do either of them any good."

"Then they'll be there till the morrow," Conan laughed, "for he'll never admit to failure." He laid two coppers on the bar. "Have you any Khorajan ale? My throat is dusty."

"Do I have Khorajan ale?" Ferian said, rummaging under the bar. "I have wines and ales you have never heard of. Why, I have wines and ales *I* have never heard of." He drew out a dusty clay crock, filled a leathern jack, and made the coppers disappear as he pushed the mug in front of Conan. "Khorajan ale. How stand affairs in the Gilded Bitch of the Vilayet? You had to leave in a hurry, did you?"

Conan covered his surprise by drinking deeply on the dark, bitter ale, and wiped white froth from his mouth with the back of his hand before he spoke. "How knew you I have been in Sultanapur? And why think you I left hurriedly?"

"You were seen there these ten days gone," Ferian smirked, "by Zefran the Slaver, who came through here on his way back to Khawarism." It was the tavernkeeper's major fault that he liked to let men know how much he knew of what they had been about. One day it would gain him a knife between his ribs. "As for the rest, I know naught save that you stand there with the dust of hard riding on you, and you were never the one to travel for pleasure. Now, what can you tell me?"

Conan drank again, pretending to think on what he could tell. The fat man was known to trade knowledge for knowledge, and Conan had one piece of it he knew was not yet in Aghrapur, unless someone had grown wings to fly it there ahead of him.

"The smuggling is much abated in Sultanapur," the Cimmerian said finally. "The Brotherhood of the Coast is in disarray. They sweat in the shadows, and stir not from their dwellings. 'Twill be months before so much as a bale of silk passes through that city without the customs paid."

Ferian grunted noncommittally, but his eyes lit. Before the sun next rose, men who would try to fill the void in Sultanapur would pay him well.

"And what can you tell me of Aghrapur?"

"Nothing," Ferian replied flatly.

Conan stared. It was not the tapster's way to give less than value. His scrupulousness was part and parcel of his reputation. "Do you doubt the worth of what I've told you?"

" 'Tis not that, Cimmerian." The tavernkeeper sounded faintly embarrassed. "Oh, I can tell you what you can learn for yourself in a day's listening in the street. Yildiz casts his eyes beyond the border, and builds the army accordingly. The Cult of Doom gains new members every day. The—"

"The Cult of Doom!" Conan exclaimed. "What in Mitra's name is that?"

Ferian grimaced. "A foolishness, is what it is. They're all over the streets, in their saffron robes, the men with shaven heads."

"I saw some dressed so," Conan said, "chanting to a tambourine."

" 'Twas them. But there's naught to them, despite the name. They preach that all men are doomed, and building up earthly treasures is futile." He snorted and scrubbed at his piggish nose with a fat hand. "As for earthly treasure, the cult itself has built up quite a store. All who join give whatever they possess to the Cult. Some young sons and daughters of wealthy merchants, and even of nobles, have given quite a bit. Not to mention an army of rich widows. There've been petitions to the throne about it, from relatives and such, but the cult pays its taxes on time, which is more than can be said of the temples. And it gives generous gifts to the proper officials, though that is not well known." He brightened. "They have a compound, almost a small city, some small distance north, on the coast. Could I find where within their treasures are kept ... well, you are skillful enough to make your fortune in a single night."

"I'm a thief no more," Conan said. Ferian's face fell. "What else can you tell me of the city?"

The fat man sighed heavily. "These days I know less than the harlots, whose customers sometimes talk in their sleep. In these three months past, two thirds of those who have given me bits and pieces, servants of nobles and of those high in the Merchant's Guild, have been murdered. What you have told me is the best piece of intelligence I have had in a month. I owe you," he added reluctantly. He was not one to enjoy indebtedness. "The first thing I hear that you might use to advantage, I will place in your hands."

"And I will hear it before anyone else? Let us say two days before?"

"Two days! As well as a year. Knowledge spoils faster than milk under a hot sun."

"Two days," Conan said firmly.

"Two days, then," the other man muttered.

Conan smiled. Breaking his word was not among Ferian's faults. But this matter of the murders, now. . . . "It seems beyond mere chance that so many of your informants should die in so short a time."

"No, friend Conan." To the Cimmerian's surprise, Ferian refilled his mug without asking payment. That was not like him. Perhaps he hoped to pay off his debt in free drink, Conan thought. "Many more have died than those who had a connection to me. There is a plague of murder on Aghrapur. More killings in these three months than in the whole year before. Were it not for the sorts who die, I might think some plot was afoot, but who would plot against servants and Palace Guards and the like? 'Tis the hand of chance playing fickle tricks, no more."

"Conan!" came a shout from the stairs at the rear of the common room. The big Cimmerian looked around.

Emilio stood on the bottom step with his arm around a slender girl in gauds of brass and carnelian and a long, narrow strip of red silk wound about her in such a way as almost to conceal her breasts and hips. She half supported him as he swayed drunkenly, which was no easy task. He was a big man, as tall as Conan, though not so heavily muscled. He was handsome of face, with eyes almost too large for a man. His eyes and his profile, he would tell anyone who would listen, drew women as honey drew flies.

"Greetings, Emilio," Conan called back. "No longer dressing as an old woman, I see." To Ferian he added, "We'll talk later." Taking his mug, he strolled to the staircase.

Emilio sent the girl on her way with a swat across her pert rump, and eyed Conan woozily. "Who told you that tale? Ferian, I'll wager. Fat old sack of offal. Not true, I tell you. Not true. I simply left Zamora to seek rich—" he paused to belch "—richer pastures. You're just the man I want to see, Cimmerian."

Conan could sense an offer of cooperation coming. "We no longer follow the same trade, Emilio," he said.

Emilio did not seem to hear. He grabbed the arm of a passing serving girl, ogling her generous breasts as he did. "Wine, girl. You hear?" She nodded and sped off, deftly avoiding his attempted pinch; he tottered and nearly fell. Still staggering, he managed to fall onto a stool at an empty table and gestured drunkenly toward another. "Sit, Conan. Sit, man. Wine'll be here before you know it."

"Never before have I seen you so drunk," Conan said as he took the stool. "Are you celebrating, or drowning sorrows?"

The other man's eyes had drifted half shut. "Do you know," he said dreamily, "that a blonde is worth her weight in rubies here? These Turanian men will kill to have a fair-haired mistress. Does she have blue eyes, they'll kill their mothers for her."

"Have you turned to slaving, then, Emilio? I thought better of you."

Instead of answering, the other man rambled on.

"They have more heat in them than other women. I think it's the hair. Gods put color in a woman's hair, they must have to take some of her heat to do it. Stands to reason. Davinia, now, she's hotter than forge-fire. That fat general can't take care of her. Too much army business." Emilio's snicker was at once besotted and lascivious. Conan decided to let him run out of wind. "So I take care of her. But she wants things. I tell her she doesn't need any necklace, beautiful as she is, but she says a sorcerer laid a spell on it for a queen. Centuries gone this happened, she claims. Woman wears it, and she's irresistible. Thirteen rubies, she says, each as big as the first joint of a man's thumb, each set on a moonstone-crusted seashell in gold. Now that's worth stealing." He snickered and leaned toward Conan, leering. "Thought she'd pay me for it with her body. Set her straight on that. I already have her body. Hundred gold pieces, I told her. Gold, like her hair. Softest ever I tangled my hand in. Softest skin, too. Buttery and sleek."

The serving girl returned to set a mug and wine-jar on the table, and stood waiting. Conan made no move to pay. *He* had no hundred gold pieces coming to him. The girl poked Emilio in the ribs with her fist. He grunted, and stared at her blearily.

"One of you pays for the wine," she said, "or I take it back."

"No way to treat a good customer," Emilio muttered, but he rooted in his pouch until he came up with the coins. When she had gone he stared at the Cimmerian across the table. "Conan! Where did you come from? Thought I saw you. It's well you are here. We have a chance to work together again, as we used to."

"We never worked together," Conan said level-ly. "And I thieve no more."

"Nonsense. Now listen you close. North of the city a short distance is an enclosure containing much wealth. I have a commission to steal a—to steal something from there. Come with me; you could steal enough to keep you for half a year."

"Is this enclosure by any chance the compound of the Cult of Doom?"

Emilio rocked back on his seat. "I thought you were fresh come to the city. Look you, those seven who supposedly entered the compound and were never seen again were Turanians. These local thieves have no skill, not like us. They'd last not a day in Shadizar or Arenjun. Besides, I think me they did not go to the compound at all. They hid, or died, or left the city, and men made up this story. People will do that, to make a place they do not know, or do not like, seem fearful."

Conan said nothing.

Ignoring his mug, Emilio swept up the clay wine-jar, not lowering it until it was nearly drained. He leaned across the table, pleading in his voice. "I know exactly where the—the treasure is to be found. On the east side of the compound is a garden containing a single tower, atop which is a room where jewelry and rarities are kept. Those fools go there to look at them. The display is supposed to show them how worthless gold and gems are. You see, I know all about it. I've asked questions, hundreds of them."

"If you've asked so many questions, think you that no one knows what you intend? Give it over, Emilio."

A fur-capped Hyrkanian stepped up to the table, the rancid odor of his lank, greased hair overpowering the smells of the tavern. A scar led from the missing lower lobe of his left ear to the corner of his mouth, pulling that side of his face into a half-smile. From the corner of his eye the Cimmerian saw four more watching from across the room. He could not swear to it, but he thought he had encountered these five earlier in the day.

The Hyrkanian at the table spared only a glance to Conan. His attention was on Emilio. "You are Emilio the Corinthian," he said gutturally. "I would talk with you."

"Go away," Emilio said without looking at him. "I know no Emilio the Corinthian. Listen to me, Conan. I would be willing to give you half what I get for the necklace. Twenty pieces of gold."

Conan almost laughed. Dead drunk Emilio might be, but he still thought to cheat his hoped-for partner.

"I would talk with you," the Hyrkanian said again.

"And I said go away!" Emilio shouted, his face suddenly suffusing with red. Snatching the wine-jar, he leaped to his feet and smashed it across the Hyrkanian's head. With the last dregs of the wine rolling down his face, the scarred nomad collapsed in a welter of clay fragments.

"Crom!" Conan muttered; a deluge of rank-smelling men in fur caps was descending on them.

Conan pivoted on his buttocks, his foot rising to meet a hurtling nomad in the stomach. With a gagging gasp the man stopped dead, black eyes goggling as he bent double. The Cimmerian's massive fist crashed against the side of his head, and he crumpled to the floor.

Emilio was wallowing on the floor beneath two of the Hyrkanians. Conan seized one by the back of his sheepskin coat and pulled him off of the Corinthian thief. The nomad spun, a dagger in his streaking hand. Surprise crossed his face as his wrist slapped into Conan's hand. The Cimmerian's huge fist traveled no more than three handspans, but the fur-capped nomad's bootheels lifted from the floor, and then he collapsed beside his fellow.

Conan scanned the room for the fifth Hyrk-anian, but could not find the remaining nomad anywhere. Emilio was getting shakily to his feet while examining a bloody gash on his should-er. Ferian was heading back toward the bar, carrying a heavy bungstarter. Another instant and Conan saw a pair of booted feet stretched out from behind a table.

"You get them out of here," Ferian shouted as he reached the bar and thrust the heavy mallet out of sight. "You dirtied my floor, now you clean it. Get them out of here, I say!"

Conan seized one of the unconscious men by the heels. "Come on, Emilio," he said, "unless you want to fight Ferian this time."

The Corinthian merely grunted, but he grabbed another of the nomads. Together they dragged the unconscious men into the street, shadowed with night, now, and left them lying against the front of the rug dealer's shop.

As they laid out the last of the sleeping men— Conan had checked each to make sure he still breathed—Emilio stared up at the waxing pearles-cent moon and shivered.

"I've an evil feeling about this, Conan," he said. "I wish you would come with me."

"You come with me," Conan replied. "Back in-side where we'll drink some more of Ferian's wine, and perhaps try our luck with the girls."

"You go, Conan. I—" Emilio shook his head. "You go." And he staggered off into the night.

"Emilio!" Conan called, but only the wind answered, whispering down shadowed streets. Muttering to himself, the Cimmerian returned to the tavern.

III

When Conan came down to the common room of the Blue Bull the next morning, the wench with the beads in her hair accompanied him, clutching his arm to her breast, firm and round through its thin silk covering, letting her swaying hip bump his thigh at every step.

Brushing her lips against his massive shoulder, she looked up at him smokily through her lashes. "Tonight?" She bit her lip and added, "For you, half price."

"Perhaps, Zasha," he said, though even at half price his purse would not stand many nights of her. And those accursed beads had quickly gotten to be an irritation. "Now be off with you. I've business." She danced away with a saucy laugh and a saucier roll of her hips. Mayhap his purse could stand *one* more night.

The tavern was almost empty at that early hour. Two men with sailors' queues tried to kill the pain of the past night's drink with still more drink, while morosely fingering nearly flat purses. A lone strumpet, her worknight done at last and her blue silks damp with sweat, sat in a corner with her eyes closed, rubbing her feet.

At the bar Ferian filled a mug with Khorajan ale before he was asked.

"Has aught of worth come to your ear?" Conan asked as he wrapped one big hand around the leathern jack. He was not hopeful, since the fat tavernkeeper had once more failed to demand payment.

"Last night," the stout man said, concentrating on the rag with which he rubbed the wood of the bar, "it was revealed that Temba of Kassali, a dealer in gems who stands high in the Merchant's Guild, has been featuring Hammaran Temple Virgins at his orgies, with the result that fourteen former virgins and five priestesses have disappeared from the Temple, likely into a slaver's kennels. Temba will no doubt be ordered to give a large gift to the Temple. Last night also twenty-odd murders took place, that I have heard of so far, and probably twice so many that have not reached my ears. Also, the five daughters of Lord Barash were found by their father entertaining the grooms of his stable and have been packed off into the Cloisters of Vara, as has the Princess Esmira, or so 'tis rumored."

"I said of worth," the Cimmerian cut off. "What care I for the virgins or princesses? Of worth!"

Ferian gave a half-hearted laugh and studied his bit of scrub cloth. "The last is interesting, at least. Esmira is the daughter of Prince Roshmanli, closest to Yildiz's ear of the Seventeen Attendants. In a city of sluts she is said to be a virgin of purest innocence, yet she is being sent away to scrub floors and sleep on a hard mat till a husband can be found." Suddenly he slammed his fist down on the bar and spat. The spittle landed on the wood, but he seemed not to see it. "Mitra's Mercies, Cimmerian, what expect you? It's been but one night since I told you I know nothing. Am I a sorcerer to conjure knowledge where there was none? An you want answers from the skies, ask old Sharak over there. He—" Suddenly his eye lit on the globule of spit. With a strangled cry he scrubbed at it as if it would contaminate the wood.

Conan looked about for the astrologer he had known in Shadizar. The bent old man, wearing what seemed to be the same frayed and patched brown tunic he had worn in Shadizar, was lowering himself creakily to a stool near the door. His white hair was thinner than ever, and as always he leaned on a long blackwood staff, which he claimed was a staff of power, though no one had ever seen any magicks performed with it. Wispy mustaches hung below his thin mouth and narrow chin, and he clutched a rat's-nest of scrolls in his bony fingers.

Ferian gave the bar one more scrub and eyed it suspiciously. "I like not this owing, Cimmerian," he muttered.

"I like not being owed." Conan's icy blue eyes peered into the fulvous ale. "After a time I begin to think I will not be repaid, and I like that even less."

"I pay my debts," the other protested. "I'm a fair man. 'Tis known from Shahpur to Shadizar. From Kuthchemes to—"

"Then pay me."

"Black Erlik's Throne, man! What you told me may be worth no more than the wind blowing in the streets!"

Conan spoke as quietly as a knife leaving its scabbard. "Do you call me liar, Ferian?"

Ferian blinked and swallowed hard. Of a sudden, the Cimmerian seemed to fill his vision. And he remembered with a sickly sinking of his stomach that among the muscular youth's more uncivilized traits was a deadly touchiness about his word.

"No, Conan," he laughed shakily. "Of a certainty not. You misunderstand. I meant just that I do not know its value. Nothing more than that."

"An you got no gold for that information last night," Conan laughed scornfully, "I'll become a priest of Azura."

Ferian scowled, muttered under his breath, and finally said, "Mayhap I have some slight idea of its worth."

A smile showed the big Cimmerian's strong white teeth. The tavernkeeper shifted uncomfortably.

"An you know its worth, Ferian, we can set some other payment than what was first agreed."

"Other payment?" Despite his plump cheeks, the innkeeper suddenly wore a look of rat-like suspicion. "What other payment?" Conan took a long pull of ale to let him steep. "What other payment, Cimmerian?"

"Lodgings, to begin."

"Lodgings!" Ferian gaped like a fish in surprise and relief. "Is that all? Of course. You can have a room for . . . for ten days."

"A fair man," Conan murmured sardonically. "Your best room. Not the sty I slept in last night."

The fat man snickered greasily. "Unless I misread me the look on Zasha's face, you did little sleeping." He cleared his throat heavily at the look on Conan's face. "Very well. The best room."

"And not for ten days. For a month."

"A month!"

"And some small information."

"This is in place of the information!" Ferian howled.

"Information," Conan said firmly. "I'll not ask to be the only one to get it, as we first spoke of, but for that month you must keep me informed, and betimes."

"I have not even agreed to the month!"

"Oh, yes. Food and drink must be included. I have hearty appetites," he laughed. Tipping up his mug, he emptied it down his throat. "I'll have more of that Khorajan."

Ferian clutched at his shiny scalp as if wishing he had hair to pull out by the roots. "Do you want anything else? This tavern? My mistress? I have a daughter somewhere—in Zamora, I think. Do you want me to find her and bring her to your bed?"

"Is she pretty?" Conan asked. He paused as if considering, then shook his head. "No, the lodgings and the rest will be enough." Ferian spluttered, his beady eyes bulging in his fat face. "Of course," the Cimmerian continued, "you could continue in my debt. You do understand I'd want just the right piece of information, do you not? 'Twas good value I gave, and I'll expect the same in return. It would be well if you found it quickly." A growl had entered his voice, and his face had slowly darkened. "You know we barbars are not so understanding as you civilized men. Why, if a tenday or two passed with you silent, I might think you wished to take advantage of me. Such would make me angry. I might even—" His big hands abruptly clutched the bar as if he intended to vault it.

Ferian's mouth worked for a moment before he managed to shout "No!" and seized Conan's hand

in his. "Done," he cried. "It's done. The month and
the rest. Done!"

"Done," Conan said.

The fat innkeeper stared at him. "A month," he
moaned. "My serving wenches will spend the
whole time in your bed. You keep your hands off
them, Cimmerian, or I'll get not a lick of work
from the lot of them. You've taken advantage of
me. Of my good nature."

"I knew not that you had one, Ferian. Mayhap if
you take a physic it will go away."

"Mitra be thanked that most of you Cimmerians
like your god-forsaken frozen wastes. Did any
more of you accursed blue-eyed devils come
south, you would own the world."

"Be not so sour," Conan said chidingly. "I'll
wager you got twenty times so much for what I
told you as what my staying here will cost."

Ferian grunted. "Just keep your hands off my
serving wenches, Cimmerian. Go away. Am I to
make up what you cost me, I cannot stand here all
day talking to you. Go talk to Sharak."

The young Cimmerian laughed, scooping up his
mug of dark ale. "At least he can tell me what the
stars say." When he left the bar, Ferian was still
spluttering over that.

The astrologer peered at Conan dimly as he
approached the table where the old man sat; then
a smile creased his thin features. The skin of his
visage was stretched taut over his skull. "I
thought I saw you, Conan, but these eyes. . . . I am
no longer the man I was twenty years ago, or even
ten. Sit. I wish that I could offer you a goblet of
wine, but my purse is as flat as was my wife's
chest. May the gods guard her bones," he added in

the careless way of a man who has said a thing so many times that he no longer hears the words.

"No matter, Sharak. I will buy the wine."

But as Conan turned to signal, one of the wenches bustled to the table and set a steaming bowl of lentil stew, a chunk of coarse bread and a pannikin of wine before the astrologer. The food set out, she turned questioningly toward the muscular youth. Abruptly her dark, tilted eyes went wide with shock, and she leaped into the air, emitting a strangled squawk. Sharak began to cackle. The wench glared at the aged man then, rubbing one buttock fitfully, darted away.

Sharak's crowing melded into a fit of coughing, which he controlled with difficulty. "It never does," he said when he could speak, "to let them start thinking you're too old to be dangerous."

Conan threw back his black-maned head and roared with laughter. "You'll never get old," he managed finally.

"I'm a dotard," Sharak said, digging a horn spoon into the stew. "Ferian says so, and I begin to think he is right. He gives me a bowl of stew twice a day, else I would eat only what I scavenge in the garbage, as many must in age. He is almost my only patron, as well. In return for the stew I read his stars. Every day I read them, and a more boring tale they could not tell."

"But why no patrons? You read the stars as a scribe reads marks on parchment. Never once did you tell me wrong, though your telling was at divers times none too clear to me."

" 'Tis these Turanians," the old man snorted. "Ill was the day I journeyed here. Half the stars they name wrongly, and they make other errors.

Important errors. Those fools in this city who call themselves astrologers had the gall to charge me with unorthodoxy before the Guild. 'Twas no more than luck I did not end at the stake. The end result is the same, though. Without the Guild's imprimatur, I would be arrested if I opened a shop. The few who deal with me are outlanders, and they come merely because I will tell their stars for a mug of wine or a loaf of bread instead of the silver piece the others charge. Did I have a silver piece, I would return to Zamora on the instant." With a rueful grunt he returned to spooning the stew into his mouth.

Conan was silent a moment. Slowly he dug into his pouch and drew out a silver piece, sliding it across the rough boards. "Tell my horoscope, Sharak."

The gaunt old man froze with his spoon half-raised to his face. He peered at the coin, blinking, then at Conan. "Why?"

"I would know what this city holds for me," the young Cimmerian said gruffly. "I hold you better than any Guildsman of Aghrapur, and so worth at least the footing they demand. Besides," he lied, "my purse is heavy with coin."

Sharak hesitated, then nodded. Without touching the coin, he fumbled through his scrolls with his left hand, all the while absently licking traces of stew from the fingers of his right. When those scrolls he wanted were spread out atop the table, he produced a wax tablet from beneath his patched tunic. The side of a stylus scraped the wax smooth. Nose almost touching the parchments, he began to copy arcane symbols with deft strokes.

"Do you not need to know when I was born, and

such?" Conan asked.

"I remember the details of your natal chart," the other replied with his eyes on the parchment, "as if it were drawn on the insides of my eyelids. A magnificent chart. Unbelievable. Hmm. Mitra's Chariot is in retrograde."

"Magnificent? You have never told me of any magnificence before."

Sighing, Sharak swiveled his head to gaze at the big youth. "Unbelievable, I called it as well, and you would not believe did I tell you. Then you would not believe anything else I told you, either, and I could do you no good. Therefore I do not tell you. Now, will you allow me to do what you have paid me for?" He did not wait for a reply before turning his eyes back to the scrolls. "Aha. The Bloodstar enters the House of the Scorpion this very night. Significant."

Conan shook his head and quaffed deeply on his dark ale. Was Sharak attempting to inflate his payment? Perhaps the habit of trying to do so was too deeply ingrained to lose.

He busied himself with drinking. The common room was beginning to fill, with queued sailors and half-naked trulls for the most part. The wenches were the most interesting, by far. One, short, round-breasted and large-eyed in her girdle of coins and gilded wristlets and torque, made him think of Yasbet. He wished he could be certain she was safe at home. No, in truth he wished her in his bed upstairs, but, failing that, it was best if she were at home, whatever her greeting from Fatima. Could he find her again, it would of a certainty brighten his days in Aghrapur. Let Emilio talk of his blonde—what was her name? Davinia?—as if she were the exotic these Turanians thought her. In his own opinion it was women with large eyes who had the fires smouldering within, even when they did not know it themselves. Why—

"I am done," Sharak said.

Conan blinked, pulled from his reverie. "What?" He looked at the wax tablet, now covered with scribbled symbols. "What does it say?"

"It is unclear," the old astrologer replied, tugging at one of his thin mustaches with bony fingers. "There are aspects of great opportunity and great danger. See, the Horse and the Lion are in conjunction in the House of Dramath, while the Three Virgins are—"

"Sharak, I would not know the House of Dramath from the house of a rugmaker. What does it mean?"

"What does it mean?" Sharak mimicked. "Always 'what does it mean?' No one wants to know the truly interesting part, the details of how. . . . Oh, very well. First of all: there is a need to go back in order to go forward. To become what you will become, you must become again what you once were."

"That's little help," Conan muttered. "I have been many things."

"But this is most important. This branching, here, indicates that if you fail to do so, you will never leave Aghrapur alive. You have already set events in motion."

The air in the tavern seemed suddenly chill. Conan wished the old man had not been right so often before. "How can I have set events in motion? I've been here barely a day."

"And spoken to no one? Done nothing?"

Conan breathed heavily. "Does it speak of gold?"

"Gold will come into your hands, but it does not seem to be important, and there is danger attached."

"Gold is always important, and there is always danger attached. What of women?"

"Ah, youth," Sharak murmured caustically. "You will soon be entangled with women—two, it seems here—but there is danger there as well."

"Woman are always at least as dangerous as gold," Conan replied, laughing.

"One is dark of hair, and one pale-haired."

The Cimmerian's laughter faded abruptly. Pale-haired? Emilio's Davinia? No! That would almost certainly mean aiding Emilio in his theft, and that had been left behind. But he was to 'become what he had been.' He forced the thought away. He was done with thieving. The astrologer's reading must mean something else.

"What more?" he asked harshly.

" 'Tis not my fault if you like it not, Conan. I merely read what is writ in the stars."

"What more, I said!"

Sharak sighed heavily. "You cannot blame me if. . . . There is danger here connected in some fashion to a journey. This configuration," he pointed to a row of strangely bent symbols scribed in the wax, "indicate a journey over water, but these over here indicate land. It is unclear."

" 'Tis all unclear, an you ask me of it." Conan muttered.

"It becomes less clear. For instance, here the color yellow is indicated as of great importance."

"The gold—"

"—is of small import, no matter your feeling on it. And there is more danger tied to this than to the gold."

The big Cimmerian ground his teeth audibly. "There is danger to breathing, to hear you tell it."

"I can well believe it so, to look at this chart. As to the rest, the number thirteen and the color red are of some significance, and are linked. Additionally, this alignment of the Monkey and the Viper indicates the need of acting quickly and decisively. Hesitate, and the moment will be lost to you. And that will mean your death."

"What will come, will come, old man," Conan snapped. "I'll not be affrighted by stars, gods, or demons."

Sharak scowled, then pushed the silver piece back across the table. "If my reading is so distasteful to you, I cannot take payment."

The muscular youth's anger dropped to a simmer instantly. " 'Tis no blame of yours whether I like the reading you give or no. You take the money, and I'll take your advice."

"I am four score and two years of age," the astrologer said, suddenly diffident, "and never in all that time have I had an adventure." He gripped his knobbly staff, leaning against the table. "There is power in this, Cimmerian. I could be of aid."

Conan hid a smile. "I've no doubt of it, Sharak. An I need such help, I will call on you, have no fear. There is one thing you might do for me now. Know you where I might find Emilio at this hour?"

"That cankerous boaster?" Sharak said disdainfully. "He frequents many places of ill repute, each worse than the last." He reeled off the names of a dozen taverns and as many brothels and gaming halls. "I could help you look for him, if you really think he's needed, though what use he could be I do not know."

"When you finish supping, you can search the hells."

"I would rather search the brothels," the old man leered.

"The hells," Conan laughed, getting to his feet. Sharak returned grumbling to his stew.

As he turned toward the door, the Cimmerian's eyes met those of a man just entering, hard black eyes in a hard black face beneath the turban-wrapped spiral helmet of the Turanian army. Of middling height, he moved with the confidence of a larger man. The striping on his tunic marked him as a sergeant. Ferian hurried, frowning, to meet the dark man. Soldiers were not usually habitués of the Blue Bull.

"I am seeking a man called Emilio the Corinthian," the sergeant said to Ferian.

Conan walked out without waiting for the innkeeper's reply. It had nothing to do with him. He hoped.

IV

Conan entered the seventh tavern with never so much as a wobble of his step, despite the quantity of wine and ale he had ingested. The large number of wenches lolling about the dim, dank common room, rouged and be-ringed, their silks casually disarrayed, told him that a brothel occupied the upper floors of the squat stone building. Among the long tables and narrow trestle-boards crowding the slate floor, sailors rubbed shoulders with journeymen of the guilds. Scattered through the room were others whose languid countenances and oiled mustaches named them high-born no less than their silk tunics embroidered in gold and silver. Their smooth fingers played as free with the strumpets as did the sailors' calloused hands.

The Cimmerian elbowed a place at the bar and tossed two coppers on the boards. "Wine," he commanded.

The barkeeper gave him a rough clay mug, filled to the brim with sour-smelling liquid, and scooped up the coins. The man was wiry and snake-faced, with heavy-lidded, suspicious eyes and a tight, narrow mouth. He would not be one to answer questions freely. Another drinker called, and the tapster moved off, wiping his hands on a filthy apron that dangled about his spindly shanks.

Conan took a swallow from his mug and grimaced. The wine was thin, and tasted as sour as it smelled.

As he eyed the common room, a strangely garbed doxy caught his gaze. Sleek and sinuous, she had climbed upon a trestle-board to dance for half a dozen sailors who pawed her with raucous shouts, running their hands up her long legs. Her oiled breasts were bare, and for garb she wore but a single strip of silk, no wider than a man's hand, run through a narrow gilded girdle worn low on the roundness of her hips, to fall to her ankles before and behind. The strangeness was that an opaque veil covered her from just below her hot, dark eyes to her chin. The sisterhood of the streets might paint their faces heavily, but then never covered them, for few men would take well to the discovery that their purchase was less fair of visage than they had believed. But not only was this woman veiled, he now saw no less than three others so equipped.

Conan caught the tavernkeeper's tunic sleeve as he passed again. "I've never seen veiled strumpets before. Do they cover the marks of the pox?"

"New come to Aghrapur, are you?" the man said, a slight smile touching his thin mouth.

"A short time past. But these women?"

" 'Tis rumored," the other smirked, "that some women highly born, bored with husbands whose vigor has left them, amuse themselves by disporting as common trulls, wearing veils so those same husbands, who frequent the brothels as oft as any other men, will not recognize them. As I say, 'tis but a rumor, yet what man will pass the chance to have a lord's wife beneath him for a silver piece?"

"Not likely," Conan snorted. "There would be murder done when one of those lords discovered that the doxy he'd bought was his own wife."

"Nay. Nay. The others flock about them, but not the lordlings. What man would risk the shame of knowing his wife had been bought?

It was true, Conan saw. Each veiled woman was the center of a knot of sailors or dockworkers or tradesmen, but the nobles ignored them, looking the other way rather than acknowledge their existence.

"Try one," the snake-faced man urged. "One silver piece, and you can see for yourself if she moves beneath you like a noblewoman."

Conan drank deeply, as if considering. Had he been interested in dalliance, it was in his mind that better value would come from an honest strumpet than from a nobly born woman pretending to be such. The tapster had none of the fripperies of the panderer about him—he did not sniff a perfumed pomander or wear more jewelry than any three wenches—but no doubt he took some part of what was earned on the mats above the common room. He might talk more easily if he thought Conan a potential patron. The Cimmerian lowered his mug.

"It's a thing to think on," he chuckled, eying a girl nearby. A true daughter of the mats, this one, in an orange-dyed wig with her face as bare as her wiggling buttocks. "But I seek a friend who was supposed to meet me. I understand he frequents this place betimes."

The tavernkeeper drew back half a step, and his voice cooled noticeably. "Look around you. An he is here, you will see him. Otherwise. . . ." He shrugged and turned to walk away, but Conan reached across the bar and caught his arm,

putting on a smile he hoped was friendly. "I do not
see him, but I still must needs find him. He is
called Emilio the Corinthian. For the man who can
tell me where to find him, I could spare the price
of one of these wenches for the night." If Sharak
was correct—and he always was—Conan *had* to
find Emilio, and what word he had thus far gar-
nered was neither copious nor good.

The tapster's face became even more snake-like,
but his lidded eyes had flickered at Emilio's name.
"Few men must pay for the whereabouts of a
friend. Mayhap this fellow—Emilio, did you say
his name is? —is no friend of yours. Mayhap he
does not wish to meet you. Ashra! Come rid me of
this pale-eyed fool!"

"I can prove to you that I know him. He is—"

A massive hand landed on the Cimmerian's
broad shoulder, and a guttural voice growled,
"Out with you!"

Conan turned his head enough to look coldly at
the wide hand, its knuckles sunken and scarred.
His icy azure gaze traveled back along a hairy arm
as big around as most men's legs. And up. This
Ashra stood head and shoulders taller even than
Conan himself, and was half again as broad with
no bit of fat on him. For all the scarring of his
hands, the huge man's broad-nosed face was un-
marked. Conan thought few could reach high
enough to strike it.

He attempted to keep his tone reasonable.
Fighting seldom brought information. "I seek a
man this skinny one knows, not trouble. Now un-
hand me and—"

For an answer the big man jerked at Conan's
shoulder. Sighing, the Cimmerian let himself be

spun, but the smile on Ashra's face lasted only
until Conan's fist hooked into his side with a loud
crack of splintering ribs. Shouting drinkers
scrambled out of the way of the two massive men.
Conan's other fist slammed into the tall man, and
again he felt ribs break beneath his blow.

With a roar Ashra seized the Cimmerian's head
in both of his huge hands and lifted Conan clear of
the floor, squeezing as if to crush the skull he held,
but a wolfish battle-light shone in Conan's eyes.
He forced his arms between Ashra's and gripped
the other's head in turn, one hand atop it, the
other beneath the heavy chin. Slowly he twisted,
and slowly the bull neck gave. Panting, Ashra
suddenly loosed his hold, yet managed to seize
Conan about the chest before he could fall. Hands
locked, he strained to snap the Cimmerian's spine.

The smile on Conan's face was enough to chill
the blood. In the time it took three grains of sand
to fall in the glass, he knew, he could break
Ashra's neck, yet a killing would of a certainty gag
the tapster's mouth. Abruptly he released his grip.
Ashra laughed, thinking he had the victory. Conan
raised his hands high, then smashed them, palms
flat, across the other's ears.

Ashra screamed and staggered back, dropping
the Cimmerian to clutch at his bleeding ears.
Conan bored after him, slamming massive fists to
the ribs he had already broken, then a third blow
to the huge man's heart. Ashra's eyes glazed, and
his knees bent, but he would not fall. Once more
Conan struck. That never-struck nose fountained
blood, and Ashra slowly turned, toppling into a
table that splintered beneath him. Once the pros-
trate man stirred as if to rise, then was still.

A murmuring crowd gathered around the fallen man. Two men grabbed his ankles, grunting as they dragged the massive weight away. More than one wench eyed Conan warmly, licking her lips and putting an extra sway in her walk, among them those with veiled faces. He ignored them and turned back to the business at hand, to the tapster.

The snake-faced innkeeper stood behind the bar wearing an expression almost as stunned as Ashra's. A bung-starter dangled forgotten in his hand.

Conan took the heavy mallet from the slack grip and held it up before the man's eyes, fists touching in the middle of the thick handle. The muscles of his arms and shoulders knotted and bunched; there was a sharp crack, and he let the two pieces fall to the bar.

The tavernkeeper licked his thin lips. He stared at Conan as if at a wonderment. "Never before have I seen the man Ashra could not break in two wit his bare hands," he said slowly. "But then, even he couldn't have. . . ." His gaze dropped to the broken mallet, and he swallowed hard. "Have you a mind to employment? The job held by that sack of flesh they're hauling off is open. A silver piece a day, plus a room, food, drink, and your choice of any wench who has not a customer. My name is Manilik. How are you called?"

"I am no hauler of tosspots," Conan said flatly. "Now tell me what you know of Emilio."

Manilik hesitated, then gave a strained laugh. "Mayhap you do know him. I'm careful of my tongue, you see. Talk when you shouldn't, and you're apt to lose your tongue. I don't waggle mine."

"Waggle it now. About Emilio."

"But that is the problem, stranger. Oh, I know of Emilio," he said quickly, as Conan's massive fist knotted atop the bar, "but I know little. And I've not seen him these three days past."

"Three days," Conan muttered despondently. Thus far he had found many who knew Emilio, but none who had seen the Corinthian these three days past. "That boasting idiot is likely gazing into a mirror or rolling with that hot-blooded Davinia of his," he growled.

"Davinia?" Tewfik sounded startled. "If you know of her, perhaps you truly *do* know. . . ." He trailed off with a nervous laugh under Conan's icy eyes.

"What do *you* know of Davinia, Tewfik?"

The innkeeper shivered, so quietly was that question asked. It seemed to him the quiet of the tomb, mayhap of *his* tomb an he answered not quickly. Words bubbled from him as water from a spring.

"General Mundara Khan's mistress, bar-, ah, stranger, and a dangerous woman for the likes of Emilio, not just for who it is that keeps her, but for her ambition. 'Tis said lemans have bodies, but not names. This Davinia's name is known, though. Not two years gone, she appeared in Aghrapur on the arm of an ivory trader from Punt. The trader left, and she remained. In the house of a minor gem merchant. Since then she's managed to change her leash from one hand to another with great dexterity. A rug merchant of moderate wealth, the third richest ship owner in the city, and now Mundara Khan, a cousin of King Yildiz himself, who would be a prince had his mother not been a concubine."

The flow of talk slowed, then stopped. Greed and fear warred on Manilik's face, and his mouth was twisted with the pain of giving away what he might, another time, have sold.

Conan laughed disparagingly and lied. "Can you not tell me more than is known on every street corner? Why, I've heard strumpets resting their feet wager on whether the next bed Davinia graces will be that of Yildiz." He searched for a way to erase the doubt that still creased the tavern-keeper's face. "Next," he said, "you'll tell me that as she chooses her patrons only to improve herself, she must risk leaving her master's bed for her own pleasures." How else to explain Emilio, and this Davinia so clearly a woman intent on rising?

Manilik blinked. "I had no idea so much was so widely known. It being so, there are those who will want to collect what the Corinthian owes before Mundara Khan has him gelded and flayed. He had better have the gold he has bragged of, or he'll not live to suffer the general's mercies."

"He mentioned gold, did he?" Conan prompted.

"Yes, he. . . ." The heavy-lidded eyes opened wide. "Mean you to say it's a lie? Four or five days, he claimed, and he would have gold dripping from his fingers. An you *are* a friend of the Corinthian, warn him clear most particularly of one Narxes, a Zamoran. His patience with Emilio's excuses is gone, and his way with a knife will leave your friend weeping that he is not dead. Narxes likes well to make examples for others who might fail to pay what they owe. Best you tell him to keep quiet about my warning, though. I've no wish for the Zamoran to come after me before Emilio finishes him."

"I will tell him," Conan said drily. Manilik was

licking his narrow lips, avarice personified. As soon as he could, the tavernkeeper would have a messenger off to this Narxes. Whether it was Narxes or Emilio who survived, Manilik would claim it was his warning that tipped the balance. But Conan did not mean to add to the Corinthian thief's troubles. "So far as I know, the gold will be his, as he claims."

The innkeeper shrugged. "If you say it, then I believe it, stranger." But his voice carried a total lack of conviction.

Conan left with a wry smile, but just outside he stopped and leaned against the doorjamb. The lowering sun was a bloody ball on the rooftops. Moments later a slender, dark-haired serving wench darted from the inn, pulling a cloak of coarse brown wool about her. He caught the girl's arm, pulling her aside. The wench stared up at him, dark eyes wide and mouth hanging open.

"You are the one Manilik is sending to Narxes," he said.

She straightened defiantly—she came no higher than Conan's chest—and glared. "I'll tell you naught. Loose me."

Releasing his grip, he half pushed her toward the street. "Go then. Never before have I seen anyone run to have her throat slit."

The girl hesitated, rubbing her arm and eying the passing carts rumbling over the cobblestones. Sailors and tradesmen thronged between the high-wheeled vehicles. A quick dash and she could be lost among them. Instead she said, "Why should Narxes wish to harm me? I've never had a copper to wager at his tables. The likes of me'd never get past the door."

"You mean you don't know?" Conan said incredulously. "That alters matters."

"Know what? What matters?"

"I heard Manilik say he was sending a girl to Narxes for. . . ." He let his voice trail off, shaking his head. "No, it's no use. Better you do not know. You couldn't escape, anyway."

She laughed shakily. "You're trying to frighten me. I am just to tell Narxes that Manilik has word for him. What did you hear?" Conan was silent, frowning as if in thought, until she stepped closer and laid a trembling hand on his arm. "You must tell me! Please?"

"Not that it will do you any good," Conan said, feigning reluctance. "Narxes will find you no matter how far you run."

"My parents have a farm far from the city. He'd never find me there. Tell me!"

"Narxes has been selling young girls to the Cult of Doom for sacrifices," he lied, and invented some detail. "You'll be strapped to an altar, and when your throat is cut the blood will be gathered in a chalice, then—"

"No!" She staggered back, one hand to her mouth. Her face had a greenish cast, as if she were about to be sick. "I've never heard that the Cult of Doom makes such sacrifices. Besides, the use of freeborn for sacrifices is forbidden by law."

"How will anyone ever know, once you're safely dead and your body tossed to the sea?" He shrugged. "But if you do not believe me, then seek out Narxes. Perhaps he will explain it to you on your way to the compound of the Cult."

"What am I to do?" she moaned, taking quick steps first in one direction then another. "I have no money, nothing but what I stand in. How am I to get to my parents' farm?"

Sighing, Conan dug a fistful of coppers from his pouch. Emilio would repay him, or he would know the reason why. "Here, girl. This will see you there."

"Thank you. Thank you." Half-sobbing, she snatched the coins from his outstretched hand and ran.

Not even a kiss for gratitude, Conan thought grumpily as he watched her disappear down the teeming street. But with luck Manilik would not discover for at least a day that his plans had gone awry. A day to find Emilio without worrying about finding him dead. The story he had concocted for the girl had sounded even more convincing than he had hoped. With a satisfied smile he started down the street.

In the dimnesses that foreshadowed dusk he did not notice the shaven-headed man in saffron robes, standing in the mouth of an alley beside the inn he had just left, a man who watched his going with interest.

V

Night filled the ivory-walled compound of the Cult of Doom. No dimmest flicker of light showed, for those of the Cult rose, worked, ate and slept only by command. No coppers were wasted on tapers. In an inner room, though, where Jhandar met with those who followed him most faithfully, bronze lion lamps illumined walls of alabaster bas-relief and floors mosaicked in a thousand colors.

The forty saffron-robed men who waited beneath the high vaulted ceiling knelt as Jhandar entered, each touching a dagger to his forehead. "Blessed be Holy Chaos," they intoned. "Blessed be disorder, confusion, and anarchy."

"Blessed be Holy Chaos," the mage replied perfunctorily. He was, as always, robed as they.

He eyed the lacquered tray of emerald and gold that had been placed on a small tripod table before the waiting men. His hands moved above the two-score small, stone bottles on the tray, fingers waving like questing snakes' tongues, as if they could sense the freshness of the blood within those stoppered containers.

One of the men shifted. "The kills were all made within the specified hours, Great Lord."

Jhandar acknowledged him only with an irritated flick of an eyelid. Of course those killed had died as he had commanded, at the hour he had

commanded. Those who knelt before him did not
know why the deaths must occur so, nor even why
they must collect the blood while their victims'
hearts still beat. They believed that they knew a
great deal, but what they knew was how to obey.
For Jhandar's purposes, that was enough.

"Go," the necromancer commanded. "Food and
drink await you. Then sleep. Go."

"Blessed be Holy Chaos," they chanted and,
rising, filed slowly from the room.

Jhandar waited until the heavy bronze door had
clanged shut behind them before speaking again.
"Che Fan," he said. "Suitai. Attend me."

Two men, tall, lean, and robed in black,
appeared as if materializing from air. It would
have taken a quick eye to see the turning panel of
stone in the wall from behind which they had
stepped. But then, even a quick eye would have
stared so at the men as to miss everything else.
Even in Aghrapur, they were unusual. Their black
eyes seemed to slant, and their skin was the color
of parchment left in the sun till it yellowed, yet so
smooth that it gave no hint of age. Like as twins
they were, though, the man called Che Fan was
perhaps a fingerbreadth the taller. By birth and
training they were assassins, able to kill with no
more than the touch of a hand.

Suitai took the tray, while Che Fan hurried to
open a small wooden door, lacquered and polished
to mirror brightness. Jhandar swept through,
followed by the two men. The passage beyond was
narrow, brightly lit by gold lamps dangling from
wall sconces, and empty. The shaven-headed mage
kept his tame killers out of sight, for there might
be those who would know them for what they

were. Even the Chosen saw them but rarely.

The narrow corridor led to a chamber, in the center of which was a large circle of bare dirt, with dead sterility. Great fluted columns supported the domed alabaster ceiling, and surrounding the barren earth were thirteen square pillars truncated at waist height.

As he had done many times before, Suitai began setting out the stone bottles on the hard-packed dirt. He made four groups of five, each group forming a cross.

"Great Lord." Che Fan spoke in a hoarse whisper. "We follow as you command, yet our existence is empty."

Jhandar looked at him in surprise. The two assassins never spoke unless spoken to. "Would you prefer to be where I found you?" he asked harshly.

Che Fan recoiled. He and Suitai had been walled up alive within the Khitan fortress where Jhandar had been imprisoned. Accidentally the necromancer had freed them in his own escape, and they had sworn to follow him. He was not certain they believed he could actually return them to their slow death in Khitai, but they seemed to.

"No, Great Lord," the Khitan said finally. "But we beg, Suitai and I, that we be allowed to use our talents in your service. Not since. . . ." His voice trailed off. Suitai glanced up from placing the last of the bottles, then studiously avoided looking at either of the other two men again.

Jhandar's face darkened. To speak of the distant past was one thing, to speak of the near past another. He disliked being reminded of failure and ignominy. Effort went into keeping his voice

normal, but it still came out like the grate of steel
on rock. "Fool! Your *talents*, as you call them,
destroy the essence of the man, as you well know.
There is naught left for me to summon when you
kill. When I need your abilities again, *if* I need
them again, I will command you. Unles you wish
to step within the circle and be commanded now?"

Suitai stumbled hurriedly from the patch of
dirt. "No, Great Lord," Che Fan replied hastily. "I
beg forgiveness for my presumption." As one, the
two assassins bowed low.

Jhandar left them so for a moment, then spoke.
"Rise. In the days ahead there will be labors to
sate even your desires. Now get you gone until I
call again. I have my own labors to perform."

As they bowed their way from his presence, he
put them from his awareness. There were more
important matters which needed all of his attention.

From beneath his robes he produced a piece of
black chalk. Atop four of the pillars, equidistantly
spaced about the circle, he marked the ancient
Khitan ideograms for the four seasons, chanting
as he did in a language not even he understood,
though he well understood the effect of the words.
Next were drawn the ideograms for the four hu-
mors, then the four elements, and all the while he
intoned the primordial spells. But one of the short,
square pillars remained. He drew the symbol for
life, then quickly, over it, the symbol of death.

A chill rose in the air, till his words came in
puffs of white, and his voice took on a hollow
aspect, as though he called from a vast deep. Mist
roiled over the circle of earth, blue and flecked
with silver, like the mist above the Pool of the

Ultimate, yet pale and transparent. The hairs on Jhandar's arms and legs stirred and rose. He could feel the Power flowing through him, curling around his bones.

In the center of the mist light flashed, argent and azure lightning. In silence the air of the chamber quivered, as to a monstrous clap of thunder. Within the circle every stone jar shattered into numberless grains of dust, and the parched dirt drank blood. The tenuous vapors above began to glow.

Never ceasing his incantation, Jhandar sought within himself for the root of the Power that coursed his veins, seized on it, bent it to his bidding. With every fiber of his being he willed a summoning, he commanded a summoning, he *forced* a summoning.

Blood-clotted earth cracked and broke, and a hand reached up from the crack to claw at the surface, a hand withered and twisted, its nails like claws, its skin a mottled moldy gray-green. In another blood-soaked place the ground split, and monstrously deformed hands dug upward, outward. Then another, and another. A slavering panting beat its way up from below the surface. Inexorably drawn by Jhandar's chant, they dug their way from the bowels of the earth, stumpy misshapen creatures bearing little resemblance to humankind, for all they were the summoned corporeal manifestations of the essences of murdered men and women. There were no distinctions now between male and female. Neuter all, they were, with hairless mottled skin stretched tightly over domed skulls whose opalescent eyes had seen the grave from inside. Their lipless mouths emitted a cacophony of howls and lamentations.

Jhandar stopped his chant, reluctantly felt the Power pour from him like water from a ewer. As the Power went, so did the mist within the circle. The ravening creatures turned to him, seeming to see him for the first time, their cries rising.

"Be silent!" he shouted, and all sound was gone as if cut off with a knife.

He it was who had summoned; they could not but obey, though some glared at him with hellborn fury. Some few always did.

"Hear you my words. Each of you will return to the house that you served in life." A low moan rose and was stilled. "There, in incorporeal form, you will watch, and listen. What your former masters and mistresses do not want known, you will tell to me when I summon you again. Nothing else will you do unless I command." That last was necessary, he had learned, though there was little they could do without being told to.

"I hear," came the muttering moans, "and obey."

"Then by the blood and earth and Power of Chaos by which I summoned you, begone."

With a crack of inrushing air the twisted shapes disappeared.

Jhandar smiled when he left the chamber. Already he knew more of the secrets of Turan than any ten other men. Already, with a whisper in the proper ear of what the owner of that ear would die to keep secret, he influenced decisions at the highest levels. Nay, he *made* those decisions. Soon the throne itself would bow to his will. He would not demand that his position as true ruler of

Turan be made known to all. That he ruled would be enough. First Turan, then perhaps Zamora, and then. . . .

"Great Lord."

Reverie broken, Jhandar glared at the shaven-headed man who had accosted him in a main corridor of his palatial quarters. Lamps of gold and silver, made from melted-down jewelry provided by new members of the Cult, cast glittering lights from walls worked in porphyry and amber.

"Why do you disturb me, Zephran?" he demanded. Not even the Chosen were allowed to approach him unbidden.

"Forgive me, Great Lord," Zephran answered, bowing low, "but I had a most distressing encounter in the city near dusk."

"Distressing encounter? What are you blathering about? I have no time for foolishness."

"It was a barbarian, Great Lord, who spoke of sacrifices within the Cult, of the altar and the use of blood."

Jhandar clutched his robes in white-knuckled fists. "Hyrkanian? He was Hyrkanian?"

"Nay, Great Lord."

"He must have been."

"Nay, Great Lord. His skin was pale where not bronzed by the sun, and his eyes were most strange, as blue as the sea."

Jhandar sagged against the wall. In Hyrkania, across the Vilayet Sea, he had first founded the Cult, first created and confined a Pool of Chaos. He would have welded the scattered Hyrkanian tribes of fierce horsemen into a single force that moved at his word. He would have launched such a wave of warriors as would have washed over

Turan and Zamora and all to the West until it came to the sea. He would have. . . .

But the spirit manifestations had not been properly controlled. They had managed to communicate to the living what occurred within the compound he was building, and the tribesmen had ridden against him, slaughtering his followers. Only by loosing the Power, turning a part of the Hyrkanian steppes into a hell, had he himself managed to escape. They believed in blood vengeance, those Hyrkanians. Deep within him was the seed of fear, fear that they would follow him across the sea. Ridiculous, he knew, yet he could not rid himself of it.

"Great Lord," Zephran said diffidently, "I do not understand why filthy Hyrkanians should concern you. The few I have seen in—"

"You understand nothing," Jhandar snarled. "This barbarian. You killed him?"

Zephran shifted uneasily. "Great Lord, I . . . I lost him in the night and the crowd among the taverns near the harbor."

"Fool! Roust your fellows from their beds! Find that barbarian! He must die! No! Bring him to me. I must find out how many others know. Well, what are you waiting for? Go, fool! Go!"

Zephran ran, leaving Jhandar staring at nothing. Not again, the necromancer thought. He would not fail again. He would pull the world down in ruins if need be, but he would not fail.

VI

Conan descended to the common room of the Blue Bull taking each step with care. He did not truly believe that his head would crack if he took a misstep, but he saw no reason to take a chance. The night before had turned into a seemingly endless procession of tavern after tavern, of tankard after tankard. And all he had gotten for his trouble was a head like a barrel.

He spotted Sharak, digging eagerly into a bowl of stew, and winced at the old man's enthusiasm. With a sigh he dropped onto a bench at the astrologer's table.

"Do you have to be so vigorous about that, Sharak?" the Cimmerian muttered. "It's enough to turn a man's stomach."

"The secret is clean living," Sharak cackled gleefully. "I live properly, so I never have to worry about a head full of wine fumes. Or seldom, at least. And it brings me luck. Last night, asking about for Emilio, I discovered that the strumpets of this city fancy Zamoran astrology. And do you know why?"

"What did you find out about Emilio, Sharak?"

"Because it's foreign. They think anything imported must be better. Of course, some of them want to pay in other coin than gold or silver." He cackled again. "I spent the night in the arms of a wench with the most marvelous—"

"Sharak. Emilio?"

The gaunt old man sighed. "If *you* wanted to boast a bit, I wouldn't stop you. Oh, very well. Not that I discovered much. No one has seen him for at least two nights. Three different people, though— two of them trulls—told me Emilio claimed he would come into a great deal of gold yesterday. Perhaps someone did him in for it."

"I'd back Emilio against any man in this city," Conan replied, "with swords, knives or bare hands." But there was no enthusiasm in his voice. He was sure now that Emilio was dead, had died while trying to steal the necklace. And while dead drunk, at that. "I should have gone with him," he muttered.

"Gone where?" Sharak asked. "No matter. More than one was counting on his having this gold. I myself heard the gamester Narxes make such dire threats against Emilio as to put me off eating." He shoveled more stew into his mouth. "Then there's Nafar the Panderer, and a Kothian moneylender named Fentras, and even a Turanian soldier, a sergeant, looking for him. As he still lives, he's left Aghrapur, and wisely so."

"Emilio intended to steal from the compound of the Cult of Doom, Sharak. I think me he tried two nights past."

"Then he is dead," Sharak sighed. "That place has acquired a bad name among the Brotherhood of the Shadows. Some thieves say 'tis doom even to think of stealing from them."

"He meant to steal a necklace of thirteen rubies for a woman with blonde hair. He wanted me to aid him."

The old astrologer tossed his spoon into the

bowl of stew. "Mayhap your chart. . ." he said slowly. "These eyes are old, Conan. 'Tis possible what I saw was merely an effect of your association with Emilio."

"And it's possible men can fly without magic," Conan laughed ruefully. "No, old friend. Never have I known you to make a mistake in your star-reading. The meaning was clear. I must enter that compound and steal the necklace."

Conan's bench creaked as a man suddenly dropped onto it beside him. "And I must go with you," he said. Conan looked at him. It was the hard-eyed, black-skinned Turanian army sergeant he had seen asking after Emilio. "I am called Akeba," the sergeant added.

The big Cimmerian let his hand rest lightly on the worn leather hilt of his broadsword. " 'Tis a bad habit, listening to other men's conversation," he said with dangerous quietness.

"I care not if you steal every last pin from the cult," Akeba said. His hands rested on the table, and he seemed to take no notice of Conan's sword. " 'Twas rumored this Emilio did not fear to enter that place, but I heard you say he is dead. I have need to enter the compound, and need of a man to guard my back, a man who does not fear the cult. If you go there, I will go with you."

Sharak cleared his throat. "Pray tell us why a sergeant of the Turanian army would want to enter that compound in secret."

"My daughter, Zorelle." Akeba's face twisted momentarily with pain. "She was taken by this Mitra-accursed cult. Or joined, I know not which. They will not allow me to speak to her, but I have seen her once, at a distance. She no longer looks as she did before falling into their hands. Her face is cold, and she does not smile. Zorelle wore a smile always. I will bring her out of there."

"Your daughter," Conan snorted. "I must needs go with stealth. The stealth of two men is the tenth part that of one. Add the need to drag a weeping girl along. . . ." He snorted again.

"How will you steal so much as a drink of water if I summon my men to arrest you?" Akeba demanded.

Conan's fist tightened on his sword hilt. "You will summon no one from your grave," he growled. Akeba reached for his own blade, and the two men began to rise.

"Be not fools!" Sharak said sharply. "You, Akeba, will never see your daughter again if your skull is cloven in this tavern. And Conan, you know the dangers of what you intend. Could not another sword be of use?"

"Not that of a blundering soldier," Conan replied. His eyes were locked with those of the Turanian, blue and black alike as hard as iron. "His feet are made for marching, not the quiet of thieving."

"Three years," Akeba said, "I was a scout against the Ibarri mountain tribes, yet I still have my life and my manhood. From the size of you, *you* look to be as quiet as a bull."

"A scout?" the Cimmerian said thoughtfully. The man had some skill at quietness, then. Perhaps Sharak had a point. It was all too possible that he *could* use another blade. Besides, killing a soldier would make it near impossible for him to remain in Aghrapur.

Conan lowered himself slowly back to the

bench, and Akeba followed. For a moment their eyes remained locked; then, as at a signal, each loosed his grip on his sword.

"Now that is settled," Sharak said, "there is the matter of oaths to bind us all together in this enterprise."

"Us?" Akeba said with a questioning look.

Conan shook his head. "I still do not know if this soldier is coming with me or not, but I *do* know that you are not. Find yourself a wench who wants her stars read. I can recommend one here, if you mind not a head full of beads."

"Who will watch your horses," Sharak asked simply, "while you two heroes are being heroic inside the compound? Besides, Conan, I told you I've never had an adventure. At my age, this may be my last chance. And I do have this." He brandished his walking staff. "It could be useful."

Akeba frowned. "It's a stick." He looked at Conan.

"The thing has magical powers, the Cimmerian said, and dropped his eyelid.

After a moment the dark man smiled faintly. "As you say." His face grew serious. "As to the compound, I would have this thing done quickly."

"Tonight," Conan said. "I, too, want it done."

"The oaths," Sharak chimed in. "Let us not forget the oaths."

The three men put their heads together.

VII

Leaving Sharak beneath a tree to mind the horses, Conan and Akeba set out through the night in a crouching run for the alabaster-walled compound of the Cult of Doom. Within those walls ivory towers thrust into the night, and golden-finialed purple domes were one with the dark amethystine sky. Scudding clouds cast shifting moon-lit shadows, and the two men were but two shades in the night. A thousand paces distant, the Vilayet Sea beat itself to white froth against the rocky shore.

At the base of the wall they quickly unlimbered the coiled ropes they carried across their shoulders. Twin grapnels, well padded with cloth, hurtled into the air, caught atop the wall with muffled clatters.

Massive arms and shoulders drew Conan upward with the agility of a great ape. At the top of the wall he paused, feeling along that hard, smooth surface. Akeba scrambled up beside him and, without pausing to check the top of the wall, clambered over. Conan's dismay that the other had done so—it was the error of a greenling thief—was tempered by the fact that there were no shards of pottery and broken stone set in the wall to rip the flesh of the unwary.

Conan pulled himself over the wall and, holding

his grapnel well out to one side, let himself fall. He took the shock of the drop by tucking a shoulder under and rolling, coming to his feet smoothly. He was in a landscaped garden, exotic shrubs and trees seemingly given life by the moving shadows. Akeba was hastily coiling his rope.

"Remember," Conan said, "we meet at the base of the tallest tower in the compound."

"I remember," Akeba muttered.

There had been more than a little discussion over which man's task was to be carried out first. Akeba feared that, in stealing the necklace, Conan might rouse guards, while Conan was sure the sergeant's daughter could not be rescued without raising an alarm. The women's quarters were certain to be guarded, while Emilio had intimated that the necklace was unguarded. It had been Sharak who effected a compromise: Conan would go after the necklace while Akeba located the women's quarters. Then they would meet and together solve the problem of getting Zorelle out. Agreement had been more reluctant on Akeba's part than on Conan's. The Cimmerian was not certain he needed a companion on this venture, for all Sharak's urging.

With a last doubtful glance at the Turanian, Conan hurried away, his pantherine stride carrying him swiftly through the night. He remembered well Emilio's description of the necklace's location. The topmost chamber of the lone tower in a garden on the east side of the compound. They had entered over the east wall, and looming out of the night ahead was a tower, square and tall. He slowed to a walk, approaching it with silent care.

A short distance away he stopped. There was enough light from the moon, barely, with which to see.

Of smooth greenstone, surrounded by a walk of dark tiles some seven or eight paces in width, the tower had no openings save an open arch at ground level and a balcony around its top. The onion-dome roof glittered beneath the moon as if set with gems.

It was the lack of guards that worried the Cimmerian. True, the avowed purpose of the tower room was to teach the Cult's disciples the worthlessness of wealth, but nothing in Conan's near twenty years led him to believe than any sane man would leave wealth unwatched and unprotected by iron bars and locks.

The tower walls were polished, offering no crevices for fingers or toes, not even those of one familiar with the sheer cliffs of Cimmeria. He looked down. The tiles of the walk were scribed in an unusual pattern of tiny crosshatches. Any one of them could be the trigger to a trap, letting onto pits filled with Kothian vipers or the deadly spiders of the Turanian steppes.

He had seen such before. Yet the place for that sort of device was before the archway. There a marble-laid path led toward the tower, stopping at the edge of the tiles. Kneeling, he examined the joining and smiled. The marble slab stood two fingerwidths higher than the tiles, and its lip was shiny, as if something were often rubbed against it. And from that low angle he could see two lines of wear, spaced at the width of the marble, stretching toward the tower arch. Here was located the trap—it did not matter what it was—

and something was laid atop these tiles to make a way for the members of the cult to enter the tower. So much, he thought, for the worthlessness of wealth.

Cocking an ear for sounds elsewhere in the compound, he strode down the marble walk away from the tower, counting his steps. Silence. At least Akeba had raised no alarm as yet. At forty paces he turned around. The tower he could see dimly, but the arch that would be his target was no more than a smudge at its base. Hastily he refastened his sword belt around his chest and over one shoulder, so the nubby leather sheath hung down his back. It would not do to have the blade tangle in his feet at the wrong time.

With a deep breath he began to run, legs driving, broad chest heaving like a bellows in the effort for speed and more speed. The width of tiles was clear, then the archway. Almost on the instant he felt the edge of the marble beneath his boot and sprang, flying through the night air. With a thump his toes landed just inside the arch. He tottered on the edge of toppling back, fingers scrabbling for the rim of the archway. For an infinite moment he hung poised to drop into the trap. Then, slowly, he drew himself into the tower.

Laughing softly, he drew his sword and moved deeper inside. Try to keep a Cimmerian out, he thought.

On the ground level of the tower were several rooms, but the doors to all of them were locked. Still, what he wanted was above, and a spiraling stone stair led up from a central antechamber. Sword questing ahead, he climbed careful step by careful step. The first trap did not mean there were not others. Without incident, though, he came to the top of the stair, and to the chamber atop the tower.

Hammered silver on the domed roof reflected and magnified the moonlight, turning it into palely useful illumination that filtered into the chamber. Half-a-dozen archways, worked in delicate filigree, let onto the narrow-railed balcony. Open cabinets, lacquered over gilded scrollwork, stood scattered about the mosaicked floor, displaying priceless jewels on velvet cushions. A crown of rubies and pearls, fit for any king. A single emerald as big as a man's fist. A score of finger-long matched sapphires, carved in erotic figures. More and more till the eyes of a mendicant priest oath-sworn to poverty would have lit with greed.

And there was the necklace, with its thirteen flawless rubies glowing darkly in the silvery light. Conan appraised it with a practiced eye before slipping it into his pouch. Perhaps it *would* make the woman who wore it irresistible to men, but then, most women seemed to believe gems of great-enough cost would do that, magic or no. This Davinia would get a bargain for her hundred gold pieces, in any case. His gaze ran around the room once more. Here was treasure worth ten thousand gold pieces. Ten times ten thousand. Ferian had been right; he could carry enough from this place to make him a rich man.

With difficulty but no regret, he put the thought firmly aside. He had turned from thieving, and what he did this night made no difference in that. But if he looted this chamber of all he could carry, he knew it would not be so easy to leave that life again. And he did not doubt that whatever gold he got for these things would last no longer than the gold he had received for other thefts. Such coin never stayed long.

"I hoped you would not come."

Conan spun, sword raised, then lowered it with a grin. "Emilio! I thought you were dead, man. You can have this Mitra-accursed necklace, and be welcome to it."

The tall Corinthian came the rest of the way up the stairs into the tower-top chamber. He had sword and dagger in hand. " 'Tis a fit punishment, do you not think, guarding forever that which I intended to steal?"

Hair stirred on the back of Conan's neck. "You are ensorceled?"

"I am dead," Emilio replied, and lunged.

Conan dodged aside, and the other's blade passed him to shatter the treasure-laden shelves of a cabinet. Snake-like, Emilio whirled after him, but he circled to keep cabinets between them.

"What foolishness is this you speak?" he demanded. "I see a man before me, not a shade."

Emilio's laugh was hollow. "I was commanded to kill all who came to this tower in the night, but naught was said against speaking." He continued to move in slow deadliness; Conan moved the other way, keeping a lacquered cabinet between them. "I was taken in this very chamber, with the necklace in my hand. So near did I come. For my pains a hollow ponaird was thrust into my chest. I watched my heart's blood pump into a bowl, Cimmerian."

"Crom," Conan muttered, tightening his grip on his sword. To kill a friend was ill, even one spell-caught and commanded to slay, yet to kill was better than to die at that friend's hands.

"Jhandar, whom they call Great Lord, took life from me," Emilio continued, neither speeding nor slowing his advance. "Having taken it, he forced some part of it back into this body that once was mine." His face twisted quizzically. "And this creature that once was Emilio the Corinthian must obey. It must . . . obey."

Abruptly Emilio's foot lashed out against the lacquered cabinet. In a crash of snapping wood it toppled toward the young Cimmerian. Conan leaped back, and Emilio charged, boots splintering delicate workmanship, carelessly scattering priceless gems.

Conan's blade flashed upward, striking sparks from the other's descending steel. Dagger darting to slide beneath Conan's ribs, the Corinthian's wrist slapped into his hand and was seized in an iron grip. Locked chest to chest they staggered out onto the balcony. Conan's knee rose, smashing into Emilio's crotch, but the reanimated corpse merely grunted. Risking freeing the Corinthian's sword, Conan struck with his hilt into Emilio's face. Now the other man fell back. Conan's blade slashed the front of his old friend's tunic, and Emilio leaped back again. Abruptly the backs of his legs struck the railing, and for an instant he hung there, arms waving desperately for balance. And then he was gone, without a cry. A sickening thud came from below.

Swallowing hard, Conan stepped to the rail and looked toward a ground that seemed all flitting shadows. He could make out no detail, but that Emilio had lived through the fall—if, indeed, he had lived before he fell—was beyond his belief. It was ill to kill a friend, no matter the need. There could be no luck in it.

Resheathing his sword, he hurried down the stairs. At the archway he stopped. Emilio's body lay sprawled just outside, and its fall had triggered the trap. From the archway to the marble path, thin metal spikes the length of a man's forearm had thrust up through the tiles. Four of them transfixed the Corinthian.

"Take a pull on the hellhorn for me," Conan muttered.

But there was still Akeba to meet, and no time for mourning. Quickly he picked his way between the spikes and set out at a dead run for the landmark they had chosen, the tallest tower in the compound, its high golden dome well visible even by moonlight.

Abruptly a woman's scream pierced the night, and was cut off just as suddenly. With an oath Conan drew his sword and redoubled his speed. That cry had come from the direction of the gold-topped tower.

Deep in the compound a gong sounded its brazen alarm, then a second and a third. Distant shouts rose, and torches flared to life.

Conan dashed into the shadows at the base of the tower, and stopped to stare in amazement. Akeba was there, holding a slender sable-skinned beauty in saffron robes, one arm pinning her arms, his free hand covering her mouth. Large dark eyes glared fiercely at him from above the soldier's fingers.

"This is your daughter?" Conan asked, and Akeba nodded, an excited smile splitting his face.

"Zorelle. I could not believe my luck. She was fetching water to the women's quarters. No one saw me."

The shouts had grown louder, and the torches now seemed to rival the stars in number.

"That does not seem to matter, at the moment," Conan said drily. "It will be no easy task to remove ourselves from this place, much less a girl who doesn't seem to want to go."

"I am taking her out of here," the Turanian replied, his voice hard.

"I did not suggest otherwise." He would not leave any woman to the mercies of Emilio's destroyer. "But we must . . . hsst!" He motioned for silence.

An atavistic instinct rooted deep inside the Cimmerian shouted that he was being watched by inimical eyes, eyes that drew closer by the moment. But his own gaze saw nothing but deceptively shifting shadows. No. One shadow resolved itself into a man in black robes. Even after Conan was certain, though, he found it difficult to keep his eyes on that dim figure. There was something about it that seemed to prevent the eye from focusing on it. The hairs on his neck rose. There was sorcery of a kind here, sorcery most foul and unnatural throughout this place.

"Mitra!" Akeba swore suddenly, jerking his hand from his daughter's mouth. "She bit me!"

Twisting in his loosened grasp, she raked at his face with her nails. At the distinct disadvantage of struggling with his own daughter, he attempted to keep his grip on her while avoiding being blinded. Under the circumstances it was an unequal fight.

In an instant she was free and running. And screaming.

"Help! Outsiders! They are trying to take me! Help!"

"Zorelle!" Akeba shouted, and ran after her.

"Zandru's Hells!" Conan shouted, and followed.

Of a sudden the black-robed man was before the girl. Gasping, she recoiled.

The strange figure's hand reached out, perhaps to brush against her face. Her words stopped on the instant, and she dropped as if her bones had melted.

"Zorelle!" The scream from Akeba held all the anguish that could be wrung from a man's throat.

Primitive instinct, primed now, reared again in Conan. Diving, he caught Akeba about the waist and pulled him to the ground. The air hummed as if a thousand hornets had been loosed. Arrows sliced through the space where they had stood, toward the man in black. And before Conan's astounded gaze the man, hands darting like lightning, knocked two shafts aside, seized two more from the air, then seemed to slide between the rest and disappear.

Close behind their arrows came half-a-score Hyrkanians, waving short horn bows and curved yataghans as they ran. Two veered toward Conan and Akeba, but another shouted gutturally, "No! Leave them! 'Tis Baalsham we want!" The squat Hyrkanians ran on into the night.

Shaking his head, Conan got slowly to his feet. He had no notion what was happening, and was, in fact, not sure that he wanted to know. Best he got on about his business and left the rest to those already involved. Screams had been added to the shouts in the distance, and the pounding of hundreds of panic-stricken feet. Fire stained the sky as a building exploded in flame.

Akeba crawled on hands to knees to his daughter. Cradling her in his arms, he rocked back and forth, tears streaming down his flat cheeks. "She is dead, Cimmerian," he whispered. "He but touched her, yet she. . . ."

"Bring your daughter," Conan told him, "and let us go. We have no part in what else happens here this night."

The Turanian lowered Zorelle carefully, drew his tulwar and examined the blade. "I have blood to avenge, a man to kill." His voice was quiet, but hard.

"Revenge takes a cool head and a cold heart," Conan replied. "Yours are both filled with heat. Remain, and you will die, and likely never see the man who killed her."

Akeba twisted to face the Cimmerian, his black eyes coals in a furnace. "I want blood, barbar," he said hoarsely. "If need be, I will begin with yours."

"Will you leave Zorelle for the worms and the ravens, then?"

Akeba squeezed his eyes shut and sucked in a long, hissing breath. Slowly he returned his blade to its sheath and, stooping, gathered his daughter in his arms. When he straightened his face and voice were without expression. "Let us be gone from this accursed place, Cimmerian."

A score of saffron-robed men and women appeared out of the dark and fled past as if terror driven. None glanced at the two men, one holding a girl's body in his arms.

Twice more as they headed for the wall they saw clusters of cult members, running mindlessly. Behind them the shouts and screams had become a solid wave of sound. Two fires now licked at the sky.

They ran into the bushes near where they had crossed the wall, and, like a covey of quail, cult members burst from hiding. Some fled shrieking; others tried to dash past the two men, almost trampling them.

Conan cuffed a pair of shaven-headed men aside and shouted, "Go Akeba! Take her on!" He knocked another man sprawling, seized a woman to toss her aside . . . and stopped. It was Yasbet.

"You!" she shouted.

Without pausing, Conan threw her over his shoulder and scrambled on, scattering the few who remained to try to hinder him. Yasbet's feet fluttered in futile kicking, and her small fists pounded at his broad back.

"Let me down!" she screamed. "You have no right! Loose me!" They reached the wall; he let her down. She stared at him with the haughtiness of a dowager queen. "I will forget this if you go now. And for the kindness you did me earlier, I'll not tell—" She broke off with a shriek as he bent to cut a strip from her robe with his dagger. In a trice her hands were bound behind her, and before she could more than begin another protest he added a gag and a hobble between her ankles.

Akeba had taken care of the grapnels. Two ropes dangled from the top of the wall. "Who is she?" he asked, jerking his head toward Yasbet.

"Another wench who should not be left to this cult," Conan replied. "Climb up. I'll attend to your daughter so you can draw her after you."

The Turanian hesitated, then said, "The live girl first. There may not be time for both." Without waiting for a reply he scrambled up one of the ropes.

Despite her struggles, Conan fastened the end of the rope about Yasbet beneath her arms. In moments her muffled squeals were rising into the air. Hurriedly he did the same to Zorelle's body with the other rope. As he was pulled up, he waited, watching and listening for Hyrkanians, for cult members, for almost anything, considering the madness of the night. He listened and waited. And waited. Akeba had to climb down on the outside, he knew, and free one of the girls before he could return atop the wall and lower a rope to Conan, but it seemed to be taking a very long time.

The rope end slapped the wall in front of his face, and he could not stop a sigh of relief. At the top of the wall he found himself face to face with Akeba. "For a time there," he said, "I almost thought you'd left me."

"For a time," Akeba replied flatly, "on the ground outside with my daughter, I almost did."

Conan nodded, and said only, "Let us go while we can."

Dropping to the ground they picked up the women—Conan Yasbet and Akeba Zorelle—and ran for Sharak and the horses. The cacophony of conflict still rose within the compound behind them.

VIII

The red glare of fire in the night glinted on Jhandar's face as he turned from the window. The shouts of initiates carrying water to fight the blazes rang through the compound, but one building, at least, was too far gone in flame to be saved.

"Well?" he demanded.

Che Fan and Suitai exchanged glances before the first-named spoke. "They were Hyrkanians, Great Lord."

The three men stood in the antechamber to Jhandar's apartments. The austerity of decoration that the necromancer invoked for his garb was continued here. Low, unadorned couches dotted the floor that was, if marble, at least plain and bare of rugs, as the walls were bare of tapestries and hangings.

"I know they were Hyrkanians!" Jhandar snarled-ed. "I could hear them shouting, 'Death to Baalsham!' Never did I think to hear that name again."

"No, Great Lord."

"How many were there?"

"Two score, Great Lord. Perhaps three."

"Three score," Jhandar whispered. "And how many yet live?"

"No more than a handful, Great Lord," Che Fan replied. "Well over a score perished."

"Then perhaps a score still live to haunt me," Jhandar said pensively. "They must be found.

There will be work for the two of you, then, you may be sure."

"Great Lord," Suitai said, "there were others in the compound tonight. Not Hyrkanians. One wore the helmet of a Turanian soldier. The other was a tall man, pale of skin."

"A barbarian?" Jhandar asked sharply. "With blue eyes?"

"Blue eyes?" Suitai asked incredulously, then recovered himself. "It was dark, Great Lord, and with the fighting I could not draw near enough to see. But they robbed the Tower of Contemplation, taking the necklace of thirteen rubies and slaying the thief you set there as guard." He hesitated. "And they killed one of the initiates, Great Lord. The girl Zorelle."

The necromancer made a dismissive gesture. He had marked the girl for his bed, in time, but her life or death was unimportant. But the necklace, now. The thief had come for that same bit of jewelry. There had to be a link there.

"Wait here," he snarled.

Carefully shutting doors behind him, he made his way to the column-lined outer hall, where waited half a score of the Chosen, Zephran among them. They thought they stood as his bodyguard, though either of the Khitan assassins could have killed all ten without effort. They bowed as he appeared. He motioned to Zephran, who approached, bowing again.

"Go to the Tower of Contemplation," Jhandar commanded. "There you will find the body of the one I set to guard that place. Bring the body to the Chamber of Summoning."

"At once, Great Lord." But Zephran did not

move. He wished to ingratiate himself with the Great Lord Jhandar. "It was the Hyrkanians, Great Lord. Those I spoke to you about, I have no doubt."

Jhandar's cheek twitched, but otherwise his face was expressionless. "You knew there were Hyrkanians in Aghrapur?" he said quietly.

"Yes, Great Lord." Sweat broke out on Zephran's forehead. Suddenly he was no longer certain it had been a good idea to speak. "Those . . . those I spoke to you of. Surely you remember, Great Lord?"

"Bring the body," Jhandar replied.

Zephran bowed low. When he straightened the necromancer was gone.

In his antechamber Jhandar massaged his temples as he paced, momentarily ignoring the Khitans. The fool had known of the Hyrkanians and yet said nothing! Of course, he had set no watch for them, warned none of the Chosen to report their appearance. To guard against them was to expect them to come, and did he expect them to come, then they would. It was the way of such things. The proof was in himself. He had not been able to destroy his own belief that they would appear. And they *had* come.

Carefully Jhandar gathered the powders and implements he would need. Dawn was but a few hours distant, now, and in the light of the sun he had few abilities beyond those of other mortals. He could not call on the Power at all while the sun shoned. He could not summon the spirit manifestations then, though commands previously given still held, of course. Perhaps he should summon them now, set them to find the Kyrkan-

ians. No. What he intended would sap much of his
strength, could it be done at all. He was not
certain he would be physically able to perform
both rituals, and what he intended was more
important. He knew something of the Hyrkanians,
nothing of the tall barbarian. The unknown threat
was always more dangerous than the known.

He motioned the Khitans to follow. A sliding
stone panel in the wall let into a secret passage,
dim and narrow, that led down to the chamber
containing the circle of barren earth. The
Chamber of Summoning.

Quickly the corpse was brought to him there, as
if Zephran thought to mitigate his transgressions
with haste, and arranged by the Khitans under
Jhandar's direction, spreadeagled in the center of
the circle. At a word the Chosen withdrew, while
the mage studied on what he was about. He had
never done the like before, and he knew no rituals
to guide him. There was no blood to manifest the
spirit of the man; there had been no blood in that
body since its first death. After that there had
been a tenuous connection between that spirit and
the body, a connection enforced by his magic, but
the second death, at the tower, had severed even
that. Still, what he intended must be attempted.

While the Khitans watched Jhandar chose three
pillars, spaced equidistantly around the circle. On
the first he chalked the ideogram for death, and
over it that for life. On the second, the ideogram
for infinity covered that of nullity. And on the last,
order covered chaos.

Spreading his arms, he began to chant, words
with meanings lost in the mists of time ringing
from the walls. Almost immediately he could feel

the surge of Power, and the near uncontrollability of it. His choice of symbols formed a dissonance, and if inchoate Power could know fury, then there was fury in the Power that flowed through Jhandar's bones.

Silver-flecked blue mist coalesced within the circle, roiling, swirling away from the posts he had marked. He willed it not to be so, and felt the resistance ripping at his marrow. Agony most torturous and exquisite. It would be as he willed. It would be. Through a red haze of pain he chanted.

Slowly the mists shifted toward, rather than away from, those three truncated pillars, touching them, then rushing toward them. Suddenly there was a snap, as from a spark leaping from a fingertip on a cold morning, but ten thousand times louder, and bars of silver-blue light, as bright as the sun, linked the posts. Chaos, forced into a triangle, the perfect shape, three sides, three points—three, the perfect number of power. Perfect order forced on ultimate disorder. Anathema, and anathema redoubled. And from that anathema, from that perversion of Chaos, welled such Power that Jhandar felt at any moment he would rise and float in the air. Sweat rolled down his body, plastering his saffron robes to his back and chest.

"You who called yourself Emilio the Corinthian," Jhandar intoned. "I summon you back to this clay that was you. By the powers of Chaos enchained, and the powers of three, I summon you. I summon you. I summon you."

The triangle of light flared, and within the circle the head of Emilio's corpse rolled to one side. The mouth worked raggedly. "Noooo!" it moaned.

Jhandar smiled. "Speak, I command you! Speak, and speak true! You came to steal a necklace of rubies?"

"Yes." The word was a pain-filled hiss.

"Why?"

"For . . . Da-vin-ia."

"For a woman? Who is she?"

"Mis-tress . . . of . . . Mun-da-ra . . . Khan."

The mage frowned. He had tried for some time to 'obtain' one of General Mundara Khan's servants, so far without success. The man stood but a short distance from the throne. Could he be taking an interest in Jhandar, as the necromancer took in him? Impossible.

"Do you know a tall barbarian?" he demanded. "A man with pale skin and blue eyes who would also try to steal that necklace."

"Co-nan," came the moaned reply. The head of the corpse twitched and moved.

Jhandar felt excitement rising in him. "Where can I find this Conan?"

"Noooo!" The head rolled again, and one arm jerked.

"Speak, I command!" The triangle of chaotic light grew brighter, but no sound came from the body.

"Speak!" Brighter.

"Speak!" Brighter.

"Speak! I command you to speak!" Brighter, and brighter still.

"I . . . am . . . a maaan!"

As the wail came, the light suddenly flared, crackling like lightning and wildfire together. Jhandar staggered back, hands thrown up to shield his eyes. Then the light was gone, and the Power, and the body. Only a wisp of oily black smoke drifting toward the ceiling remained.

"Freeee. . . ." The lone, thin word dissipated with the smoke, and naught remained of Emilio the Corinthian.

Weariness rolled into Jhandar's bones as the Power left. Despite himself, he sagged and nearly fell. There would be no summoning of spirit manifestations this night. That meant a full day must pass before he could send those incorporeal minions searching for the Hyrkanians, and for the barbarian. Conan. A strange name. But there was the woman, Davinia. There could be use in her, both for finding the barbarian and beyond. General Mundara Khan's mistress.

With a tired hand he motioned the Khitans to help him to his chambers.

IX

The palace of Mundara Khan was of gray marble and granite, relieved by ornate gardens from which rose towers of ivory and porphyry, while alabaster domes whitely threw back the sun. The guards who stood before its gates with drawn tulwars were more ceremonial than otherwise, for an attack on the residence of the great General Mundara Khan was as unlikely as one on the Royal Palace of King Yildiz. But the guards were numerous enough to cause trouble, especially if a handsome young man should announce that he had come to see the general's mistress.

Conan had no intention of entering by a guarded gate, though. Finding a tall, spreading tree near the garden wall, well out of the guards' sight, he pulled himself up into its thick branches. One, as thick as his leg, ran straight toward the garden, but it was cut cleanly, a bit higher than the wall but well short of it. The top of *this* wall was indeed set with razor shards of obsidian. Within the garden, slate walks and paths of red brick wound through the landscaping, and in the garden's center was a small round outbuilding of citron marble, cupolaed and columned, gossamer hangings stirring in the breeze at its windows and archways.

Arms held out to either side for balance, he ran

along the limb, leaped, and dropped lightly inside the garden.

Moving carefully, eyes watchful for guards or servants, he hurried to the yellow structure. It was of two stories, the ground level walled about entirely with gauze-hung archways. Within those arches, the glazed white tiles of the floor were covered with silken pillows and rare Azerjani rugs. Face down on a couch in the center of the room lay a woman, her pale, generous curves completely bare save for the long golden hair that spilled across her shoulders. Above her a wheel of white ostrich plumes revolved near the ceiling, a strap of leather disappearing through a hole above.

Conan swore to himself. A servant must be occupying the floor above, to turn the crank that in turn rotated the plumes. Still, he would not turn back. His calloused hand moved aside delicate hangings, and he entered.

For a time he stood enjoying his view of her, a woman of satiny rounded places. "Be not alarmed, Davinia," he said at last.

With a yelp of surprise the blonde rolled from the couch, long legs flashing, and snatched up a length of pale blue silk that she clutched across her breasts. The nearly transparent silk covered her ineffectually to the ankles.

"Who are you?" she demanded furiously. High cheekbones gave her face a vulpine cast.

"I am called Conan. I come in the place of Emilio the Corinthian."

Fury fading into consternation, she wet her full lips hesitantly. "I know no one of that name. If you

come from Mundara Khan, tell him his suspicions
are—"

"Then you do not know this, either," Conan said,
fishing the ruby necklace from his pouch and
dangling its gold-mounted length from his finger-
tips. He chuckled to watch her face change again,
deep blue eyes widening in shock, mouth working
wordlessly.

"How. . .," she fumbled. "Where. . . ." Her voice
dropped to a whisper. "Where is Emilio?"

"Dead," he said harshly.

She seemed neither surprised nor dismayed.
"Did you kill him?"

"No," he replied with only partial untruth.
Emilio's true death had come before their meeting
in the tower. "But he is dead, and I have brought
you the necklace you want."

"And what do you wish in return?" Her voice
was suddenly warm honey, and her arm holding
the strip of blue had lowered until pink nipples
peered at him, seeming nestled in the silk. He did
not think it an accident.

Smiling inside, Conan replied, "Emilio spoke of
one hundred pieces of gold."

"Gold." Her tinkling laughter dismissed gold as
trivial. Rounded hips swaying, she moved closer.
Then, suddenly, she was pressed tightly against
his chest. In some fashion the silk had disappeared. "There are many things of more interest to a man like you than gold," she breathed,
snaking an arm around his neck. "Of much more
interest."

"What of he who turns the fan?" he asked.

"He has no tongue to tell what he hears," she

murmured. "And no one will enter without being commanded, except Renda, my tirewoman, who is faithful to me."

"Mundara Khan?"

"Is far from the city for two nights. Can you only ask questions, barbarian?"

She tried to pull his head down for a kiss, but he lifted her, kissing her instead of being kissed. When she moaned softly deep in her throat, he let her drop.

"What," she began as her heels thudded to the floor, but he spun her about, and his hard palm flattened her buttocks. With a shrill squeal she tumbled head over heels among the cushions, long, bare legs windmilling in the air.

"The gold first, Davinia," he laughed.

Struggling to her knees, she threw a cushion at his head. "Gold?" she spat. "I'll summon the guards and—"

"—And never see the necklace again," he finished for her. She frowned fretfully. "Either I will escape, taking it with me, or the guards will take me, and the necklace, to Mundara Khan. He will be interested to find his leman is receiving jewelry from such as me. You did say he was suspicious, did you not?"

"Erlik blast your eyes!" Her eyes were blue fire, but he met them coolly.

"The gold, Davinia."

She glared at him a time longer, then, muttering to herself, crawled over the cushions. Carefully keeping her back to him she lifted a tile set in the floor and rummaged beneath.

She need not have bothered, he thought. With

the view he had as she knelt there, he would not have looked away to survey the treasure rooms of King Yildiz.

Finally she replaced the tile and turned to toss a bulging purse before him. It clanked heavily when it hit the floor. "There," she snarled. "Leave the necklace and go."

That was an end to it. Or *almost*, he thought. He had the gold—the amount did not matter—the tellings of Sharak's star-charts had been fulfilled. But the woman had thought to use him, as she had tried to use Emilio. She had threatened him. The pride that only a young man knows drove him now.

"Count it," he demanded. She stared at him in disbelief, but he thrust a finger at the purse. "Count it. It would pain me, and you, to discover you'd given me short weight."

"May the worms consume your manhood," she cried, but she made her way to the purse and emptied it, rondels of gold ringing and spinning on the white tiles. "One. Two. Three. . . ." As she counted each coin she thrust it back into the small sack, as viciously as though each coin was a dagger that she was driving into his heart. Her acid eyes remained on his face. ". . . .One hundred," she said at last. Tying the cords at the mouth of the purse, she hurled it at him.

He caught the gold-filled bag easily in one hand, and tossed the necklace to her. She clutched it to her breasts and backed away, still on her knees, eying him warily.

He saw no shimmers of magic when she touched the necklace, but by all the gods she was a bit of flesh to dry a man's mouth and thicken his throat.

He weighed the purse in his hand. "To feel this," he said, "no one would suspect that you counted five coins twice."

"It is . . . possible I made an error," she said, still moving away. "An it is so, I'll give you the five gold pieces more."

Conan dropped the purse on the floor, unbuckled his sword belt and let it fall atop the gold.

"What are you doing?" she asked doubtfully.

" 'Tis a heavy price to pay for a wench," he replied, "but as you do not want to pay what you agreed, I'll take the rest in your stock in trade."

A strangled squawk rose from her throat, and she tried to scramble away. He caught her easily, scooping her up in his muscular arms. She attempted to fend him off, but he pulled her to him as easily as if she had not tried at all. Her hands were caught inside the circle of his arms, her full breasts flattened against his broad chest.

"Think you," she gasped, "that I'll lie with you after what has passed here? After you've struck me, called me strumpet, manhandled me. . . ." Her angry words gave way to protesting splutters.

"Mundara Khan is old," Conan said softly. He trailed one finger down her spine to the swell that began her buttocks. "And fat." He brought the finger up to toy with a strand of golden hair that lay on her cheek. "And he often leaves you alone, as now." She sighed, and softened against him. Blue eyes peered into blue eyes, and he said quietly, "Speak, and I will go. Do you want me to go?"

Wordlessly she shook her head.

Smiling, Conan laid her on the couch.

X

Conan was still smiling when he strolled into the Blue Bull much later in the day. Davinia had been *very* lonely indeed. He knew it was madness to dally with the mistress of a general, but he knew his own weakness where women were concerned, too. He was beginning to hope the army took Mundara Khan from Aghrapur often.

The common room was half-filled with the usual crowd of sailors, laborers and cutpurses. Sharak and Akeba shared a table in one corner, conversing with their heads close together, but instead of joining them, Conan went to the bar.

Ferian greeted him with a scowl, and began scrubbing the bar top even faster than before. "I've nothing for you yet, Cimmerian. And I want you to get that wench out of here."

"Is she still secured in my room?" Conan demanded. Yasbet had become no more reasonable about being rescued for finding herself in a waterfront tavern.

"She's there," the innkeeper said sourly, "but I'd sacrifice in every temple in the city if she disappeared. She near screamed the roof off not a glass gone. Thank all the gods she's been quiet since. That's no trull or doxie, Cimmerian. Men are impaled for holding her sort against their will."

"I'll see to her," Conan replied in a soothing

tone. "You keep your eyes and ears open."

He hurried upstairs, listening to what suddenly seemed an ominous silence from his room. The latch-cord on his door was still tied tightly to a stout stick. A man might break the cord and lift the latch inside, but for Yasbet it should have been as good as an iron lock. Unless she had managed to wriggle through the window. Surely that small opening was too narrow even for her, but. . . . Muttering oaths beneath his breath, Conan unfastened the cord and rushed in.

A clay mug, hurled by Yasbet's hand, shattered against the door beside his head. He ducked beneath the pewter basin that followed and caught her around the waist. It was difficult to ignore what a pleasant armful she made, even while her small fists pounded at his head and shoulders. He caught her wrists, forcing them behind her back and holding them there with one hand.

"What's gotten into you, girl? Did that cult addle your wits?"

"Addle my. . . .!" She quivered with supressed anger. "They thought I had worth. And they treated me well. You brought me here bound across a horse and imprisoned me without so much as word. Then you went off to see that strumpet."

"Strumpet? What are you talking about?"

"Davinia." She growled the name. "Isn't that what she's called? That old man—Sharak?—came up to try to quiet me. He told me you'd gone to see this . . . woman. And you have the same smug look on your face that my father wears when he's just visited his zenana."

Mentally Conan called down several afflictions,

all of them painful, on Sharak's head. Aloud he said, "Why should you care if I visit twenty women? Twice now I've saved your fool life, but there's naught between us."

"I did not say there was," she said stoutly, but her shoulders sagged. Cautiously he released her wrists, and she sat down dejectedly on the roughly built bed, no more than straw ticking covered with a coarse blanket, with her hands folded in her lap. "You saved my life once," she muttered. "Perhaps. But this other was naught but kidnap."

"You did not see what I saw in that place, Yasbet. There was sorcery there, and evil."

"Sorcery!" She frowned at him, then shook her head. "No, you lie to try to stop me from returning."

He muttered under his breath, then asked, "How did you end up with them? When you ran away from me I thought you were going home." He grinned in spite of himself. "You were going to climb over the garden wall."

"I did," she muttered, not meeting his eye. "Fatima caught me atop the wall and locked me in my room." She shifted her seat uncomfortably, and the remnants of an unpleasant memory flitted across her face.

Conan was suddenly willing to wager that locking her in her room was not all that the amah had done. Barely suppressing his chuckle, he said, "But that's no reason to run away to something like this cult."

"What do you know of it?" she demanded. "Women labor on an equal footing with men there, and can rise equally, as well. There are no rich or poor in the cult, either."

"But the cult itself is rich enough," he said drily. "I've seen some of its treasures."

"Because you went there to steal!"

"And I saw a man ensorceled to his death."

"Lies!" she cried, covering her ears with her palms. "You'll not stop me returning."

"I'll leave that to your father. You're going back to him if I have to leave you at his door bound hand and foot."

"You don't even know who he is," she said, and he had the impression that she just stopped herself from sticking her tongue out at him.

"I'll find out," he said with an air of finality.

As he got to his feet she caught his wrist in both of her hands. Her eyes were large with pleading. "Please, Conan, don't send me back to my father. He . . . he has said I am to be married. I know the man. I will be a wife, yes, honored and respected. And locked in his zenana with fifty other women."

He shook his head sympathetically, but said only, "Better that than the cult, girl."

He expected her to make a break for the door as he left, but she remained sitting on the bed. Retying the latch cord, he returned to the common room. Akeba and Sharak barely looked up when he took a stool at their table.

". . .And so I tell you," Sharak said, tapping the table with a bony finger for emphasis, "that any attempt at direct confrontation will be disaster."

"What are you two carrying on about?" Conan asked.

"How we are to attack the Cult of Doom," Akeba replied shortly. His eyes bore the grim memory of the night before. "There must be a way to bring this Jhandar down." His face twisted with distaste. "I am told they call him Great Lord, as if he were a king."

"And the Khitan, of course," Sharak added. "But Jhandar—he is leader of the cult—must have given the man orders. His sort do not kill for pleasure, as a rule."

Conan was more than a little bewildered. "Khitan? His sort? You seem to have learned a great deal in the short time I've been gone."

" 'Twas not such a short time," Sharak leered. "How was she?" At the look on Conan's face he hastily cleared his throat. "Yes. The Khitan. From Akeba's description of the man who . . . well, I'm sure he was from Khitai, and a member of what is called the Brotherhood of the Way. These men are assassins of great skill." A frown added new creases to his face. "But I still cannot understand what part the Hyrkanians played."

"I've never heard of any such Brotherhood," Conan said. "In truth, I no more than half believe Khitai exists."

"They were strange to me, also," Akeba said, "but the old man insists they are real. Whatever he is, though, I will kill him."

"Oh, they're real, all right," Sharak said. "By the time your years number twice what they do now, you'll begin to learn that more exists beneath the sky than you conceive in your wildest flights of fancy or darkest nightmares. The two of you must be careful with this Khitan. They of the Brotherhood of the Way are well versed in the most subtle poisons, and can slay with no more than a touch."

"That I believe," Akeba said hoarsely, "for I saw it." He tilted up his mug and did not lower it till it was dry.

"You, especially, must take care, Conan," the astrologer went on. "I know well how hot your head can be, and that fever can kill you. This assassin—"

Conan shook his head. "This matter of revenge is Akeba's, not mine."

Sharak squawked a protest. "But, Conan! Khitan assassins, revenge, Hyrkanians, and the gods alone know what else! How can we turn our backs on such an adventure?"

"You speak of learning," Conan told him. "You've still to learn that adventure means an empty belly, a cold place to sleep, and men wanting to put a dagger in your ribs. I find enough of that simply trying to live, without seeking for it."

"He is right," Akeba said, laying a hand on the old man's arm. "I lost a daughter to the Grave-digger's Guild this morn. I have reason to seek vengeance, but he has none."

"I still think it a poor reason to stand aside," Sharak grumbled.

Conan shared a smile with Akeba over the old man's head. In many ways Sharak qualified as a sage, but in some he was far younger than the Cimmerian.

"For now," Conan said, "I think what we must do is drink." Nothing would ever make Akeba forget, but at least the memory could be dulled until protecting scars had time to form. "Ferian!" he bellowed. "A pitcher of wine! No, a bucket!"

The innkeeper served them himself, a pitcher of deep red Solvanian in each hand and a mug for Conan under his arm. "I have no buckets," he said drily.

"This will do," Conan said, filling the mugs all around. "And take something up to my room for the girl to eat."

"Her food is extra," Ferian reminded him.

Conan thought of the gold weighting his belt, and smiled. "You'll be paid." The tapster left, muttering to himself, and Conan turned his attention to the astrologer. "You, Sharak," he said sharply.

Sharak spluttered into his wine. "Me? What? I said nothing."

"You said too much," the Cimmerian said. "Why did you tell Yasbet I was going to see Davinia? And what *did* you tell her, anyway?"

"Nothing," the old man protested. "I was trying to quiet her yelling—you said not to gag her—and I thought if she knew you were with another woman she wouldn't be afraid you were going to ravish her. That's what women are always afraid of. Erlik take it, Cimmerian, what was wrong with that?"

"Just that she's jealous," Conan replied. "I've talked to her but twice and never laid a hand on her, but she's jealous."

"Never laid a hand on her? You tied her like a sack of linen," Akeba said.

"It must be his charm," Sharak added, his face impossibly straight.

" 'Tis funny enough for you two," Conan said darkly, "but I was near brained with my own washbasin. She. . . ."

As rude laughter drowned Conan's next words, Ferian ran panting up to the table.

"She's gone, Cimmerian!" the tavernkeeper gasped. "I swear by Mitra and Dagon I don't believe she could squeeze through that window, but she did."

Conan sprang to his feet. "She cannot have been gone long. Akeba, Sharak, will you help me look?"

Akeba nodded and rose, but Sharak grimaced. "An you don't want her, Cimmerian, why not leave her for someone who does?"

Without bothering to reply Conan turned to go, Akeba with him. Sharak followed hastily, hobbling with his staff.

Once in the street, the three men separated, and for near a turn of the glass Conan found nothing but frustration. Hawkers of cheap perfumes and peddlers of brass hairpins, fruit vendors, potters, street urchins, —none had seen a girl, so tall, large-breasted and beautiful, wearing saffron robes and possibly running. All he found were blank looks and shaken heads. No few of the strumpets suggested that he could find what he was looking for with them, and some men cackled that they might keep the girl themselves, did they find her, but their laughter faded to nervous sweating under his icy blue gaze.

As he returned to the stone-fronted tavern, he met Akeba and Sharak. At the Turanian's questioning glance he shook his head.

"Then she's done with," the astrologer said. "My throat needs cool wine to soothe it after all the people I've questioned. I'll wager Ferian has given our Solvanian to someone else."

The pitchers remained on the table where they had left them, but Conan did not join in the drinking. Yasbet was not done with, not to his mind. He found it strange that that should be so, but it was. Davinia was a woman to make a man's blood boil;

Yasbet had heated his no more than any other pretty wench he saw in passing. But he had saved her life, twice, for all her denials. In his belief that made him responsible for her. Then too, she needed him to protect her. He was not blind to the attractions she had for a man.

He became aware of a Hyrkanian approaching the table, stooped and bowed of leg, his rancid smell preceding him. His coarse woolen trousers and sheepskin coat were even filthier than was usual for the nomads, if such was possible. Two paces short of them he stopped, his long skinny nose twitching as if prehensile and his black eyes on the Cimmerian. "We have your woman," he said gutturally, then straightened in alarm at the blaze of rage that lit Conan's face.

Conan was on his feet with broadsword half-drawn before he himself realized that he had moved.

Akeba grasped his arm. Not the sword arm; he was too old a campaigner for that. "Hear him out before you kill him," he urged.

"Talk!" Conan's voice grated like steel on bone.

"Tamur wants to talk with you," the Hyrkanian began slowly, but his words came faster as he went. "You fought with some of us, though, and Tamur does not think you will talk with us, so we take your woman until you talk. You will talk?"

"I'll talk," Conan growled. "And if she's been harmed, I'll kill, too. Now take me to her."

"Tonight," was the thick reply.

"Now!"

"One turn of the glass after the sun sets, someone will come for you." The Hyrkanian eyed Akeba and Sharak. "For you alone."

The last length of Conan's blade rasped from its worn shagreen sheath.

"No, Conan," Sharak urged. "Kill him, and you may never find her again."

"They would send another," Conan said, but after a moment he tossed his sword on the table. "Leave me before I change my mind," he told the nomad, and, scooping up one of the wine pitchers, tilted back his head in an effort to drain it. The Hyrkanian eyed him doubtfully, then trotted from the tavern.

XI

Davinia stretched luxuriously as gray-haired Renda's fingers worked perfumed oils into the smooth muscles of her back. There was magic in the plump woman's hands, and the blonde woman needed it. The big barbarian had been more than she bargained for. And he had intimated that he would return. He had not named a time but that he would return was certain. Her knowledge of men told her so. Though it was but a few turns of the glass since Conan had left her, a tingling frisson of anticipation rippled through her at the thought of long hours more in his massive arms. To which gods, she wondered, should she offer sacrifices to keep Mundara Khan from the city longer?

A tap at the door of Davinia's tapestry-hung dressing chamber drew Renda's hands from her shoulders. With a petulant sigh, the sleek blonde waited impatiently until her tiring woman returned.

"Mistress," Renda said quietly, "there is a man to see you."

Careless of her nakedness, Davinia sat up. "The barbarian?" She confided everything in her tiring woman. Almost everything. Surely Conan would not dare enter through the gates and have himself announced, yet simply imagining the risk of it excited her more than she would have believed possible.

"No, mistress. It is Jhandar, Great Lord of the Cult of Doom."

Davinia blinked in surprise. She was dimly aware of the existence of the cult, though she did not concern herself unduly with matters of religion. Why would a cult leader come to her? Perhaps he would be amusing.

"A robe, Renda," she commanded, rising.

"Mistress, may I be so bold—"

"You may not. A robe."

She held out her arms as Renda fastened about her a red silken garment. Opaque, she noted. Renda always had more thought for her public reputation—and thus her safety—than did she.

Davinia made a grand entrance into the chamber where Jhandar waited. Slaves drew open the tall, ornately carved doors for her to sweep through. As the doors were closed she posed, one foot behind the other, one knee slightly bent, shoulders back. The man half-reclined on a couch among the columns. For just an instant her pose lasted, then she continued her advance, seeming to ignore the man while in fact she studied him. He no longer reclined, but rather sat on the edge of the couch.

"You are . . . different than I expected," he said hoarsely.

She permitted herself a brief smile, still not looking directly at him. Exactly the effect she had tried for.

He was not an unhandsome man, this Jhandar, she thought. The shaven head, however, rather spoiled his looks. And those ears gave him an unpleasantly animalistic countenance.

For the first time she faced him fully, lips carefully dampened with her tongue, eyes on his in an adoring caress. She wanted to giggle as she watched his breath quicken. Men were so easily manipulated. Except, perhaps, the barbarian. She hastily pushed aside the intruding thought. Carefully, she made sure of a breathy tone.

"You wish to see me . . . Jhandar, is it not?"

"Yes," he said slowly. Visibly he caught hold of himself. His breath still came rapidly, but there was a degree of control in his eyes. A degree. "Have you enjoyed the necklace, Davinia?"

"Necklace?"

"The ruby necklace. The one stolen from me only last night."

His voice was calm, so conversational that it took a moment for the meaning of his words to enter her. Shock raced through her. She wondered if her eyes were bulging. The necklace. How could she have been so stupid as not to make the connection the moment Jhandar was announced? It was that accursed barbarian. She seemed able to concentrate on little other than him.

"I have no idea of what you speak," she said, and was amazed at the steadiness of her voice. Inside she had turned to jelly.

"I wonder what Mundara Khan will say when he knows you have a stolen necklace. Perhaps he will inquire, forcefully, into who gave such a thing to his mistress."

"I bought—" She bit her tongue. He had flustered her. It was not supposed to happen that way. It was she who disconcerted men.

"I know that Emilio was your lover," he said quietly. "Has Conan taken his place there, too?"

"What do you want?" she whispered. Desperately she wished for a miracle to save her, to take him away.

"One piece of information," he replied. "Where may I find the barbarian called Conan?"

"I don't know," she lied automatically. The admission already made was one too many.

"A pity." He bit off the words, sending a shiver through her. "A very great pity."

Davinia searched for a way to deflect him from his purpose. All that passed through her mind, echoing and re-echoing, was 'a very great pity.'

"You may keep the necklace," he said suddenly.

She stared at him in surprise. He did not have complete control of himself still, she saw. He had continually to lick dry lips, and his eyes drank her in as a man in the desert drank water. "Thank you. I—"

"Wear it for me."

"Of course," she said. There was still a chance.

She left the room as regally as she had entered, but once outside, before the slaves had even closed the doors, she ran—despite the fact that to be languid at all times was one mark of a properly cared-for mistress.

Renda, arranging the pillows on Davinia's bed, leaped as her mistress dashed into the chamber. "Mistress, you startled me!"

"Tell me what you know of this Jhandar," Davinia panted, as she dropped to her knees and began rooting in her jewel chest. "Quickly. Hurry!"

"Little is known, mistress," the plump tire-woman said hesitantly. "The cult professes—"

"Not that, Renda!" Tossing bits of jewelry left and right, she came up with the stolen necklace clutched in her fist. Despite herself, she breathed a sigh of relief. "Mitra be thanked. Tell me what the servants and slaves know, what their masters will not know for half a year more. Tell me!"

"Mistress, what has he. . . ." She broke off at Davinia's glare. "Jhandar is a powerful man in Turan, mistress. So it is whispered among the servants. And 'tis said he grows more powerful by the day. Some say the increase in the army was begun by him, by his telling certain men, who in turn convinced the king, that it should be so. Of course, it is well known that King Yildiz has long dreamed of empire. He would not have taken a great deal of telling."

"Still," Davinia murmured, "it is a display of power." Mundara Khan had never swayed the king for all his blood connections to the throne. "How does he accomplish it?"

"All men have secrets, mistress. Jhandar makes it his business to learn their secrets. To keep their secrets, most men will agree to any suggestion Jhandar makes." She paused. "Many believe he is a sorcerer. And the cult does have immense wealth."

"How immense?"

"It may rival that of King Yildiz."

A look of intense practicality firmed Davinia's face. This situation, which had seemed so frightening, might yet be turned to her advantage. "Fetch me a cloak," she commanded. "Quickly."

When she returned to Jhandar, surprise was plain on his countenance. A cloak of fine scarlet wool swathed her from her neck to the ground.

"I do not understand," he said, anger mounting in his voice. "Where is the necklace?"

"I wear it for ,you." She opened the cloak, revealing the rubies caressing the upper slopes of her breasts. And save for the necklace, her sleek body was nude.

Only for an instant she held the cloak so. Even as he gasped, she pulled it closed. But then, rising on her toes, she spun so that her hips flashed whitely beneath flaring crimson. Around the room she danced, offering him brief tantalizing glimpses, but never so revealing as the first.

She finished on her knees before him, the scarlet cloth lowered to bare pale shoulders and the rubies nestled in her sweat-slick cleavage. Masking her triumph with care, she met his gaze. His face was flushed with desire. And now for the extra stroke.

"The man Conan," she said, "told me that he stays at the Blue Bull on the Street of the Lotus Dreamers, near the harbor."

For a moment he stared at her, uncomprehending; then he lurched to his feet. "I have him," he muttered excitedly. "An the Hyrkanians are found. . . ." All expression fled from his face as he regarded her. "Men have no use for lemans who lie," he said.

She replied with a smile. "A mistress owes absolute truth and obedience to her master." Or at least, she thought, a mistress should make him believe he had those things. "But you are not my master. Yet."

"I will take you with me," he said thickly, but she shook her head.

"The guards would never let me go. There is an old gate at the rear of the palace, however, unused and unguarded. I will be there with my serving woman one turn of the glass past dark tonight."

"Tonight. I will have men there to meet you."
Abruptly he pulled her to her feet, kissing her
brutally.

But not so well as Conan, she thought as he left.
It was a pity the barbarian was to die. She had no
doubt that was what Jhandar intended. But
Jhandar was a step into her future; Conan was of
the past. As she did with all things past, she put
him out of her mind as if he had never existed.

XII

The common room of the Blue Bull grew crowded as the appointed hour drew near, raucous with the laughter of doxies and drunken men. Conan neither laughed nor drank, but rather sat watching the door with his two friends.

"When will the man come?" Sharak demanded of the air. "Surely the hour has passed."

Neither Conan nor Akeba answered, keeping their eyes fastened to the doorway. The Cimmerian's hand on his sword hilt tightened moment by long moment till, startlingly, his knuckles cracked.

The old astrologer flinched at the sound. "What adventure is this, sitting and waiting for Mitra knows how long while—"

"He is here," Akeba said quietly, but Conan was already getting to his feet.

The long-nosed Hyrkanian stood in the doorway beckoning to Conan, casting worried glances out into the night.

"Good luck be with you, Cimmerian," Akeba said quietly.

"And with you," Conan replied.

As he strode across the common room, he could hear the astrologer's querulous voice. "Why this talk of luck? They but wish to talk."

He did not listen for Akeba's answer, if answer there was. More than one man taken to a meeting in the night had never left it alive.

"Lead on," he told the Hyrkanian, and with one more suspicious look up and down the street the nomad did so.

Twilight had gone, and full night was upon the city. A pale moon hung like a silver coin placed low above the horizon. Music and laughter drifted from a score of taverns as they passed through yellow pools of light spilling from their doors, and occasionally they heard shouts of a fight over women or dice.

"Where are you taking me?" Conan asked.

The Hyrkanian did not answer. He chose turnings seemingly at random, and always he cast a wary eye behind.

"My friends will not follow," Conan told him. "I agreed to come alone."

"It is not your friends I fear," the Hyrkanian muttered, then tightened his jaws and looked sharply at the muscular youth. Thereafter he would not speak again.

Conan wondered briefly who or what it was the man *did* fear, but his own attention was split between watching for the ambush he might be entering and unraveling the twists and turns through which he was taken. When the fur-capped man motioned him through a darkened doorway and up a flight of wooden stairs, he was confident—and surprised—that for all the roundabout way they had gone the Blue Bull was almost due north, no more than two streets away. It was well to be oriented in case the meeting came to a fight after all.

"You go first," Conan said. Expressionless, the nomad complied. Loose steps creaked alarmingly beneath his tread. Conan eased his sword in its scabbard, and mounted after him.

At the top of the stairs a door let into a room lit by two guttering tallow lamps set on a rickety table. The rancid smell of grease filled the room. Including his guide, half a score sheepskin-coated Hyrkanians watched him warily, though none put hand to weapon. One Conan recognized, the man with the scar across his cheek, he over whose head Emilio had broken the wine jar.

"I am called Tamur," Scarface said. "You are Conan?" With his guttural accent he mangled the name badly.

"I am Conan," the young Cimmerian agreed shortly. "Where is the woman?"

Tamur gestured, and two of the others opened a large chest sitting against a wall. They lifted out Yasbet, bound in a neat package and gagged with a twisted rag. Her saffron robes were mud-stained and torn, and dried tracks of tears traced through the dust on her cheeks.

"I warned this one," Conan grated. "If she is hurt, I'll—"

"No, no," Tamur cut in. "Her garments were so when we took her, behind the inn where you sleep. Had we ravaged your woman, would we show her to you so and yet expect you to talk with us?"

It was possible. Conan remembered the narrowness of the window through which she had had to wriggle. "Loose her feet."

Producing a short, curved dagger, one of the nomads cut the ropes at Yasbet's ankles. She tried to stand and, with a gag-muffled moan, sat on the lid of the chest in which she had been confined. The Hyrkanian looked questioningly at Conan,

and motioned with the knife to her still-bound
wrists, and her gag, but the muscular youth shook
his head. Based on past experience he would not
risk what she might say or do if freed. She gave
him an odd look, but, surprisingly, remained still.

"You were recognized in the enclosure of Baalsham," Tamur said.

"Baalsham?" Conan said. "Who is Baalsham?"

"You know him as Jhandar. What his true name
is, who can say?" Tamur sighed. "It will be easier
if I begin at the beginning."

He gave quick orders, and a flagon of cheap
wine and two rough clay mugs were produced.
Tamur sat on one side of the table, Conan on the
other. The Cimmerian noted that the other
nomads were careful not to move behind him and
ostentatiously kept their hands far from swords.
It was a puzzlement. Hyrkanians were an arrogant
and touchy people, by all accounts little given to
avoiding trouble in the best of circumstances.

He accepted a mug of wine from Tamur, then
forgot to drink as he listened.

"Five years gone," the scar-faced nomad began,
"the man we call Baalsham appeared among us,
he and the two strange men with yellow skins. He
performed some small magicks, enough to be
accepted among the tribal shamans, and began to
preach much as he does here, of chaos and in-
evitable doom. Among the young men his teachings caught hold, for he called the western nations
evil and said it was the destiny of the Hyrkanian
people once more to ride west of the Vilayet Sea.
And this time we were to sweep the land clean."

"A man of ambitions," Conan muttered. "But
failed ambitions, it seems."

"By the thickness of a fingernail. Not only did Baalsham gather about him young warriors numbering in the thousands, but he began to have strange influence in the Councils of the Elders. Then creatures were seen in the night—like demons, or the twisted forms of men—and we learned from them that they were the spirits of murdered men, men of our blood and friendship, conjured by Baalsham and bound to obey him. Their spying was the source of his powers in the Councils."

Yasbet made a loud sound of denial through her gag, and shook her head violently, but the men ignored her.

"I've seen his sorcery," Conan said, "black and foul. How was he driven out? I assume he did not leave of his own accord."

"In a single night," Tamur replied, "ten tribes rose against him. The very spirits that had warned us, shackled by his will, fought us, as did the young warriors who followed him." He touched the scar on his cheek. "This I had from my own brother. The young warriors—our brothers, our sons, our cousins—died to the last man, and even the maidens fought to the death. In the end our greater numbers carried the victory. Baalsham fled, and with his fleeing the spirits disappeared before our eyes. To avoid bloodshed among the tribes, the Councils decreed that no man could claim blood right for the death of one who had followed Baalsham. Their names were not to be spoken. They had never existed. But some of us could not forget that we had been forced to spill the same blood that flows in our own veins. When traders brought rumors of the man called Jhandar and the Cult of Doom, we knew him for Baalsham. Two score and ten crossed the sea to seek our forbidden vengeance. Last night we failed, and now we number but nineteen." He fell silent.

Conan frowned. "An interesting tale, but why have you told it to me?"

The nomad's face twisted with reluctance. "Because we need your help," he said slowly.

"My help?" Conan exclaimed.

Tamur hurried on. "When the palace Baalsham was building was overrun, powers beyond the mind were loosed. The very ground melted and flowed like water. That place is now called the Blasted Lands. For three days and three nights the shamans labored to contain that evil. When they had constructed barriers of magic, the boundaries of the Blasted Lands were marked, and a taboo laid. No one of the blood may pass those markers and live. There must be devices of sorcery within, devices that could be turned against Baalsham. He could not have taken all when he fled. But no Hyrkanian may go to bring them out. No Hyrkanian." He looked at the big Cimmerian with intensity.

"I am done with Jhandar," Conan said.

"But is he done with you, Conan? Baalsham's enmity does not wither with time."

Conan snorted. "What care I for his enmity? He does not know who I am or where I am to be found. Let his enmity eat at him like foxes."

"You know little of him," Tamur said insistently. "He—"

With a loud crack the floorboards by Conan's feet splintered, and a twisted gray-green hand reached through the opening to grasp his ankle.

"The spirits have come!" one of the nomads cried, eyes bulging, and Yasbet began to scream through her gag. The other men drew weapons, shouting in confusion.

Conan scrambled to his feet, trying to pull his leg free, but those leathery fingers held with preternatural strength. Another deformed hand broke through the boards, reaching for him, but his sword leaped from its sheath and arched down. One hand dropped to the floor; the other still gripped him. But at least, he thought, steel would slice them.

With his sword point he pried the fingers loose from his ankle. Even as that hand fell free, though, the head of the creature, with pointed ears and dead, haunted eyes above a lipless gash of a mouth, smashed up through the floor in a shower of splintered wood. Handless arms stretched out to the hands lying on the floor. The mold-colored flesh seemed to flow, and the hands were once more attached to the arms. The creature began to tear its way up into the room, ripping the sturdy floor apart as if its boards were rotted.

Suddenly another set of hands smashed through a wall, seizing a screaming Hyrkanian, tearing at his flesh. Conan struck off the head of the first creature, but it continued to scramble into the room even while its head spun glaring on the floor. A third head broke through the floor, and a hand followed to seize Yasbet's leg. With a shriek, she fainted.

Conan caught her as she fell, cutting her free of the creature that held her. There was naught to do in that room but die.

"Flee!" he shouted. "Get out!"

Tossing Yasbet over his shoulder like a sack of meal, he scrambled out the window to drop to the street below.

Struggling Hyrkanians fought to follow. Screams from that suddenly hellish room rose to a crescendo, pursuing the big Cimmerian as he ran with his burden. As abruptly as it had begun, the screaming ceased. Conan looked back, but he could see nothing in the blackness.

A low moan broke from Yasbet, stirring on his shoulder. Remembering the tenacity of the hand that had gripped him, he lowered her to the ground and bent to feel along her leg. His fingers encountered the lump of leathery skin and sinew; it writhed at his touch. With an oath he tore it from her flesh and hurled it into the night.

Yasbet groaned, and opened her eyes. "I . . . I had a nightmare," she whispered.

" 'Twas no dream," he muttered. His eyes searched the dark for pursuit. "But it is done." He hoped.

"But those demons . . . you mean that they were real?" Sobs welled up in her. "Where did they come from? Why? Oh, Mitra protect us," she wailed.

Clamping a hand over her mouth, he growled, "Quiet yourself, girl. Were I to wager on it, I'd stack my coin on Jhandar's name. And if you continue screeching like a fishwife, his minions will find us. We may not escape so easily again." Cautiously he took his hand away; she scrambled to her feet, staring at him.

"I do not believe you," she said. "Or those smelly Hyrkanians." But she did not raise her voice again.

"There is evil in the man," he said quietly. "I've seen the foulest necromancy from him, and I doubt not this is more of his black art."

"It cannot be. The cult—"

"Hsst!"

The thump of many feet sounded down the street. Pulling Yasbet deeper into the shadows, Conan waited with blade at the ready. Dim figures appeared, moving slowly from the way he had come. The smell of old grease drifted to him.

"Tamur?" he called softly.

There were mutters of startlement, and the flash of bare blades in the dark. Then one figure came closer. "Conan?"

"Yes," the Cimmerian replied. "How many escaped?"

"Thirteen," Tamur sighed. "The rest were torn to pieces. You must come with us, now. Those were Baalsham's spirit creatures. He will find you eventually, and when he does. . . ."

Conan felt Yasbet shiver. "He cannot find me," he said. "He does not even know who to look for."

Suddenly another Kyrkanian spoke. "A fire," he said. "To the north. A big fire."

Conan glanced in that direction, a deathly chill in his bones. It *was* a big fire, and unless he had lost his way entirely the Blue Bull was in the center of it. Without another word he ran, pulling Yasbet behind him. He heard the nomads following, but he cared not if they came or stayed.

The street of the Lotus Dreamers was packed with people staring at the conflagration. Flames from four structures whipped at the night, and reflected crimson glints from watching faces. One, the furthest gone, was the Blue Bull. Someone had formed a chain of buckets to the nearest cistern, Ferian among them, but it was clear that some goodly part of the district would be destroyed before the blaze was contained, most likely by pulling down buildings to surround the fire and letting it burn itself out.

As Conan pushed through the crowd of on- lookers, a voice drifted to him.

"I hit it with the staff, and it disappeared in a cloud of black smoke. I told you the staff had magical powers."

Smiling for what seemed the first time in days, Conan made his way toward that voice. He found Akeba and Sharak, faces smudged with smoke, sitting with their backs against the front of a potter's shop.

"You are returned," Sharak said when he saw the big Cimmerian. "And with the wench. To think we believed it was you who would be in danger this night. I killed one of the demons."

"Demons?" Conan asked sharply.

Akeba nodded. "So they seemed to be. They burst through the walls and even the floors, tearing apart anyone who got in their way." He hesitated. "They seemed to be hunting for someone who was not there."

"Me," Conan said grimly.

Yasbet gasped. "It cannot be." The men paid her no mind.

"I said that he would find you," Tamur said, appearing at Conan's side. "Now you have no choice but to go to Hyrkania."

"Hyrkania!" Sharak exclaimed.

Regretfully, Conan nodded agreement. He was committed, now. He must destroy Jhandar or die.

XIII

In the gray early morning Conan made his way down the stone quay, already busy with lascars and cargo, to the vessel that had been described to him. *Foam Dancer* seemed out of place among the heavy-hulled roundships and large dromonds. Fewer than twenty paces in length, she was rigged with a single lateen sail and pierced for fifteen oars a side in single banks. Her sternpost curved up and forward to assume the same angle as her narrow stem, giving her the very image of agility. He had seen her like before, in Sultanapur, small ships designed to beach where the King's Custom was unlikely to be found. They claimed to be fishing vessels, to the last one, these smugglers, and over this one, as over every smuggler he had seen, hung a foul odor of old fish and stale ship's cooking.

He walked up the gangplank with a wary eye, for the crews of such vessels invariably had a strong dislike for strangers. Two sun-blackened and queued seamen, stripped to the waist, watched him with dark unblinking eyes as he stepped down onto the deck.

"Where is your captain?" he began, when a surreptitious step behind made him whirl.

His hand darted out to catch a dagger-wielding arm, and he found himself staring into a sharp-nosed face beneath a dirty red-striped head scarf.

It was the Iranistani whose companions he had been forced to kill his first day in Aghrapur. And if he was a crew member, then as like as not the other two had been as well. The Iranistani opened his mouth, but Conan did not wait to hear what he had to say. Grabbing the man's belt with his free hand, Conan took a running step and threw him screaming over the rail into the harbor. Sharpnose hit the garbage-strewn water with a thunderous splash and, beating the water furiously, set out away from the ship without a backward glance.

"Hannuman's Stones!" roared a bull-necked man, climbing onto the deck from below. Bald except for a thin black fringe, he wore a full beard fanning across his broad chest. His beady eyes lit on Conan. "Are you the cause of all the shouting up here?"

"Are you the captain?" Conan asked.

"I am. Muktar, by name. Now what in the name of Erlik's Throne is this all about?"

"I came aboard to hire your ship," Conan said levelly, "and one of your crew tried to put a dagger in my back. I threw him into the harbor."

"You threw him into the. . . ." The captain's bellow trailed off, and the went on in a quieter, if suspicious, tone. "You want to hire *Foam Dancer*? For what?"

"A trading voyage to Hyrkania."

"A trader! You?" Muktar roared with laughter, slapping his stout thighs.

Conan ground his teeth, waiting for the man to finish. The night before he, Akeba and Tamur had settled on the trading story. Never a trusting people, the Hyrkanians had become less tolerant of strangers since Jhandar, but traders were still permitted. Conan thought wryly of Davinia's gold. When the cost of trade goods, necessary for the disguise, was added to the hiring of this vessel, there would not be enough left for a good night of drinking.

At last Muktar's mirth ran its course. His belly shook a last time, and cupidity lit his eyes. "Well, the fishing has been very good of late. I don't think I could give it up for so long for less than, say, fifty gold pieces."

"Twenty," Conan countered.

"Out of the question. You've already cost me a crewman. He didn't drown, did he? An he did, the authorities will make me haul him out of the harbor and pay for his burial. Forty gold pieces, and I consider it cheap."

Conan sighed. He had little time to waste. If Tamur was right, they had to be gone from Aghrapur by nightfall. "I'll split the difference with you," he offered. "Thirty gold pieces, and that is my final offer. If you do not like it, I'll find another vessel."

"There isn't another in port can put you ashore on a Hyrkanian beach," the captain sneered.

"Tomorrow, or the next day, or the next, there will be." Conan shrugged unconcernedly.

"Very well," Muktar muttered sourly. "Thirty gold pieces."

"Done," Conan said, heading for the side. "We sail as soon as the goods are aboard. The tides will not matter to this shallow draft."

"I thought there was no hurry," the bearded man protested.

"Nor is there," Conan said smoothly. "Neither is

there any need to waste time." Inside, he wondered if they would get everything done. There
simply *was* no time to waste.

"Speak on," Jhandar commanded, and paced
the bare marble floor of his antechamber while he
listened.

"Yes, Great Lord," the young man said, bowing.
"A man was found in one of the harbor taverns, an
Iranistani who claimed to have fought one who
must be the man Conan. This Iranistani was a
sailor on a smuggler, *Foam Dancer*, and it seems
that this ship sailed only a few hours past bearing
among its passengers a number of Hyrkanians, a
huge blue-eyed barbarian, and a girl matching the
description of the initiate who disappeared the
night of the Hyrkanians' attack." He paused,
awaiting praise for having ferreted out so much so
quickly.

"The destination, fool," Jhandar demanded.
"Where was the ship bound?"

"Why, Hyrkania, or so it is said, Great Lord."

Jhandar squeezed his eyes shut, massaging his
temples with his fingers. "And you did not think
this important enough to tell me without being
asked?"

"But, Great Lord," the disciple faltered, "since
they have fled . . . that is. . . ."

"Whatever you discover, you will tell me," the
necromancer snapped. "It is not for you to decide
what is important and what is not. Is there aught
else you have omitted?"

"No, Great Lord. Nothing."

"Then leave me!"

The shaven-headed young man backed from

Jhandar's presence, but the mage had already dismissed him from his mind. He who had once been known as Baalsham moved to a window. From there he could see Davinia reclining in the shade of a tree in the gardens below, a slave stirring a breeze for her with a fan of white ostrich plumes. He had never known a woman like her before. She was disturbing. And fascinating.

"I but listen at corners, Great Lord," Che Fan said behind him, "yet I know that already there is talk because she is not treated as the rest."

Jhandar suppressed a start and glanced over his shoulder at the two Khitans. Never in all the years they had followed him had he gotten used to the silence with which they moved. "If wagging tongues cannot be kept still," he said, "I will see that there are no tongues to wag."

Che Fan bowed. "Forgive me, Great Lord, if I spoke out of my place."

"There are more important matters afoot," Jhandar said. "The barbarian has sailed for Hyrkania. He would not have done so were he merely fleeing. Therefore he must be seeking something, some weapon, to use against me."

"But there is nothing, Great Lord," Suitai protested. "All was destroyed."

"Are you certain of that?" Jhandar asked drily. "Certain enough to risk all of my plans? I am not. I intend to secure the fastest galley in Aghrapur, and the two of you will sail on the next tide. Kill this Conan, and bring me whatever it is he seeks."

"As you command, Great Lord," the Khitans murmured together.

All would be well, Jhandar told himself. He had come too far to fail now. Too far.

XIV

Gray seas rolled under *Foam Dancer's* pitching bow, and a mist of foam carried across her deck. The triangular sail stood taut against the sky, where a pale yellow sun had sunk halfway from zenith to western horizon. At the stern a seaman, shorter than Conan but broader, leaned his not inconsiderable weight against the steering oar, but the rest of the crew for the most part lay sprawled among the bales of trade goods.

Conan stood easily, one hand gripping a stay. He was no sailor, but his time among the smugglers of Sultanapur had at least taught his stomach to weather the constant motion of a ship.

Akeba was not so fortunate. He straightened from bending over the rail—as he had done often since the vessel left Aghrapur—and said thickly, "A horse does not move so. Does it never stop?"

"Never," Conan said. But at a groan from the other he relented. "Sometimes it will be less, and in any case you will become used to it. Look at the Hyrkanians. They've made but a single voyage, yet show no illness."

Tamur and the other nomads squatted some distance in front of the single tail mast, their quiet murmurs melding with the creak of timbers and cording. They passed among themselves clay wine jugs and chunks of ripe white cheese, barely interrupting their talk to fill their mouths.

"I do not want to look at them," Akeba said, biting off each word. "I swear before Mitra that I know not which smells worse, rotted fish or mare's milk cheese."

Nearby, in the waist of the ship, a few of the sailors listened to Sharak. ". . .Thus did I strike with my staff of power," he gestured violently with his walking staff, "slaying three of the demons in the Blue Bull. Great were their lamentations and cries for mercy, but for such foul-hearted creatures as they I would know no mercy. Many more would I have transmuted to harmless smoke, blown away on the breeze, but they fled before me, back to their infernal regions, casting balls of fire to hinder my pursuit, as I. . . ."

"Did he truly manage to harm one of the creatures?" Conan asked Akeba. "He has boasted of that staff for years, but never have I seen more from it than support for a tired back."

"I know not," Akeba said. He was making a visible effort to ignore his stomach, but his dark face bore a greenish pallor. "I saw him at the first, leaping about like a Farthii fire-dancer and flailing with his stick at whatever moved, then not again till we had fled to the street. Of the fire, however, I do know. 'Twas Ferian. He threw a lamp at one of the demons, harming the creature not at all, but scattering burning oil across a wall."

"And burned down his own tavern," Conan chuckled. "How it will pain him to build anew, though I little doubt he has the gold to do it ten times over."

Muktar, making his way aft from the necessary —a plank held out from the bow on a frame—

paused by Conan. His beady eyes rolled to the sky, then to the Cimmerian's face. "Fog," he said, then chewed his thought a moment before adding, "by sunset. The Vilayet is treacherous." Clamping his mouth shut as though he had said more than he intended, he moved on toward the stern in a walk that would have seemed rolling on land, but here exactly compensated for the motion of the deck.

Conan grimly watched him go. "The further we sail from Aghrapur, the less he talks and the less I trust him."

"He wants the other half of his gold that you hold back. Besides, with the Hyrkanians we out-number his crew."

Mention of the gold was unfortunate. After he paid the captain, Conan would have exactly eight pieces of gold in his pouch. In other times it would have seemed a tidy sum, but not so soon after having had a hundred. He found himself hoping to make a profit on the trade goods, and yet thoughts of profits and trading left a taste in his mouth as if he had been eating the Hyrkanians' ripest cheese.

"Mayhap," he said sourly. "Yet he would feed us to the fish and return to his smuggling, were he able. He— What's the matter, man?"

Eyes bulging, Akeba swallowed rapidly, and with force. "Feed us to—" With a groan he doubled over the rail again, retching loudly and emptily. There was naught left in him to come up.

Yasbet came hurrying from the stern, casting frowns over her shoulder as she picked her way quickly among coiled ropes and wicker hampers of provisions. "I do not like this Captain Muktar," she announced to Conan. "He leers at me as if he would see me naked on a slave block."

Conan had declared her saffron robe unsuited for a sea voyage, and she had shown no reluctance to rid herself of that reminder of the cult. Now she wore a short leather jerkin, laced halfway up the front, over a gray wool tunic, with trousers of the same material and knee-high red boots. It was a man's garb, but the way the coarse wool clung to her form left no doubt there was a woman inside.

"You've no need to fear," Conan said firmly. Perhaps he should have a talk with Muktar in private. With his fists. And the captain was not the only one. His icy gaze caught the leering glances of a dozen sailors directed at her.

"I've no fear of anything so long as you are with me," she said, and innocently pressed a full breast against his arm. At least, he thought it was innocently. "But what is the matter with Akeba, Conan?" She herself had showed no effects from the roughest seas.

"He's ill."

"I am so sorry. Perhaps if I brought him some soup?"

"Erlik take the woman," Akeba moaned faintly.

"I think not just now," Conan laughed. Taking Yasbet's arm he led her away from the heaving form on the rail and seated her on an upturned keg before him. His face was serious now.

"Why look you so glum, Conan?" she asked.

"An there is trouble," he said quietly, "here or ashore, stay close to me, or to Akeba if you cannot get to me. Sick or not, he'll protect you. Does the worst come, Sharak will help you escape. He is no fighter, but no man lives so long as he without learning to survive."

A small frown creased her forehead. When he

was done, she exclaimed, "Why do you speak as if you might not be with me?"

"No man knows what comes, girl, and I would see you safe."

"I thought so," she said with a warmth and happiness he did not understand. "I wished it to be so."

"As a last resort, trust Tamur, but only if there is no other way." He thought the nomad was the best of the lot, the least likely to betray a trust, but it was best not to test him too far. As the ancient saying held, he who took a Hyrkanian friend should pay his burial fee beforetime. "Put no trust in any of the rest, though, not even if it means you must find your way alone."

"But you will be here to protect me," she smiled. "I know it."

Conan growled, at a loss to make her listen. By bringing her along, for all he had done it for the best, he had exposed her to danger as great as Jhandar's, if different in kind. How could he bring that home to her? If only she were capable of her own protection. Her own. . . .

Rummaging in the bales of trade goods, the Cimmerian dug out a Nemedian sica, its short blade unsharpened. The Hyrkanian nomads liked proof that a sword came to them fresh from the forge, such proof as would be given by watching the first edge put on blunt steel.

He flipped the shortsword in the air, catching it by the blade, and thrust the hilt at Yasbet. She stared at it wonderingly.

"Take it, girl," he said.

Hesitantly she put a hand to ⊔he leather-wrapped hilt. He released his grip, and she gasped, almost dropping the weapon. " 'Tis heavy," she said, half-laughing.

"You've likely worn heavier necklaces, girl. You'll be used to the weight in your hand before we reach Hyrkania."

"Used to it?"

Her yelp of consternation brought chortles and hoots from three nearby sailors. The Hyrkanians looked up, still eating; Tamur's face split into an open grin.

Conan ignored them as best he could, firmly putting down the thought of hurling one or two over the side as a lesson for the others. "The broadsword is too heavy," he said, glowering at the girl. "Tulwar and yataghan are lighter, but there is no time to teach the use of either before we land. And learn the blade you will."

She stared at him silently with wide, liquid eyes, clutching the sword to her breasts with both hands.

Raucous laughter rolled down the deck, and Muktar followed close behind the sound of his merriment. "A woman! You intend to teach a woman the sword?"

Conan bit back an oath, and contended himself with growling, "Anyone can learn the sword."

"Will you teach children next? This one," Muktar crowed to his crew, "will teach sheep to conquer the world." Their mirth rose with his, and their comments became ribald.

Conan ground his teeth, his anger flashing to the heat of a blade in the smith-fire. This fat, lecherous ape called itself a man? "A gold piece says in the tenth part of a glass I can teach her to defeat any of these goats who follow you!"

Muktar tugged at his beard, the smile now twisting his mouth into an emblem of hatred. "A gold piece?" he sneered. "I'd wager five on the ship's cook."

"Five," Conan snapped. "Done!"

"Talk to her, then, barbar." The captain's voice was suddenly oily and treacherous. "Talk to the wench, and we'll see if she can uphold your boasting."

Already Conan was wishing his words unsaid, but the gods, as usual in such cases, did not listen. He drew Yasbet aside and adjusted her hands on the sword hilt.

"Hold it so, girl." Her hand was unresisting—and gripped with as much strength as bread dough, or so it seemed to him. She had not taken her eyes from his face. "Mitra blast your hide, girl," he growled. "Clasp the hilt as you would a hand."

"You truly believe that I can do this," she said suddenly. There was wonder in her voice, and on her face. "You believe that I can learn to use a sword. And defeat a man."

"I'd not have wagered on you, else," he muttered, then sighed. "I have known women who handled a blade as well as any man, and better than most. 'Tis not a weapon of brute muscle, as is an axe. The need is for endurance, and agility and quickness of hand. Only a fool denies a woman can be agile, or quick."

"But—to defeat a man!" she breathed. "I have never even held a sword before." Abruptly she frowned at the blade. "This will not cut. Swords are supposed to cut. Even I know that."

Conan mouthed a silent prayer. "I chose it for

that reason, for practice. Now it will serve you better than another. The point can still draw blood, but you'll not kill this sailor by accident, so I'll not have to kill Muktar."

"I see," she said, nodding happily. Her face firmed, and she started past him, but he seized her arm.

"Not yet, wench," he laughed softly. "First listen. These smugglers are deadly with a knife, especially in the dark, but they are no warriors in the daylight." He paused for that to sink in, then added. "That being so, were this a true fight, he would likely kill you in the space of three breaths."

Dismay painted her face. "Then how—"

"By remembering that you can run. By encouraging his contempt for you, and using it."

"I will not," she protested hotly. "I have as much pride as any man, including you."

"But no skill, as yet. You must win by trickery, and by surprise, for now. Skill will come later. Strike only when he is off balance. At all other times, run. Throw whatever comes to hand, at his head or at his feet, but never at his sword for those objects he will easily knock aside. Let him think that you are panicked. Scream if you wish, but do not let the screaming seize you."

"I will not scream," she said sullenly.

He suppressed a smile. "It would but make him easier to defeat, for he would see you the more as a woman and the less as an opponent."

"But the sword. What do I do with the sword?"

"Beat him with it," he said, and laughed at her look of complete uncomprehension. "Think of the sword as a stick, girl." Understanding dawned on

her features; she hefted the sica with both hands
like a club. "And forget not to poke him," he
added. "Such as these usually think only to hack,
forgetting a sword has a point. You remember it,
and you'll win."

"How long will you talk to the wench?" Muktar
shouted. "Your minutes are gone. An you talk
long enough, perhaps Bayan will grow old, and
even your jade can defeat him."

Beside the bearded sea captain stood a wiry
man of middle height, his sun-darkened torso
stripped to the waist. With his bare tulwar he
drew gleaming circles of steel, first to one side
then the other, a tight smile showing yellowed
teeth.

Conan's heart sank. He had hoped Muktar
would indeed choose his fat ship's cook, or one of
the bigger men of the crew, so as to intimidate
Yasbet with her opponent's sheer size. Thus
Yasbet's agility would count for more. Even if it
meant eating his words, he could not allow her to
be hurt. A bitter taste on his tongue, he opened his
mouth to end it.

Yasbet strode out to meet the seaman before
Conan could speak, shortsword gripped in her two
small hands. She fixed the man with a defiant
glare. "Bayan, are you called?" she sneered.
"From the look of you, it should be Baya, for you
have about you a womanish air."

Conan stood with his mouth still open, staring at
her. Had the wench gone mad?

Bayan's dark eyes seemed about to pop from his
narrow head. "I will make you beg me to prove my
manhood to you," he snarled.

"Muktar!" Conan called. Yasbet looked at him,

pleading in her eyes, and despite himself he changed what he had been about to say. "This is but a demonstration, Muktar. No more. Does he harm her, you'll die a heartbeat after he does."

The bearded man jerked his head in a reluctant nod. Leaning close to Bayan he began whispering with low urgency.

The wiry sailor refused to listen. Raising his curved blade on high, he leaped toward Yasbet, a snarling grimace on his face and a terrible ululating cry rising from his mouth.

Conan put a hand to his sword hilt.

Bayan landed before her without striking, though, and it was immediately obvious that he thought to frighten her into immediate surrender. His grimace became a gloating smile.

Yasbet's face paled, but with a shout of her own she thrust the sword into the seaman's mid-section. The unsharpened blade could not penetrate far, but the point was enough to start a narrow stream of blood, and the force of the blow bulged Bayan's eyes.

He gagged and staggered, but she did not rest. Clumsily, but swiftly, she brought the blunted blade down like a club on the shoulder of his sword arm. Bayan's scream was not of his choosing, this time. His blade dropped from a hand suddenly useless. Before the tulwar struck the deck Yasbet caught him a glancing blow on the side of the head, splitting his scalp to the bone. With a groan Bayan sank to his knees.

Conan watched in amazement as the wiry sailor tried desperately to crawl away. Yasbet pursued him across the deck, beating at his shoulders and back with the edgeless steel. Yelping, Bayan found himself against the rail. At one and the same time he tried to curl himself into a ball and claw his way through the wood to safety.

"Surrender!" Yasbet demanded, standing above him like a fury. She stabbed at Bayan's buttocks, drawing a howl and a stain of red on his dirty once-white trousers.

Hand on his dagger, Muktar started toward her, a growl rising in his throat. Suddenly Conan's blade was a shining barrier before the captain's eyes.

"She won, did she not?" the young Cimmerian asked softly. "And you owe me five gold pieces. Or shall I shave your beard at the shoulders?"

Another shriek came from Bayan; the other buttock of his trousers bore a spreading red patch as well, now.

"She won," Muktar muttered. He flinched as Conan caressed his beard with the broadsword, then almost shouted, "The wench won!"

"See that this goes no further," Conan said warningly. He got a reluctant nod in reply. When the Cimmerian thrust out his palm, the gold coins were counted into it with even greater reluctance.

"I won!" Yasbet shouted. Waving her short-sword above her head, she capered gaily about the deck. "I won!"

Conan sheathed his blade and swept her into the air, swinging her in a circle. "Did I not say that you would?"

"You did!" she laughed. "Oh, you did! On my oath, I will believe anything that you tell me from this moment. Anything."

He started to lower her feet to the deck, but her arms wove about his neck, and in some fashion he found himself kissing her. A pleasant armful, indeed, he thought. Soft round breasts flattened against his broad chest.

Abruptly he pulled her loose and set her firmly on the deck. "Practice, girl. There's a mort of practice to be done before I grind an edge on that blade for you. And you did not fight as I told you. I should take a switch to you for that. You could have been hurt."

"But, Conan," she protested, her face falling.

"Place your feet so," he said, demonstrating, "for balance. Do it, girl!"

Sullenly she complied, and he began to show her the exercises in the use of the short blade. That was the problem, he thought grimly, about setting out to protect a wench. Sooner or later you found yourself protecting her from you.

XV

Squatting easily on his heels against the pitching of the ship as it breasted long swells, Conan watched Yasbet work her blunted blade against a leather-wrapped bale of cloaks and tunics. Despite a freshening wind, sweat rolled down her face, but already she had gone ten times as long as she had managed the first day. She still wore her mannish garb, but had left off the woolen tunic, complaining that the coarse fabric scratched. The full curves of her breasts swelled at the lacings of her jerkin, threatening to burst the rawhide cords at her every exertion.

Sword arm dropping wearily, she looked at him with artistic pleading in her eyes. "Please, Conan, let me retire to my tent." That tent, no more than a rough structure of grimy canvas, had been his idea, both to keep her from the constant wetting of sudden squalls and to shelter her sleep from lustful eyes. "Please? Already I will be sore."

"There's plenty of linament," he said gruffly.

"It smells. And it stings. Besides, I cannot rub it on my back. Perhaps if you—"

"Enough rest," he said, motioning her back to the bale.

"Slaver," she muttered, but her shortsword resumed its whacking against leather.

Well over half their voyage was done. The coast of Hyrkania was now a dark line on the eastern horizon, though they had yet a way north to sail. Every day since placing the sica in her hands he had forced Yasbet to practice, exercising from gray dawn to purple dusk. He had dragged her from her blankets, poured buckets of water over her head when she whined of the midday heat, and threatened keelhauling when she begged to stop her work. He had tended and bandaged blisters on her small hands, as well, and to his surprise those blisters seemed at once a mark of pride to her and a spur.

Akeba dropped down beside him, eying Yasbet with respect. "She learns. Can you teach so well, and to a woman, there is need of you in the army, to train the many recruits we take of late."

"She has no ideas of swordplay to unlearn," Conan replied. "Also, she does exactly as I say."

"Exactly?" Akeba laughed, lifting an eyebrow. At the look on Conan's face he pulled his countenance into an expression of exaggerated blandness.

"Does your stomach still trouble you?" the youthful Cimmerian asked hopefully.

"My head and my legs now ignore the pitching," Akeba replied with a fixed grin.

Conan gave him a doubtful look. "Then perhaps you would like some well-aged mussels. Muktar has a keg of the ripest—"

"No, thank you, Conan," the Turanian said in haste, a certain tautness around his mouth. As though eager to change the subject, he added, "I have not noticed Bayan about today. You did not drop him over the side, did you?"

The Cimmerian's mouth tightened. "I overheard him discussing his plans for Yasbet, and I spoke to him about it."

"In friendly fashion, I trust. 'Tis you who
mutters that these sea rats would welcome an
excuse to slit our throats."

"In friendly fashion," Conan agreed. "He is
nursing his bruises in his blankets this day."

"Good," the Turanian said grimly. "She is of an
age with Zorelle."

"A tasty morsel, that girl," Sharak said, sitting
down on Conan's other side. "Were I but twenty
years younger I would take her from you,
Cimmerian."

Yasbet's sword clanged on the deck, drawing all
three men's eyes. She glared at them furiously. "I
am no trained ape or dancing bear that you three
may squat like farm louts and be entertained by
me!"

She stalked away, then back to snatch up the
sica—her eyes daring them to speak, as she
did—and marched down the deck to disappear
within her small tent before the mast.

"Your wench begins to develop a temper,
Conan," Sharak said, staring after her. "Perhaps
you have made a mistake in teaching her to use a
weapon."

Akeba nodded with mock gravity. "She is no
longer the shy and retiring maiden that once she
was, Cimmerian, thanks to you. Of course, I
realize that she is no longer a maiden at all, also
thanks to you, but at least you could gentle her
before she begins challenging us all to mortal
combat."

"How can you talk so?" Conan protested. "But
moments gone you likened her to your own
daughter."

"Aye," Akeba said gravely, his laughter gone. "I was much concerned with Zorelle's virtue while she lived. I see things differently now. Now she is dead, I hope that she had what joy she could of her life."

"I have not touched her," Conan muttered reluctantly, and bridled at their disbelieving stares. "I rescued her. She's innocent and alone, with none to protect her but me. Mitra's Mercies! As well ask a huntsman to pen a gazelle fawn and slay it there for sport."

Sharak hooted with laughter. "The tiger and the gazelle. But which of you is which? Which hunter, which prey? The wench has you marked, Cimmerian."

" 'Tis true," Akeba said. He essayed a slight smile. "The girl is among those aboard this vessel who think her your wench. Zandru's Nine Hells, do you think to be a holyman?"

"I may let the pair of you swim the rest of the way," Conan growled. "I tell you. . . ." His words trailed off as Muktar loomed over the three men.

The bull-necked man tugged at his beard, spread fan-shaped across his chest, and eyed Conan with speculation. "We are followed," he said finally. "A galley."

Conan rose smoothly to his feet and strode to the stern, Akeba and Sharak scrambling in his wake. Muktar followed more slowly.

"I see nothing but water," the Turanian sergeant complained, shading his eyes. Sharak muttered agreement, squinting furiously.

Conan saw the follower, though, seeming no more than a chip on the water in the distance, but with the faint sweep of motion at its sides that told of long oars straining for speed.

"Pirates?" Conan asked, Although there were many such on the Vilayet Sea, he did not truly believe those who followed were numbered among them.

Muktar shrugged. "Perhaps." He did not sound as if he believed it either.

"What else could they be?" Akeba demanded.

Muktar glanced sideways at Conan, but did not speak.

"I still see nothing," Sharak put in.

"How soon before they come up on us?" Conan said.

"Near dark," Muktar replied. He looked at the gray-green water, its long swells feathering whitely in the wind, then peered at the sky, where pale gray clouds were layered against the afternoon blue. "We may have a storm before, though. The Vilayet is a treacherous bitch."

The Cimmerian's eyes locked on the approaching ship, one huge fist thumping the rail as he thought. How to fight the battle that must come, and win? How?

"If we have a storm," the old astrologer said, "then we will hide from them in it."

"If it comes," Conan told him.

"I have counted their oarstroke," Muktar said abruptly, "and they will kill slaves if they do not slacken it. Yet I do not believe they will. No one cares enough about Hyrkanians to chase them with such vigor. And *Foam Dancer* is a small ship, not a dromond loaded to the gunnels with ivory and spices. It must be you three, or the wench. Have you the crown of Turan hidden in your bales? Is your jade a princess stolen from her father? Why do they follow so?"

"We are traders," Conan said levelly. "And you have been paid to carry us to Hyrkania and back to Turan."

"I've gotten no coin for the last."

"You will get your gold. Unless you let pirates take our trade goods. And your ship. Then all you'll receive is a slaver's manacles, an you survive."

Motioning the others to follow, the big Cimmerian left Muktar muttering into his beard and peering at the ship behind.

In the waist of the ship Conan took a place by the rail where he, too, could watch the galley. It seemed larger, now. Tamur joined them.

"It follows us," Conan said quietly.

"Baalsham," the Hyrkanian snarled at the same instant that Akeba, nodding, said, "Jhandar."

Sharak shook his staff at the galley with surprising fierceness. "Let him send his demons. I am ready for them."

Tamur's dark eyes shone. "This time we will carve him as a haunch of beef if he has a thousand demons."

Conan met Akeba's gaze. It seemed more likely that those on *Foam Dancer* would be meat on a spit.

"How many men does such a vessel carry?" the Turanian asked. "I know little of naval matters."

Conan's own knowledge of the sea was limited to his short time with the smugglers in Sultanapur, but he had been pursued by such vessels before. "There are two banks of oars to a side, but the oar-slaves will not be used to fight. A vessel of that size might carry five score besides the crew."

There was a moment of silence, broken only by the rigging lines humming in the rising wind. Then Sharak said hollowly, "So many? This adventuring begins to seem ill-suited for a man of my years."

"By the One-Father, I shall die happy," Tamur said, "an I know Baalsham goes with me into the long night."

Akeba shook his head bleakly. "He will not be on this ship. Such men send others to do their killing. But at least we shall find blood enough to pay our ferryman's fee, eh, Cimmerian?"

"It will be a glorious fight in which to die," Tamur agreed.

"I do not intend to die yet," the Cimmerian said grimly.

"The storm," Sharak said, his words holding a new excitement. "The storm will hide us." The clouds were thicker now, and darker, obscuring the lowering sun.

"Mayhap," Conan replied. "But we will not depend on that.

The god of the icy peaks and wind-ravaged crags of Conan's Cimmerian homeland was Crom, Dark Lord of the Mound, who gave a man life and will, and nothing more. It was given to each man to carry his own fate in his hands and his heart and his head.

Conan strode aft to Muktar, who still stood gazing at the galley. The bronze glint of its ram could be seen plainly now, knifing through gray swells. "Will they reach us before night falls?"

Conan asked the captain. "Or before the storm breaks?"

"The storm may never break," Muktar muttered. "On the Vilayet lightning may come from a sky where the sun was bright an instant before, or clouds may darken for days, then lift without a drop of rain. Do you lose me my ship, Cimmerian, I'll see your corpse."

"It was in my mind you were a sea captain," Conan taunted, "not an old woman wanting only to play with her grandchildren." He waited for Muktar's neck to swell with anger and his face empurple, then went on. "Listen. We may all be saved. For as long as we are able, we must run before them. Then. . . ."

As Conan spoke the dark color slowly left Muktar's face. Once he blanched, and tried to stop the Cimmerian's flow of words, but Conan would not pause for the other's objections. He pressed on, and after a time Muktar began to listen intently, then to nod.

"It may work," he said finally. "By Dagon's Golden Tail, it may just work. See to your nomads, Cimmerian." Whirling with more agility that would have seemed possible, the bulky captain roared, "To me, you whoreson dogs! To me, and listen to how I'll save your worthless hides still another time!"

"What in Mitra's name is that all about?" Akeba asked when Conan was back at the rail.

As Muktar's voice rose and fell in waves, haranguing the crew in the stern, Conan told his companions what he planned.

A grin appeared on Sharak's thin face, and he

broke into a little dance. "We have them. We have them. What a grand adventure!"

Tamur's smile was wolfish. "Whether we escape or die, this will be a thing to be told around the campfires. Come, Turanian, and show us if any remnant of Hyrkanian blood remains in you." With a wry shake of his head Akeba followed Tamur to join the other nomads.

It was done then, Conan thought. Nothing remained but . . . Yasbet. Even as her name came into his head, she was there before him. Her soft round eyes caressed his face.

"I heard," she said. "Where is my place in this?"

"I will make you a place in the midst of the bales," he told her, "where you will be safe. From archers or slingers, at least."

"I will not hide." Her eyes flashed, suddenly no longer soft. "You've taught me much, but not to be a coward!"

"You'll hide if I must bind you hand and foot. But if it comes to that, I promise you'll not sit without wincing for a tenday. Give me your sword," he added abruptly.

"My sword? No!"

She clutched the hilt protectively, but he snatched the blade from her and started down the deck. She followed in silence, hurt, tear-filled eyes seeming to fill her face.

In front of the mast the ship's grindstone, where the crew sharpened axes and swords alike, was fastened securely to the planking. Working the foot treadle, Conan set the edge of the blunt sica to the spinning stone. Sparks showered from the metal. With his free hand he dripped oil from a clay jug onto the wheel. The heat must not grow too great, or the temper of the blade would be ruined.

Yasbet scrubbed a hand across her cheek, damp with tears. "I thought that you meant to . . . that you. . . ."

"You are no woman warrior," he said gruffly. "Not in these few days. But you may have need to defend yourself, an the worst comes."

"Then you will not make me," she began, but he quelled her with an icy glance. The blood of battle was rising in him, driving out what small softness he had within. When steel was bared, the slightest remnant of gentleness could slay the one who bore it. Fiery sparks fountained from steel that was no harder than him who sharpened it.

XVI

About *Foam Dancer's* deck men rushed, readying the parts of Conan's plan. The clouds darkened above as if dusk had come two turns of the glass before its time, and wind strummed the rigging like a lute, yet no moisture fell on the deck save spume from waves shattering on the bow.

Bit by bit the galley closed the distance, a deadly bronze-beaked centipede skittering across the water, seemingly unimpeded by the rising waves through which *Foam Dancer* now labored, wallowing heavily from trough to trough. *Foam Dancer* seemed a sluggish water beetle, waiting to die.

"They busy themselves in the bows!" Muktar bellowed suddenly.

Conan finished tying the line around Yasbet's waist where she lay between stacked bales, themselves lashed firmly to the deck. "You've no fear of being washed overboard now," he told her, "no matter how violent the storm becomes."

"It's the catapult!" Muktar cried.

Conan started to turn away, but Yasbet seized his hand, pressing her lips to his calloused palm. "I shall be waiting for you," she murmured, "when the battle is done." She tugged his hand lower, and he found his fingers inside her leather jerkin, a swelling breast nestled in his hand.

With an oath he pulled his hand free, though not without reluctance. "There is no time for that now," he said roughly. Did she not realize how difficult it was for him already, he wondered, protecting a wench he longed to ravish?

"They prepare to fire!" Muktar shouted, and Conan put Yasbet from his mind.

"Now!" the young Cimmerian cried. "Cut!"

In the stern Muktar raced to the steering oar, roughly shoving aside the burly steersman to seize the thick wooden shaft himself. In the bow two scruffy smugglers drew curved swords and chopped. Lines parted with loud snaps, and the bundles of extra sailcloth Conan had had put over the side were loosed. The sleek vessel leaped forward, all but jumping from wave-top to wave-top.

Almost beneath her stern a stone fell, half-a-man-weight of granite, raising a fountain that drenched Muktar.

"Now, Muktar!" Conan shouted. Snatching an oilskin bag, he ran aft. "I said now! The rest of you watch the pots!"

The deck was dotted with scores of covered clay pots, scavenged from every corner of the ship. Some hissed as foaming water swirled around them and ran across the planking.

Cursing at the top of his lungs, Muktar heaved at the steersman's oar, its massive thickness bowing from the strain. Slowly *Foam Dancer* responded, coming around. The crew dashed to run out long sweeps, stroking and backing desperately to aid the turn.

This was the point that had made Muktar's face pale when Conan told him of it. Turned broadside to the line of waves, the vessel heeled over, further, further, till her rail lay nearly on the surface. Faces twisted with fear, the smugglers worked their oars with feverish intensity. Akeba, Sharak, and the Hyrkanians scrambled to keep the clay containers from toppling or washing over the side. For a froth-peaked gray mountain of water now rolled over the rail, till it seemed that men waded in shallows.

Among those laboring men Conan's eyes suddenly lit on Yasbet, free of her bonds, struggling among the rest of the pots. His curses were borne away by the wind, and there was no time to do anything about her.

Sluggishly but certainly *Foam Dancer's* bow came into the waves, and the vessel lifted. She did not ride easily, as she had before—there was likely water enough below decks to float a launch—but still she crested that first wave and raced on. Back toward the galley.

On the other ship, the catapult arm stood upright. If another stone had been launched, the splash of its fall had been lost in the rough seas. On the galley's decks, seeing their intended prey turn back on them, men raced about like ants in a crushed anthill. But not so many men as Conan had feared, unless they kept others below. Most of those he could make out wore the twinned gueues of sailors.

"We've lost half the pots!" Akeba shouted over the howling wind. "Gone into the sea!"

"Then ready what we have!" Conan bellowed back. "In full haste!" The Hyrkanians took up oilskin sacks, like that Conan carried.

Those on the other ship, apparently believing their quarry intended to come to grips, had now provided themselves with weapons. Swords, spears and axes bristled along the galley's rail. In its bow, men labored to winch down the catapult's arm for another shot, but too late, Conan knew; *Foam Dancer* was now too close.

Undoing the strings that held the mouth of his sack, Conan drew out its dry contents: a quiver of arrows, each with rags tied behind the head, and a short, recurved bow. Near him a Hyrkanian, already holding his bow, knocked the top from a clay crock. Within coals glowed dully, hissing from the spray that fell inside the container. A few quick puffs fanned them to crackling flame, and into that fire Conan thrust an arrow. The cloth tied to it burst into flame.

In one swift motion the big Cimmerian turned, nocked, drew and released. The fire arrow flew straight up to the galley, lodging in a mast. His was the signal. A shower of fire arrows followed, peppering the galley.

Conan fired again and again as the two ships drew closer. Though now the galley tried to veer away, *Foam Dancer* gave chase. On the galley men rushed with buckets of sand to extinguish points of flame, but two blossomed for each that died. Tendrils of fire snaked up tarred ropes, and a great square sail was suddenly aflame, the conflagration whipped by shrieking wind.

"Closer!" Conan called to Muktar. "Close under the stern!"

The bull-necked man muttered, but *Foam Dancer* curved away from her pursuit, crossing the galley's wake a short spear-throw from its stern.

Hastily Conan capped the pot of coals, edging it

into the oilskin bag with ginger respect for its blistering heat. Once the sack whirled about his head, twice, and then it arced toward the galley, dropping to its deck unnoticed by men frantically cutting away the flaming sail.

"The oil!" Conan shouted even as the sack fell. He seized another jar, this with its lid sealed in place with pitch, and threw it to smash aboard the galley. "Quickly, before the distance widens!"

More sealed pots flew toward the other vessel. Half fell into tossing water, but the rest landed on the galley's stern. The two ships diverged, but now the galley's burning sail was over the side, and her men were turning to *Foam Dancer*.

Conan pounded his fist on the rail. "Where is it?" he muttered. "Why has nothing—"

Flame exploded in the stern of the galley as spreading oil at last reached the coals that had burned out of the sack. Screams rose from the galley, and wild cheers from the men of *Foam Dancer*.

In that instant the rains came at last, a solid sheet of water that cut off all vision of the other ship. Wind that had howled now raged like a mad beast, and Muktar's vessel reeled to the hammer blows of waves that towered above her mast.

"Keep us sailing north!" Conan shouted. He had to put his mouth close to Muktar's ear to be heard, even so.

Straining at the steering oar, the bearded man shook his head. "You do not sail a storm of the Vilayet!" he bellowed. "You survive it!"

And then the wind rose, ripping away even shouted words as they left the mouth, and talk was impossible.

The wind did not abate, nor did the furious waves. Gray mountains of water, their peaks whipped to violent white spray, hurled themselves at *Foam Dancer* as if the gods themselves, angered by her name, would prove that she could not dance with their displeasure. Those who had dared to pit this cockleshell against the unleashed might of the Vilayet could do naught but cling and wait.

After an endless age, the rains began to slacken and, at last, were gone. The wind that flogged choppy waves to whitecaps became no more than stiff, and whipped away the clouds to reveal a bright gibbous moon hung in a black velvet sky, its pale light half changing day for night. There was neither sight nor hint of the galley.

"The fire consumed it," Sharak gloated. "Or the storm."

"Perhaps," Conan answered doubtfully. An the fire had not been well caught, the storm would have extinguished it. And if *Foam Dancer* could ride that tempest, then the galley, if well handled, could have too. To Muktar, who had returned the steering oar to the steersman, he said, "Find the coast. We must find how far we've gone astray."

"By dawn," the bearded man announced confidently. He seemed to feel that the battle with the sea had been his alone; the victory had put even more swagger into his walk.

Yasbet, approaching, laid a hand on Conan's arm. "I must speak with you," she said softly.

"And I with you," he replied grimly. "What in Mitra's name did you mean by—"

But she was walking away, motioning for him to follow, stepping carefully among the night-shrouded shapes of men who had collapsed where they stood from exhaustion. Growling fearsome oaths under his breath, Conan stalked after her. She disappeared into the pale shadow of her sagging tent, its heavy fabric hanging low from the pounding of the storm. Furiously jerking aside the flap, he ducked inside, and had to kneel for lack of headroom.

"Why did you leave where I put you?" he demanded. "And how? I made that knot too firm for your fingers to pick. You could have been killed, you fool wench! And you told me you'd stay there. Promised it!"

She faced his anger, if not calmly at least unflinchingly. "Indeed your fingers wove a strong knot, but the sharp blade you gave me cut it nicely. As to why, you have taught me to defend myself. How could I do that lashed like a bundle for the laundress? And I did *not* promise. I said I would be waiting for you when the battle was done. Did I not better that? I came to find you."

"I remember a promise!" he thundered. "And you broke it!"

Disconcertingly, she smiled and said quietly, "Your cloak is wet through." Delicate fingers unfastened the bronze pin that held the garment, and soft arms snaked about his neck as she pushed the cloak from his shoulders. Sensuous lips brushed the line of his jaw, his ear.

"Stop that," he growled, pushing her away. "You'll not distract me from my purpose. Had I a switch to hand, you would think yourself better off in your amah's grasp."

With an exasperated sigh she leaned on one arm, frowning at him. "But you have no switch," she said. As he stared in amazement, she undid the laces of her jerkin and drew it over her head. Full, rounded breasts swung free, shimmering satin flesh that dried his throat. "Still," she went on, "your hand is hard, and your arm strong. I have no doubt it will suffice for your—purpose, did you call it?" Boots and trousers joined the jerkin. Twisting on her knees to face away from him, she pressed her face to the deck.

Conan swallowed hard. Those lush buttocks of honeyed ivory would have brought sweat to the face of a statue, and he was all too painfully aware at that moment that he was flesh and blood. "Cover yourself, girl," he said hoarsely, "and stop this game. 'Tis dangerous, for I am no girl's toy."

"And I play no game," she said, kneeling erect again, her knees touching his. She made no move toward her garments. "I know that all aboard this vessel think I am your . . . your leman." Her cheeks pinkened; that, more than her nudity, made him groan and squeeze his eyes shut. A brief look of triumph flitted across her face. "Have I not complained to you before," she said fiercely, "about protecting me when I did not want to be protected?"

Unclenching white-knuckled fists, he pulled her to him; she gasped as she was crushed against his chest. "The toying is done, wench," he growled. "Say go, and I will go. But if you do not. . . ." He toppled them both to the deck, her softness a cushion under him, his agate blue eyes gazing into hers with unblinking intensity.

"I am no girl," she breathed, "but a woman. Stay." She wore a triumphant smile openly now.

Conan thought it strange, that smile, but she was indeed a woman, and his mind did not long remain on smiles.

XVII

From a rocky headland covered with twisted, stunted scrub, waves crashing at its base, Conan peered inland, watching for Tamur's return. The nomad had claimed that he would have horses for them all in three or four turns of the glass, but he had left at dawn, and the sun sat low in its journey toward the western horizon.

On a short stretch of muddy sand north of the headland *Foam Dancer* lay drawn up, heeling over slightly on her keel. An anchor had been carried up the beach to dunes covered with tall, sparse brown grass, its long cable holding the vessel against the waves that tugged at her stern. Cooking fires dotted the sand between the ship and the dunes. Yasbet's tent had been pitched well away from the blankets of the Hyrkanians and the sailors, scattered among their piles of driftwood.

As Conan turned back to his scanning, a plume of dust inland and to the south caught his eye. It could be Tamur, with the horses, or it could be . . . who? He wished he knew more about this land. At least the sentry he had set atop the highest of the dunes could see the dust, too. He glanced in that direction and bit back an oath. The man was gone! The dust was closer, horses plain at its base. Tamur? Or some other?

Making an effort to appear casual, he walked up the headland to where a steep downward slope led to the beach, dotted with wind-sculpted trees, their gnarled roots barely finding a grip in the rocky soil. Between the dunes and the plain lay thickets of such growth. He half-slid down that slope, still making an effort to show no haste.

At the fires he leaned over Akeba, who sat cross-legged before a fire, honing his sword. "Horsemen approach," he said quietly. "I know not if it is Tamur or others. But the sentry is nowhere to be seen."

Stiffening, the Turanian slid his honing stone into his pouch and his curved blade into its scabbard. He had removed his distinctive tunic and spiral helmet, for the Turanian army was little loved on this side of the Vilayet. "I will take a walk in the dunes. You can see to matters here?" Conan nodded, and Akeba, taking up a spade as if answering a call of nature, strolled toward the dunes.

"Yasbet!" Conan called, and she appeared at the flap of her tent. He motioned her to come to him.

She made a great show of buckling on her sword belt and adjusting its fit on her hips before making her way slowly across the sand. As soon as she was in arm's reach of him, he grabbed her shoulders and firmly sat her down in the protection of a large driftwood bole.

"Stay there," he said when she made to rise. Turning to the others, scattered among the campfires, he said, as quietly as he could and still be heard, "None of you move." Some turned their faces to him curiously, and Muktar got to his feet. "I said, 'don't move!' " Conan snapped. Such was the tone of command in his voice that the bearded captain obeyed. Conan went on quickly. "Horsemen will be here any moment. I know not who. Be still!" A Hyrkanian drew back the hand he had stretch forth for his bow, and a sailor, who had risen with a look of running on his face, froze. "Besides this, the sentry has disappeared. Someone may be watching us. Choose your place of cover and when I give the word—not yet!— seize your weapons and be ready. Now!"

In an instant the beach seemed to become deserted as men rolled behind piles of driftwood. Conan snatched a bow and quiver, and dropped behind the bole with Yasbet. He raised himself enough to barely look over it, searching the dunes.

"Why did you see to my safety before telling the others?" Yasbet demanded crossly. "All my life I have been wrapped in swaddling. I will be coddled no longer."

"Are you the hero in a saga, then?" Was that the drumming of hooves he heard? Where in Zandru's Nine Hells was Akeba? "Are you impervious to steel and proof against arrows?"

"A heroine," she replied. "I will be a heroine, not a hero."

Conan snorted. "Sagas are fine for telling before a fire of a cold night, or for entertaining children, but we are made of flesh and blood. Steel can draw blood, and arrows pierce the flesh. Do I ever see you attempting to be a hero—or a heroine— you'll think your bottom has suddenly become a drum. Be still, now."

Without taking his eyes from the dunes he felt the arrows in his quiver, checking the fletching.

"Will we die then, Conan, on this pitiful beach?" she asked.

"Of course not," he said quickly. "I'll take you

back to Aghrapur and put pearls around your neck, if I don't return you to Fatima for a stubborn wench first." Of a certainty the sound of galloping horses was closer.

For a long moment she seemed to consider that. Then suddenly she shouted, "Conan of Cimmeria is my lover, and I his! I glory in sharing his blankets!"

Conan stared at her. "Crom, girl! I told you to be still!"

"If I am to die, I want the world to know what we share."

As Conan opened his mouth, the drumming abruptly became a thunder, and scores of horses burst over the dunes, spraying muddy sand beneath their hooves, roiling in a great circle on the beach. Conan nocked an arrow, then hesitated when he saw that many of the horses had no riders. Tamur appeared out of the shifting mass of riders.

"Do not loose!" Conan shouted, striding out to meet the Hyrkanian, who swung down from his horse as Conan approached. "Erlik take you, Tamur! You could have ended wearing more feathers than a goose, riding in that way."

"Did not Andar tell you who we were?" The scarred Hyrkanian said, frowning. "I saw you set him to watch."

"He was relieving himself," Akeba said disgustedly, joining them, "and did not bother to set another in his place." He was trailed by a narrow-jawed Hyrkanian, greased mustaches framing his mouth and chin.

Tamur glared at the man, who shrugged and said, "What is there to watch for, Tamur? These

scavenging dung-rollers?" Andar jerked his head
at the mounted men, who sat their small, shaggy
horses in a loose circle about those they herded.

"You did not keep watch as you were told,"
Tamur grated. He turned and called to the other
Hyrkanians, "Does any here stand for this one?"
None answered.

Alarm flashed onto Andar's face, and he grabbed for his yataghan. Tamur spun back to the
mustached man, his blade flashing from its
scabbard, striking. Andar fell, sword half-drawn,
his nearly severed neck spurting blood into the
sand.

Tamur kicked the still-jerking body. "Take this
defiler of his mother's womb into the dunes and
leave him with the offal he thought was more important than keeping watch."

Two of the Hyrkanians seized the dead man by
his ankles and dragged him away. None of the
others so much as twitched an eyebrow. Behind
him Conan could hear Yasbet retching.

"At least you got the horses," Conan said.

"They look more like sheep," Akeba muttered.

Tamur gave the Turanian a pained look. "Perhaps, but they are the best mounts to be found on
the coast. Hark you now, Conan. These horse
traders tell me they have seen other strangers.
Give them what they ask for the mounts, and they
will tell what they know."

"What they ask," Conan said drily. "They would
not be blood kin of yours, would they, Tamur?"

The Hyrkanian looked astonished. "You are an
outlander, Cimmerian, and ignorant, so I will not
kill you. They are the scavengers and dung-rollers
Andar named them, living by digging roots and

robbing the nests of sea-birds. From time to time they loot a ship driven ashore by a storm." He thrust his blade into the sand to clean away Andar's blood. "They are no better than savages. Come, I will take you to their leader."

The men on the shaggy horses were a ragged lot, their sheepskin coats motheaten, their striped tunics threadbare and even filthier than when they were worn by seamen whose luckless vessels had ended on this coast. The leader was a stringy, weather-beaten man with one suspicious, darting eye and a sunken socket where the other had been. About his neck he wore a necklace of amethysts, half the gilding worn from the brass. It seemed one of those ships had carried a trull.

"This is Baotan," Tamur said, gesturing to the one-eyed man. "Baotan, this is Conan, a trader known in far lands and a warrior feared by many."

Baotan grunted and shifted his eye to Conan. "You want my horses, trader? For each horse, five blankets, a sword and an axe, plus a knife, a cloak, and five pieces of silver."

"Too much," Conan said.

Tamur groaned. For Conan's ear alone, he mutter, "Forget the trading, Cimmerian. 'Tis the means to destroy Baalsham we seek."

Conan ignored him. Poor traders were little respected, and a lack of respect would mean poor information if not outright lies. "For every two horses, one blanket and one sword."

Baotan showed the stumps of yellowed teeth in a grin, and climbed down from his horse. "We talk," he said.

The talk, Baotan and Conan squatting by one of the campfires, was more leisurely than Conan would have liked, yet he had to maintain his pose as a trader. Tamur produced clay jugs of sour Hyrkanian beer and lumps of mare's milk cheese. The beer made Baotan's eyes light up, but the one-eyed man gave ground grudgingly, and often stopped bargaining entirely to talk of the weather or some incident in his camp.

At last, though, the bargain was struck. The sky was beginning to darken; men dragged in more driftwood to pile on the fires. For the pack horses they needed, one sword and one blanket. For the animals they would ride, one axe and one blanket. Plus a knife for every man with Baotan and two pieces of gold for the stringy man himself.

"Done," Conan said.

Baotan nodded and began to produce items from beneath his coat. A pouch. A small pair of tongs. What appeared to be a copy of a bull's horn, half-sized and molded in clay. Before Conan's astonished gaze, Baotan stuffed herbs from the pouch into the clay horn. With the tongs, the one-eyed man deftly plucked a coal from the fire and used it to puff the herbs to a smouldering burn. Conan's jaw dropped as the man drew deeply on the horn, inhaling the pungent smoke. Tilting back his head, Baotan expelled the smoke in a long stream toward the sky, then offered the horn to Conan.

Tamur leaned close to speak in his ear. " 'Tis the way they seal a bargain. You must do the same. I told you they were savages."

Conan was prepared to believe it. Doubtfully he took the clay horn. The smouldering herbs smelled like a fire in a rubbish heap. Putting it to his mouth, he inhaled, and barely suppressed a grimace. It tasted even worse than it smelled, and felt hot enough to blister his tongue. Fighting an urge to gag, he blew a stream of smoke toward the sky.

"They mix powdered dung with the herbs," Tamur said, grinning, "to insure even burning."

From across the fire Akeba laughed. "Would you like some aged mussels, Cimmerian?" he called, near to rolling on the sand.

Conan ground his teeth and handed the clay horn back to Baotan, who stuck the horn in his mouth and began to emit small puffs of smoke. The Cimmerian shook his head. He had seen many strange customs since leaving the mountains of his homeland, but, sorcery aside, this was certainly the strangest.

When his mouth no longer felt as if he were attempting to eat a coal from the fire—though the taste yet remained—Conan said, "Have you seen any other strangers on the coast? You understand that I must be concerned with other traders."

"Strangers," Baotan said through teeth clenched around the clay horn, "but no traders." Each word came out accompanied by a puff of smoke. "They bought horses, too. No trade goods. Silver." He grinned suddenly. "They paid too much."

"Not traders," Conan said, pretending to muse. "That is strange indeed."

"Strangers are strangers. Their boat was much charred at the back, and some of them suffered from burns."

The galley. It had survived both fire and storm after all. "Perhaps we might help these men," Conan said. "How far off are they, and in which direction?"

Baotan waved a hand to the south. "Half a day. Maybe a day."

Far enough that they might not know *Foam Dancer* had also survived. But if that was so, why the horses? Perhaps there *was* something here that Jhandar feared. Conan felt excitement rising.

"Use our campfires this night," he said to Baotan. "Akeba, Tamur, we ride at first light."

Yasbet appeared from the dark to nestle her hip against Conan's shoulder. "It grows cold," she said. "Will you warm me?" Ribald laughter rose from the listening men, but, oddly, a glare from her silenced them, even Tamur and Baotan.

"That I will," Conan said, and as he rose flipped her squealing over his shoulder.

Her squeals had turned to laughter by the time they reached her tent. "Put me down, Conan," she managed between giggles. " 'Tis unseemly."

Suddenly the hair on the back of his neck rose, and he whirled, staring into the dark, at the headland.

"Are you trying to make me dizzy, Conan? What is it?"

Imaginings, he told himself. Naught but imaginings. The galley and those it carried were far to the south, sure *Foam Dancer* and all aboard had perished in the storm.

" 'Tis nothing, wench," he growled. She squealed with laughter as he ducked into the tent.

Che Fan rose slowly from the shadows where he had dropped, and peered at the beach below, dotted with campfires. There was no more to learn by watching. The barbarian was abed for the night. He made his way across the headland and down the far slope, gliding surefooted over the rough ground, a wraith in the night.

Suitai was waiting at their small fire—well shielded by scrub growth—along with the six they had chosen from the uninjured to accompany them. The men huddled silently on the far side of the fire from the Khitans. They had seen just enough on the voyage to guess that the two black-robed men carried a sort of deadliness they had never before encountered. Thus they feared greatly, and wisely, although still ignorant.

"What did you see?" Suitai asked. He sipped at a steaming decoction of herbs.

Che Fan squatted by the fire, filling a cup with the same bitter liquid as he spoke. "They are there. And they have obtained horses from that dung-beetle Baotan."

"Then let us go down and kill them," Suitai said. "It may be more difficult if we must find them again." The six who had accompanied them from the galley shifted uneasily, but the Khitans did not appear to notice.

"Not until they have found what they came to seek," Che Fan replied. "The Great Lord will not be pleased if we return with naught but word of their deaths." He paused. "We must be careful of the barbarian called Conan."

"He is but a man," Suitai said, "and will die as easily as any other."

Che Fan nodded slowly, uncertain why he had spoken such a thing aloud. And yet. . . . In his boyhood had he learned the art of appearing invisible, of hiding in the shadow of a leaf and becoming one with the night, but there was that about the muscular barbarian's gaze that seemed to penetrate all such subterfuge. That was nonsense, he told himself. He was of the Brothers of the Way, and this Conan *was* but a man. He would die as easily as any other. Yet . . . the doubts remained.

XVIII

Tugging his cloak closer about him against the brisk wind, Conan twisted on his sheepskin saddle pad to look behind for the hundredth time since dawn. Short-grassed plain and rolling hills, so sparsely grown with a single stunted tree was a startlement, revealed no sign of pursuit. Disgruntled, he faced front. The pale yellow sun, giving little warmth in the chill air, rose ahead of them toward its zenith. The Vilayet lay two nights behind. No matter what his eyes told him, deeper instinct said that someone followed, and that instinct had kept him alive at times when more civilized senses failed.

The party rode well bunched, half of the Hyrkanians leading strings of pack horses, cursing. The small beasts, seeming little larger than the hampers and bales lashed to their pack saddles, tried to turn their tails into the wind whenever they found slack in the lead ropes. The men not so encumbered kept hands near weapons and eyes swiveling in constant watch. It was not unknown for travelers to be attacked on the plains of Hyrkania. Traders were usually immune, but more than one had lost his head.

Tamur galloped his shaggy horse between Conan and Akeba. "Soon we shall be at the Blasted Lands."

"You have been saying that since we left the

sea," Conan grumbled. His temper was not improved by the way his feet dangled on either side of his diminutive mount.

"A few more hills, Cimmerian. But a few more. And you must be ready to play the trader. One of the tribes is sure to be camped nearby. Each takes its turn guarding the Blasted Lands."

"You've said that as well."

"I hope we find a village soon," Yasbet said through clenched teeth. She half stood in her stirrups then, seeing the amusement that flitted across the men's faces, sat again hastily, wincing.

Conan managed to keep a straight face. "There is liniment in one of the packs," he offered. It was not his first time to do so.

"No," she said brusquely, the same answer she had given to his other offers. "I need no coddling."

" 'Tis not coddling," he snapped, exasperated. "Anyone may use liniment for a sore . . . muscle."

"Let him rub some on," Sharak chortled. The astrologer clung to his horse awkwardly, like a stick figure placed on a pony by children. "Or if not him, wench, then let me."

"Still your tongue, old man," Akeba said, grinning. "I see you ride none too easily yourself, and I may take it in mind to coat you with so much liniment that you run ahead of us the rest of the way."

"You have done well, woman," Tamur said suddenly, surprising everyone. "I thought we would have to tie you across your saddle before the sun was high, but you have the determination of a Hyrkanian."

"I thank you," she told him, glaring at the Cimmerian. "I was not allow . . . that is, I have never ridden before. I walked, or was carried in a palanquin." She eased herself on her saddle pad and muttered an oath. Sharak cackled until he broke into a fit of coughing. "I will use the liniment this night," Yasbet said stiffly, "though I am not certain the cure won't be worse than the disease."

"Good," Conan said, "else by tomorrow you'll not be able to walk, much less—" He broke off as they topped a rise. Spread before them was a great arc of yurts. More than a thousand of the domed felt structures dotted the rolling plain like gray mushrooms. "There's the encampment you predicted, Tamur. I suppose 'tis time for us to begin acting the part of traders."

"Wait. This could be ill,' the nomad said. "There are perhaps four tribes camped here, not one. Among so many there may well be one who remembers that we swore vengeance on Baalsham despite the ban. Do they realize we have brought you here to break the taboo on the Blasted Lands. . . ." A murmur rose from the other Hyrkanians.

From the tents two score of fur-capped horsemen galloped toward them, lance points glittering in the rising sun.

"It is too late to turn back, now." Conan kicked his mount forward. "Follow me, and remember to look like traders."

"For violating a taboo," Tamur said, trailing after the Cimmerian, "a man is flayed alive, and kept so for days while other parts important to a man are removed slowly. Burning slivers are thrust into his flesh."

"Flayed?" Sharak said hollowly. "Other parts?

Burning slivers? Perhaps we could turn back after all?''

Yet he followed as well, as did the others, Yasbet riding with shoulders back and hand on sword hilt, Akeba in an apparently casual slouch above the cased bow strapped ahead of his saddle pad. The rest of the Hyrkanians came more slowly, muttering, but they came.

Tamur raised his sword hand in greeting—and no doubt to show that he did not intend to draw the weapon—as they approached the other horsemen. "I see you. I am called Tamur, and am returned to my people from across the sea, bringing with me this trader, who is called Conan.''

"I see you," the leader of the mounted nomads said, lifting his right hand. Squat and dark, mustaches thick with grease dangling below his chin, he eyed Conan suspiciously from beneath the fur cap pulled down to his shaggy brows. "I am called Zutan. It is late in the year for traders.''

Conan put on a broad smile. "Then there will be no others to compete with me.''

Zutan stared at him, expressionless, for a long moment. Then, wheeling his horse, he motioned them to follow.

The riders from the encampment spread out in two lines, one to either side of Conan and his party, escorting them—or guarding them, perhaps —into the midst of the yurts, to a large open space in the center of the crescent. People gathered around them, men in fur caps and thick sheepskin coats, women in long woolen dresses, dyed in a rainbow of colors, with hooded fur cloaks held close about them. Those males who had reached an age to be called men were uniformly surrounded by the rankness of rancid grease, and those of middle years or beyond were so weathered and leather-skinned as to make their ages all but impossible to tell. The women, however, were another matter. There were toothless crones among them, and wrinkled hags, but one and all they seemed *clean*. Many of the younger women were pretty enough for any zenana. They moved lithely to the tinkle of ankle bells beneath their skirts, and more than one set of dark, kohled eyes followed the young giant above full, smiling lips.

Sternly Conan forced himself to ignore the women. He had come for a means to destroy Jhandar, not to disport himself with nomad wenches. Nor would the need to kill father, brother, husband or lover help him. Nor would trouble with Yasbet.

As he swung down from his wooly mount, Conan leaned close to Tamur and spoke softly. "Why do the women not grease their hair also?"

Tamur looked shocked. " 'Tis a thing for men, Cimmerian." He shook his head. "Hark you. I have meant to speak on this to you for some time. Many traders adopt this custom while among us. It would aid your disguise to be seen to do so. Perhaps you could grow a mustache as well? And this washing you insist on is a womanly thing. It saps the strength."

"I will think on these things," Conan said. He noticed Akeba, a wry smile on his dark face, peering at him over his horse.

"Long mustaches," the Turanian said. "And mayhap a beard like that of Muktar."

Conan growled, but before he could reply a

sharp cry broke from Yasbet. He spun to see her half fall from her saddle-pad in attempting to dismount. Darting, he caught her before she collapsed completely to the ground.

"What ails you, wench?"

"My legs, Conan," she moaned. "They will not support me. And my . . . my. . . ." Her face reddened. "My . . . muscles are sore," she whispered.

"Liniment," he said, and she moaned again. The crowd about them stirred. Hastily he lifted her back to her feet and put her hands on her sheepskin saddle-pad. "Hold to that. You must keep your feet a moment longer." Half-sobbing, she tangled her hands in the thick wool; he turned immediately from her to more pressing matters.

Zutan pushed his way to the forefront of those watching. Four squat, bow-legged elders followed him, and the murmurs of the onlookers were stilled. "I present to you," Zutan intoned, "the trader called Co-nan. Know, Co-nan, that you are presented to the chiefs of the four tribes here assembled, to Olotan, to Arenzar, to Zoan, to Sibuyan. Know that you are presented to men who answer only to the Great King. Know this, and tremble."

It was near impossible to tell the age of any man above five-and-twenty in those tribes, but these men had surely each amassed three times so many years, if not four. Their faces were gullied rather than wrinkled, and had the color and texture of a boot left ten years in the desert sun. The hair that straggled from under their filthy fur caps was as white as bleached parchment, beneath a coating of grease, and their mustaches, just as pale, were long and thin. One had no teeth at all, muttering through his gums, while the other three showed blackened stumps when they opened their mouths. Yet the eight black eyes that peered at him were hard and clear, and there was no tremor in the bony hands that rested lightly on the hilts of their yataghans.

Conan raised his right hand in the greeting Tamur had used. What did traders say at these times, he wondered. Whatever he said, though, it had best come fast. Zutan was beginning to tug at his mustache impatiently. "I see you. I am honored to be presented to you. I will trade fairly with your people."

The four stared at him unblinkingly. Zutan's tugging at his mustache became more agitated.

What else was he supposed to say, Conan thought. Or do? Suddenly he turned his back on the chiefs and hurried back among the pack animals. Mutters sounded among the tribesmen, and the Hyrkanians who held the guide-ropes eyed him with frowns. Hastily he unroped a wicker hamper and drew out four tulwars, their hilts ivory and ebony. The blades had been worked with beeswax and acid into scenes of men hunting with bows from horseback, with silver rubbed across the etchings hammered till the argentine metal shone. Conan had raised a storm when he found the blades among the trade goods—he was still of a mind that Tamur had meant them for himself and his friends—but they had already been paid for. Now he was glad of them.

As the Cimmerian returned, two swords in each huge fist, Tamur groaned, "Not those, northerner. Some other blades. Not those."

Conan reached the four chiefs and, after a

moment, awkwardly sketched a bow. "Accept these, ah, humble gifts as a, ah, token of my admiration."

Dark eyes sparked avariciously, and the blades were snatched as if the squat men expected them to be withdrawn. The etched steel was fingered; for a time Conan was ignored. At last the chief nearest him—Conan thought he was the one called Sibuyan—looked up. "You may trade here," he said. Without another word the four turned away, still fingering their new swords.

Akeba put a hand on Conan's arm. "Come, Cimmerian. We traders must display our wares."

"Then display them. I must see to Yasbet."

As he returned to her, Conan ignored the bustle of hampers being lifted from pack saddles, of pots and knives, swords and cloaks being spread for eager eyes. The throng pressed close, many calling offers of furs, or ivory, or gold as soon as items appeared. Some of Tamur's followers began gathering the horses.

Yasbet had sagged to her hands and knees on the hard-packed ground beside her mount. Muttering an oath Conan stripped off his cloak and spread it on the ground. When he had her lying on it, face down, he removed the sheepskin saddle-pad from her horse and put it beneath her head.

"Are you all right?" he asked. "Can you stand at all?"

"I do not need to be wrapped in swaddling," she replied between clenched teeth.

"Hannuman's Stones, wench! I do not swaddle you. You must be able to ride when it is time to go."

She sighed, not looking at him. "I can neither

stand nor ride. I cannot even sit." She laughed mirthlessly.

"It is possible we may have to leave suddenly," he said slowly. "It may be needful to tie you across a saddle. And again I do not mean to mock you by that."

"I know," she said quietly. Suddenly she grasped his hand and pulled it to her lips. "You have not only my body," she murmured, "but my heart and my soul. I love you, Conan of Cimmeria."

Brusquely he pulled his hand away and stood. "I must see to the others," he muttered. "You will be all right here? It may be some time before your tent can be put up."

"I am comfortable."

Her words were so soft he barely heard them. With a quick nod he strode to where the trade goods were displayed. Why did women always have to speak of love, he wondered. The most calloused trull would do it, given a fingerbreadth of encouragement, and other women took even less. Then they expected a man to act like a giddy boy with his first hair on his chin. Or worse, like a poet or a bard.

He glanced back at Yasbet. Her face was buried in the sheepskin, and her shoulders shook as if she cried. No doubt her rump pained her. Growling wordlessly under his breath, he joined his fellows acting the trader.

Sharak bounced from nomad to nomad, always gesticulating, here offering lumps of beeswax, there pewter cups from Khauran or combs of tortoise shell from Zamboula or lengths of Vendhyan silk. Akeba was more sedate in his demonstrations of the weapons, tulwars bearing the stamp of the Royal Arsenal of Turan, glaives from far Aquilonia, and even khetens, broad-bladed battleaxes from Stygia. Tamur and his men, on the other hand, squatted to one side, passing among themselves clay jars of the ale they had gotten from men of the tribes.

Conan walked among the goods, stopping from time to time to listen to Akeba or Sharak bargain, nodding as if he agreed with what was being done. A merchant who had two men to do the actual peddling surely was not expected to do more.

The trading was brisk, but Conan was soon thinking more of quenching his thirst with a crock of ale than of his playacting. It was then that he noticed the woman.

Past her middle years, she was yet a beauty, tall and well-breasted, with large dark eyes and full red lips. Her fur-trimmed blue cloak was of fine wool, and her kirtle of green was slashed with panels of blue silk. Her necklace of intricate links was gold, not gilded brass; the brooch that held her cloak was a large emerald; and the bracelets at her wrists were of matched amethysts. And she had no eye for the perfumes or gilded trinkets that Sharak bartered away. Her gaze never left the muscular Cimmerian. An interested gaze.

Conan judged her to be the woman of a wealthy man, perhaps even of a chief. That made her just the sort of woman he should avoid, even more so than the other women of the tribe. He made sure there was nothing in his expression that she could read as invitation, and turned away to make a show of studying the goods laid out on a nearby blanket.

"You are young to be a trader," a deep female voice said behind him.

He turned to find himself face to face with the woman who had been watching him. "I am old enough," he said in a flat tone. His youth was a touchy point with him, especially with women.

Her smile was half mocking, half . . . something more. "But you are still young."

"A man must begin at some age. Do you wish to trade for something?"

"I would think you would be demonstrating the swords and spears to the men, youngling." Her gaze caressed the breadth of his shoulders, trailed like fingers across the tunic strained by the muscles of his deep chest.

"Perhaps kohl for your eyes." He snatched a small blue-glazed jar from the blanket and held it out to her. His eyes searched the crowd for a man taking an unfriendly interest in their conversation. This woman would have men after her when she was a grandmother.

"From the way that sword sits on your hip, I would name you, not merchant, but. . ." she put a finger to her lips as if in thought ". . .warrior."

"I am a trader," he said emphatically."If not kohl, perhaps perfume?"

"Nothing," she said, amusement in her eyes. "For now, at least. Later I will have something from you." She turned away, then stopped to look at him over her shoulder. "And that *is* perfume. Trader." Her laughter, low and musical, hung in the air after she had disappeared into the crowd.

With a sudden sharp crack the small jar shattered in Conan's grip.

"Erlik take all women," he muttered, brushing

shards of glazed pottery from his hand. There was nothing to be done about the smell of jasmine that hung about him in a cloud.

Grumbling, he resumed his pacing among the trade goods. Occasionally a man would glance at him in surprise, nose wrinkling, or a woman would eye him and smile. Each time he hurried furiously elsewhere, muttering ever more sulphurous oaths under his breath. A bath, he decided. When their camp was set he would bathe, and Mitra blast all the Hyrkanians if they thought it unmanly.

XIX

Throughout the day the trading continued briskly, goods from the west for goods looted from eastern caravans. As twilight empurpled the air Zutan returned. The bargaining tribespeople began to trail away at his appearance.

"I will show you to your sleeping place," the greasy-mustached Hyrkanian said. "Come." And he stalked off in the rolling walk of one more used to the back of a horse than to his own feet.

Conan set the others to repacking the trade goods, then scooped Yasbet into his arms. She was in an exhausted sleep so deep that she barely stirred as he carried her after Zutan, to a spot a full three hundred paces from the yurts.

"You sleep here," the nomad said. "It would be dangerous to leave your fires after dark. The guards do not know you. You might be injured." That thought apparently caused no pain in his heart. Traders might be necessary, his expression said, but they warranted neither the hospitality of shelter nor trust.

Conan ignored him—it was better than killing him, though less satisfying—and commanded Yasbet's tent to be erected. As soon as the stakes were driven and the ropes drawn taut, he carried her inside. She gave but a sleepy murmur as he removed her garments and wrapped her in blankets.

Perhaps sleep would help her, he thought. His

192

nose twitched at the scent of jasmine that was beginning to fill the tent. Sleep would not help him.

When he went outside, Zutan was gone. The sky grew blacker by the moment, and fires of dried dung cast small pools of light. The yurts could have been half a world away, for their lamps and fires were all inside, and the encampment of the tribes was lost in the dark. The horses had been tied to a picket line, near which the hampers of trade goods were shadowy mounds.

Straight to those mounds Conan went, rummaging through them until he found a lump of harsh soap. Thrusting it into his belt pouch, he hefted two water bags in each hand and stalked into the night. When he returned an odor of lye came from him, and it was all he could do to stop his teeth from chattering in the chill wind that whipped across the plain.

Settling crosslegged beside the fire where a kettle of thick stew bubbled, he accepted a horn spoon and a clay bowl filled to the brim.

"I am not certain that lye improves on jasmine," Akeba said, sniffing the air pointedly.

"A fine scent, jasmine," Sharak cackled. "You are a little large for a dancing girl, Cimmerian, but I do believe it became you more than your new choice." Tamur choked on stew and laughter.

Conan raised his right hand, slowly curling it into a massive fist until his knuckles cracked. "I smell nothing." He looked challengingly at each of the other three in turn. "Does anyone else?"

Chuckling, Akeba spread his hands and shook his head.

"All this washing is bad for you," Tamur said, then added quickly as Conan made to rise, "But I smell naught. You are a violent man, Cimmerian, to act so over a jest among friends."

"We will talk of other things," Conan said flatly.

Silence reigned for a moment before Sharak spoke up. "Trade. We'll talk of trade. Conan, it is no wonder merchants are men of wealth. What we bargained for today will bring at least three hundred pieces of gold in Aghrapur, yet a full two-thirds of the trade goods remain. Mayhap we should give up adventuring and become traders in truth. I have never been rich. I think I would find it pleasing."

"We are here for more important matters than gold," Conan growled. He set aside his bowl; his hunger had left him. "Know you that we have been followed since the coast?"

Tamur looked up sharply. "Baotan? I thought he had an eye for more than he received for the horses."

"Not Baotan," Conan replied.

"You looked back often," Akeba said thoughtfully, "but said nothing. And I saw no one."

Conan shook his head, choosing his words with care. "Nor did I see anyone. Still, someone was following. Or something. There was a feel . . . not human about it."

Sharak laughed shakily. "An Jhandar, or Baalsham, or whatever he chooses to call himself, has come after us to these wastes, I will think on journeying to Khitai. Or further, if there is any place further."

"Baalsham is a man," Tamur said nervously. He eyed the surrounding darkness and edged closer to the fire, dropping his voice. "But the spirits—if he has sent dead men after us. . . ."

A footstep sounded beyond the small pool of light from the fire, and Conan found himself on his feet, broadsword in hand. He was somewhat mollified to see that the others had drawn weapons as well. Even the old astrologer was shakily holding his staff out like a spear.

Zutan stepped into the light and stopped, staring at the bared steel.

Conan sheathed his blade with a grunt. "It is dangerous to leave your fires in the dark," he said.

The Hyrkanian's mustache twitched violently, but all he said was, "Samarra will see you now, Co-nan."

"Samarra!" Tamur's voice was a dry speak. "She is here?"

"Who is this Samarra?" Conan demanded. "Mayhap I do not wish to see her."

"No, Conan," Tamur said insistently. "You must. Samarra is a powerful shamaness. *Very* powerful."

"A shamaness," Sharak snorted. "Women should not be allowed to meddle in such matters."

"Hold your tongue, old man," Tamur snapped, "else you may find your manhood turned to dust, or your bones to water. She is powerful, I say." He had turned his back to Zutan and was grimacing vigorously at Conan.

The young Cimmerian eyed him doubtfully, wondering if Tamur's fear of this woman was enough to unhinge him. "Why does Samarra wish to see me?" he asked.

"Samarra does not give reasons," Zutan replied. "She summons, and those she summons come. Even chiefs."

"I will go to her," Conan said.

Tamur's groan was loud as Conan followed Zutan into the dark.

They walked to the yurts in silence. The nomad would not deign to converse with a trader, and Conan had his own thoughts to occupy him. Why did this Samarra wish to speak with him? Her sorcerous arts could have told her the true reason for his presence in Hyrkania, but only if she had purposely sought it out. In his experience of such things nothing was found unsought, and nothing was sought casually. Knowledge had its price when gained by thaumaturgical means, and though he had met sorcery and magic in many forms, never had he known it used to satisfy mere curiosity.

Had this Samarra been a man he could have first explained, then, an that did not work, slain the fellow. But it was not in him to kill a woman.

Lost in the workings of his mind, Conan started when the other halted before a huge yurt and motioned him to enter. The structure of felt stretched on wooden frames was at least twenty paces across, fit for a chief. But then, he told himself, a shamaness who could summon chiefs would certainly live as well as they. Without another glance at Zutan, he pushed open the flap and went in.

He found himself in a large chamber within the yurt, its "walls" brocaded hangings. The ground was covered by Kasmiri carpets in a riot of colors, dotted with cushions of silk. Gilded lamps hung on golden chains from the wooden frames of the roof, and a charcoal fire in a large bronze brazier provided warmth against the chill outside.

So much he had time to note, then his eyes

popped as eight girls burst from behind the
hangings. From lithe to full-bodied they ranged,
and their skins from a paleness that spoke of
Aquilonia to Hyrkanian brownness to the yellow
of well-aged ivory. Gilded bells tinkled at their
ankles as they ran giggling to surround him; such
was the whole of their costume.

His vision seemed filled by rounded breasts and
buttocks as they urged him to a place on the
cushions before the brazier. A scent of roses hung
about them.

No sooner was he seated than two darted away
to return with damp cloths to wipe his face and
hands. Another set a chased silver tray of dates
and dried apricots by his side, while a fourth
poured wine from a crystal flagon into a goblet of
beaten gold.

The music of flutes and zithers filled the
chamber; the remaining girls had taken up the in-
struments and, seating themselves cross-legged,
played. The four who had served him began to
dance.

"Where is Samarra?" he asked. "Well? Answer
me! Where is she?" The music soared, and the
dancers with it, but none spoke.

He picked up the goblet, but put it down again
untouched. Strong powders could be put in wine;
he wagered that this shamaness knew of them.
Best he neither eat nor drink till he was gone from
Samarra's dwelling place. And best he not eye the
girls too closely, either. Mayhap the shamaness
had a reason for wishing his attention occupied.
He kept a close watch on the hangings, and a hand
on his sword.

But despite his intentions he found his eyes

drifting back to the dancing girls. Graceful as gazelles they leaped, legs striding wide on air, then rolled to the carpets, hips thrusting in abandon. Sweat beaded his forehead, and he wondered if perhaps the fire in the brazier made the yurt too hot. Did this Samarra remain away much longer, he might forget himself. Even though they would not talk, these girls might be willing to disport themselves with a young northerner.

A single sharp clap sounded above the music. Immediately the girls left off playing and dancing, and dashed behind the hangings. The grin that had begun on Conan's face faded, and his hand returned to his sword as he sprang to his feet. The hangings parted, and the woman who had taunted him earlier appeared. The cloak was gone now, and long hair as black as night hung in soft waves about her shoulders. Her long kirtle clung to her curves.

"I prefer the dancing of young men," she said, "but I did not think you would share my taste."

"You?" Conan said incredulously. "You are Samarra?"

She gave a throaty laugh. "You are disappointed that I am not an aged crone, with a beak of a nose and warts? I prefer to remain as I am for as long as the arts of woman and magic combined can keep me so." Her hands smoothed the bosom of her kirtle, pulling it tight over full round breasts. "Some say I am still beautiful." Delicately wetting her lips, she moved closer. "Do you think so?"

The woman had no need of sorcery for distraction, Conan thought. The musk of her perfume seemed to snare his brain. With no more than

what was known to every woman she had his
blood inflamed, his throat thick with desire. "Why
did you send for me?" he rasped.

Her dark eyes caressed his face more sensuous-
ly than hands might have done, slid lingergly
across his broad shoulders and massive chest. Her
nostrils flared. "You washed the scent away," she
said, a touch of mocking disappointment in her
tone. "Hyrkanian women are used to men who
smell of sweat and horse and grease. That scent
would have gained you many favorable looks. But
even so you are an exotic, with your muscles and
your size and that pale skin. And those eyes." Her
slender fingers stopped a hair's breath from his
face, tracing along his cheek. "The color of the
sky," she whispered, "and as changeable. The
spring sky after a rain, the sky of a fall morning.
And when you are angry, a sky of thunder and
storms. An exotic giant. You could have your pick
of half the women in this encampment, perhaps
three or four at a time, if such is your taste."

Angrily he wrapped an arm about her, lifting
her from the ground, crushing her softness
against his chest. His free hand tangled in her
hair, and the blue eyes that stared into hers did
indeed have much of the storm in them. "Taunting
me is a dangerous game," he said, "even for a
sorceress."

She stared back unperturbed, a secretive smile
dancing on her lips. "When do you mean to enter
the Blasted Lands, outlander?"

Involuntarily his grip tightened, wringing a gasp
from her. There was naught of the sky in his gaze
now, but rather ice and steel. "It is a foolish time

to reveal your sorceries, woman."

"I am at your mercy." With a sigh that smacked of contentment she wriggled to a more comfortable position, shifting her breasts disturbingly against his hard chest. "You could break my neck merely by flexing your arm, or snap my spine like a twig. I can certainly perform no magic held as I am. Perhaps I have made myself helpless before your strength to prove that I mean you no harm."

"I think you are as helpless as a tigress," he said wryly. Abruptly he set her heels on the carpets; there was a tinge of disappointment in her eyes as she patted her hair back into place. "Speak on, woman. What suspicions caused you to bend your magic to the reason of my coming?"

"No magic except that of the mind," she laughed. "You came in company with Tamur and others who I know crossed the Vilayet to find and slay Baalsham. I know well the horror of those days, for I was one of those who laid the wards that contain what lies within the Blasted Lands."

Conan realized why Tamur had been agitated at hearing her name. "Perhaps I, wishing to trade in Hyrkania, merely took Tamur into service."

"No, Conan. Tamur has many faults, but he, and the others, swore oaths to defy the ban on Baalsham's memory and avenge their blood. That they returned with you merely means that they think to find success in the Blasted Lands. Though their oaths led them to defiance, they know that violating the taboo means death for one of Hyrkanian blood, and so sought another to do the deed."

"Then why am I not fighting for my life against your warriors?"

She answered slowly, her voice tense, as if her words held import below the surface. As if there was danger in them for her, danger that she must carefully avoid. "When the barriers were erected, I alone among the shamans believed that they were not enough. I spoke for pursuing Baalsham and destroying him, for surely if he managed to establish his evil elsewhere it would eventually return to haunt us. The others, fearing another confrontation with him, forced me—" She stopped abruptly.

"Forced you to what?" he growled. "Swear oaths? What?"

"Yes," she said, nodding eagerly. "Both oath and *geas*. Do I break that oath, I will find myself the next dawn scrubbing pots in the yurt of a most repulsive man, unable to magic the pain from a sore tooth or think beyond a desire to obey. Many take it ill that there is a line of women who use the powers, and they would as soon see it end with me." Again her words halted, but her eyes begged him to question further.

"What holds your tongue, woman? What oath did you swear?"

"It took long enough to bring you to it," she sighed, tightness draining visibly from her face. "Firstly, I can speak to no one of the oaths unless asked, and no Hyrkanian but another who, like me, sits Guardian on the Blasted Lands would ask. Betimes one or another of them likes to taunt me with it."

"So you must trick me into asking," Conan muttered.

"Exactly. For the rest, I can aid no Hyrkanian to

enter the Blasted Lands or act against Baalsham, nor can I seek out any man to do those things."

A broad smile spread over his features. "But if a man who is not a Hyrkanian seeks you out. . . ."

". . .Then I can help him. But he must be the right man, outlander. I will not risk failure." Her mouth twisted as at a foul taste. "Anator, the repulsive toad of whom I spoke, waits for me to fall into his hands. Death I would risk, but not a life with him till I am old and shriveled."

"But you will help me?" he asked, frowning.

"If you are the right man. I must consult the Fire that Burns Backwards in Time. And I must have a lock of your hair for that."

In spite of himself, he took a step back. Hair, spittle, nail parings, anything that came from the body could be used in thaumaturgies that bound the one from whom they came.

"Do you think I need magicks to bind you?" Samarra laughed, and swayed her hips exaggeratedly.

"Take it, then," he said. But a grimace crossed his face as she deftly cut a few strands from his temple with a small golden knife.

Swiftly then she opened a series of small chests against a hanging, removing her paraphernalia. The hair was ground in a small hand-mill, then mixed in an unadorned ivory bowl with the contents of half a score of vials—powders of violent hue and powerful stench, liquids that seethed and bubbled—and stirred with a rod of bone. Setting up a small golden brazier on a tripod, Samarra filled it with ashes, smoothing them with the bone rod. Chanting words unintelligible to Conan, she poured the contents of the bowl onto the dead ash, and set the bowl aside.

Her voice rose, not in volume, but in pitch, till it pierced his ears like red-hot needles. Strange flames rose from the ash, blue flames, not flickering like ordinary fire, but rolling slowly like waves of a lazy sea. Higher that unnatural fire rose with Samarra's words, to the reach of a man's arm. Unblinking she stared into its depths as she spoke the incantations. A rime of frost formed on the outside of the golden dish that held the flames.

The other fires in the chamber, the flickering lamps and blazing charcoal, sank low, as if overawed, or drained. The Cimmerian realized that his fingernails were digging into his palms. With an oath he unclenched his fists. He had seen sorcery before, sorcery directed at him with deadly intent. He would not be affrighted by this.

Abruptly Samarra's chanting stopped. Conan blinked as he looked into the golden dish; half-burned pieces of wood now nestled among ash that was less than it had been. Then Samarra set a golden lid atop the brazier, closing off the blue fire.

For a long time she stared at the brazier before turning to him. "An you enter the Blasted Lands, scores will die," she said bleakly, "among them perhaps Baalsham. And perhaps you, as well. Your bones may feed the twisted beasts that dwell trapped in that accursed place."

"Perhaps?" he said. "What means of divining is this? Even Sharak does not so hedge his star-readings about."

"The fire shows the many things which can be.

Men choose which *will* be by their decisions. What is, is like a line, but at every decision that line branches, in two directions or ten, and each of those will also branch, until numbers beyond counting are reached. I will tell you this: if you enter, you, or Baalsham, or both, will stare Erlik's minions in the eyes. But if you do not, you will surely die. A hundred lines I examined, hoping to find an escape for you, and a hundred times I saw you die, each time more horribly than the last. And if you do not enter, not only will you die. Tens upon tens of thousands will perish fighting the spread of Baalsham's evil, and every day hundreds more will walk willingly to their deaths for his necromancies. Kings and queens will crawl on their bellies to worship at his feet, and such a darkness will cover the earth as has not been seen these many thousands of years, not since the attainted days of foul Acheron."

Conan laughed mirthlessly. "Then it seems I must try to save the world, whether I will or no." His blade leaped into his hand; he tested the edge carefully. "If I must wager my life, the odds will grow no better for waiting. I will go to these Blasted Lands now."

"No," she said sharply. He opened his mouth, but she hurried on. "Night is best, it is true, but not this night. Think of the girl with you. When you have done this thing, you must go immediately, for others sit Guardian besides me, and they will soon know what has been done. But she cannot stand, much less sit a saddle."

"Then I'll tie her across it," he answered roughly. Already the battle rage was rising in him. If he was to die this night, he would not die easily.

"But if you let me bring her here, I can cure her sore flesh in a day. She will be able to ride by tomorrow night." Samarra smiled. "Many women have asked me to take the pain from a smarting rump, but this will be the first time I have used my powers for so low a purpose."

"The longer I wait, the greater the chance that someone else will remember Tamur."

"But you still cannot enter the Blasted Lands without any help. The barrier of the Outer Circle will slay only those of Hyrkanian blood, but that of the Inner Circle, where you must go if you are to find what you seek, will destroy anything that lives. I must give you special powders to spread, and teach you incantations, if you are to survive."

"Then give them to me," he demanded.

Instead she untied her silk sash and tossed it aside. "No Hyrkanian man," she said, staring him in the eye, "will look at a shamaness as a woman. I have slaves, young men, full of vigor, but full of fear, too." She began to undo the silver pins that held her garment. "They touch me because I command it, but they do so as if I might shatter, afraid of hurting or angering. Until you put your hands on me, no man in my entire life has touched me as a woman, who will not break for a little roughness in a caress. I can wait no longer." The long kirtle slid to the carpets and she stood in lush nudity, all ripe curves and womanly softness. Feet apart she faced him, defiance in her eyes, fists on the swelling of her hips, shoulders thrown back so that her breasts seemed even fuller. "There is a price for my aid. If that makes me a harlot, well, that is something I have never experienced. And I want to experience everything that a man and a woman can do to each other. Everything, Conan."

Conan let his sword fall to the ground. Battle rage had changed to a different sort of fire in his blood. "Tomorrow night will be time enough," he said hoarsely, and pulled her into his embrace.

XX

Early the next morning Conan sent a message to Akeba that the Turanian was to see to the trading that day. Soon after, Yasbet was brought to the shamaness's yurt on a litter borne by two of Samarra's muscular young male slaves. Samarra scrambled red-faced to her feet, hastily pulling a silk robe around her nudity. The slaves glared at Conan with covert jealousy.

"Conan, why am I here?" Yasbet almost wept. Lying face down on the litter, she winced at every movement. "I hurt, Conan."

"Your pain will soon be gone," he told her gently. "Samarra will see to you."

Still blushing furiously, the shamaness led the litter-bearers to another part of the yurt. Half a turn of the glass later she returned, with high color yet in her cheeks. Conan lay sprawled on the silken cushions, occupying himself with a flagon of wine.

"I gave her a sleeping potion as well," she said. "The spell took her pain away immediately, but she needs rest, and it is best if that does not come from magic. If I relieved her fatigue so, she would repay it ten times over, later. The powers always demand repayment."

All the while she spoke she remained across the chamber from him, rubbing her hands together as if in nervousness. He motioned her to him. "Come

Sit, Samarra. Do not make me play host under your roof."

For a moment she hesitated, then knelt gracefully beside him. "Everything, I said," she murmured ruefully, "but I did not mean to have my own slaves enter while I lay naked in a stupor of lust. Not to mention the woman of the man I am lying with. I feel strange to have your lover but a few paces away."

Her ardor had surprised Conan in its fierceness. "What she does not know will not harm her," he said, tugging her robe from a smooth shoulder.

She slapped his hand away. "Is that all women are to you? A tumble for the night, and no more?"

"Women are music and beauty and delight made flesh." He reached for her again. She shrugged him away, and he sighed. So much for poetry, even when it was true. "Someday I will find a woman to wed, perhaps. Until then, I love all women, but I'll not pretend to any that she is more to me than she really is. Now, are you ready to remove that robe?"

"You know not your own vigor," she protested. Attempting to stretch, she stopped with a wince. "I am near as much in need of aid for sore muscles as that poor girl."

"In that case, I might as well return to Akeba and the others," he said, getting to his feet.

"No," she cried. Ripping the robe from her, she scrambled on her knees to throw her arms around his legs. "Please, Conan. Stay. I . . . I will keep you here by brute force, if I must."

"Brute force?" he chuckled.

She gave a determined nod. Laughing, he let her topple him to the pillows.

By two glasses after sunfall he was ready to go.
Briefly he looked in on Yasbet. She slept naturally
now; the potion had worn off. He brushed her
cheek with his fingers, and she smiled without
waking.

When he returned to the larger chamber Samarra had donned her kirtle, and put on a somber
mien as well. "You have the powder?" she demanded. "You must take care not to lose it."

"It is here," he replied, touching the pouch that
hung from his belt along with sword and dagger.
Within were two small leather bags containing
carefully measured powders would weaken the
barrier of the Inner Circle enough for him to pass it,
one portion for entering and one for leaving.

"The incantation. You remember the incantation?"

"I remember. Do not worry so."

He tried to put his arms around her, but she
stepped back out of his embrace, her face a mask.
"The gods be with you, Conan." She swallowed,
and whispered, "And with all of us."

There was more help in steel than in gods,
Conan thought as he went into the night. The
moon hung bright in a cloudless sky, bathing the
countryside in pale light, filling the camp with
shadows. It seemed a place of the dead, that camp.
No one was about, and even the guard dogs
huddled close to the yurts, only lifting their heads
to whine fretfully as he passed. He gathered his
cloak against the chill of the wind, and against a
chill that was not of the wind.

Akeba, Sharak, and Tamur were waiting, as they
had agreed, east of the crescent of yurts. The rest
of the Hyrkanians remained in their small camp,

so that it should not be found empty. The horses remained in camp as well; the sound of hooves in the night might attract unwanted attention.

Tamur peered beyond Conan nervously and whispered, "She did not come with you, did she?"

"No," Conan said. Tamur heaved a heavy sigh of relief. "Let's do this and be done," he went on. "Tamur, you lead."

Hesitantly, the Hyrkanian started to the east. Akeba followed, horsebow in hand and arrow nocked, to one side of Conan. Sharak labored on the other, leaning on his staff and muttering about the footing despite the bright moonlight.

"Tamur almost did not come," Akeba said quietly, "so afraid is he of Samarra. Did he hate Jhandar one iota less, he would have ridden for the coast, instead."

"But he does hate Jhandar," Conan replied. "He will lead us true."

"I wonder you have energy for this night, Conan," Sharak snickered, "after a day and a night with this witch-woman. I saw little of her, not nearly so much as you," he paused to cackle shrilly, "but I'd say she was a woman to sap a man's strength."

"Watch your step, old man," the big Cimmerian said drily. "I've not seen you read your own stars of late. This could be the night you break your neck."

"Mitra!" Sharak swore, stumbled, and almost fell. "I have not," he went on in a shaken voice. "Not since Aghrapur. The excitement, and the adventure, and the. . . ." He stumbled, peered at the sky and muttered, "The brightness of the moon blinds me. I cannot tell one star from another."

They traveled without words, then, following the dim shape of Tamur until abruptly the Hyrkanian stopped. "There," he said, pointing to two tall shadows ahead. "Those are the marks of the barrier. I can go no closer."

Samarra had described the shadowy objects as well as telling Conan what she knew of what lay beyond them. Around the perimeter of the Outer Circle huge pillars of crude stone had been set, thrice the height of a man and four times as thick. To pass those stelae meant death for one of Hyrkanian blood.

"There is no need for me to accompany you, Conan," Sharak said. "My eyes. I would be more hindrance than help. No, I must remain here and learn what I can of our prospects from the stars." He suddenly clutched the arm of a surprised Tamur, and though the Hyrkanian tried to shake himself free, Sharak clung tightly, pulling on the other man. "Can you tell one star from another, Hyrkanian? No matter. I will tell you what to look for. Come." The two moved off to the side, Tamur still jerking futilely at his arm.

"I, at least, will come with you," Akeba said, but Conan shook his head.

"Samarra told me that any who enters other than myself will die." She had said no such thing, but what she did say convinced him that two men, or fifty, would have no better chances of survival than one, and perhaps less.

"Oh. Then I will await your return, Cimmerian. You are an odd fellow, but I like you. Fare you well."

Conan clapped the slighter man on the shoulder. "Take a pull at the hellhorn, an you get there before me, Akeba."

"What? 'Tis a strange thing to say."

"Other countries, other customs," Conan said. "It is a way of saying fare you well." His amusement faded abruptly as he eyed the stone pillars. It was time to be on with it. His blade slid from its scabbard, steel rasping on leather.

"Strange, indeed, you pale-eyed barbarians," Akeba said. "Well, you take a pull at the . . . whatever it was you said."

But Conan was already moving forward. Without pausing, the Cimmerian strode by the crude pillars, sword at the ready. As he did, a tingle passed through his body, as if nails and teeth had all been dragged across slate at once. The greatest tingle was at his waist, beneath the pouch at his belt. Samarra had warned him of this, and told him to ignore it, but he fumbled for the two smaller sacks anyway. Both were intact.

There was no growth of any kind, not even the tough grass that covered the plains of Hyrkania. The ground was smooth, yet ridged, as if it had flowed then hardened in waves. He had seen such before, where fissures had opened and the bowels of the earth had spewed forth molten rock. The moonlight here was tinged with the xanthous color of flesh gone to mold. Shadows moved furtively in that nacreous light, though no clouds crossed the moon.

Had he been the hero of a saga, he thought, he would seek out those creatures and hack his way to the Inner Circle. But the heroes of sagas always had the luck of ten men, and used it all. He went on, deeper into the Blasted Lands, moving with pantherine grace, yet carefully, as if avoiding seeking eyes. That eyes were there, or something that sensed movement, he was certain. Strange slitherings sounded from the rocks around him, and clickings, as of chitinous claws on stone. Once he did indeed see eyes, three unblinking red orbs, set close together, peering at him from the dark beside a boulder, swiveling to follow his passage. He quickened his pace. The sound of scraping claws came closer, and more quickly. A piping hiss rose, behind and either side, like the hunting cry of a pack.

Abruptly there was silence. Did the shadow creatures attack in silence, he wondered, or had they ceased their pursuit? And if they had, why? What could lie ahead that would frighten. . . .? The answer came as he skidded to a halt, a bare pace from a pillar marking the deadly Inner Circle.

Despite himself he let out a long breath. But he still lived, and perhaps fear of the barrier would hold whatever followed at bay for a time longer. Behind he heard the hissing begin again. Hastily he pulled one leather sack from his pouch and sprinkled the scintillating powder in a long line by the stone pillar. With great care he spoke the words Samarra had taught him, and a shimmering appeared in the air above the line, as wide as a man's outstretched arms and reaching nearly as high as the stone marker. Within that shimmer the barrier was weakened, not destroyed, so Samarra said. A strong man could survive passing through it. So she said.

The scraping claws were louder, and the hissing. Whatever made those sounds was almost to him. Taking a deep breath, he leaped. The hisses rose to a scream of frustrated hunger, and then he struck the shimmer. Every muscle in his body knotted and convulsed in agony. Back arched, he was hurled into the Inner Circle.

Head spinning, he staggered to his feet. Somehow he had retained his sword. If that was a weakened barrier, he thought, he wanted no part of it at full strength. He checked his pouch again. The second sack was still safe.

Whatever had hunted him had gone, suck back into those writhing shades outside the Inner Circle. The shimmer in the barrier yet held, but by the time he could count to one hundred the force of its protection would be gone. That second portion of the powder was his only way of crossing the barrier again, unless he went now. Turning his back on the shimmer, he went deeper into that twisted country.

Blasted Lands they were indeed. Here hills were split by gaping fissures, or stood in tortured remnants as if parts had been vaporized. Fumaroles bubbled and steamed, and the air was heavy with the stench of a decay so old that only sorcery could have kept it from disappearing long since. Foul vapors drifted in sheets, like noxious clouds hugging the ground; they left a feel of dampness and filth on the skin they touched.

Samarra had told him where Jhandar's unfinished palace had stood on that day when nightmares were loosed. What he might find there she could not say—the forces unleashed had been more than even the shamans could face—but it was the only place she could suggest for his search. In the midst of these hills the land had been leveled for the palace. Ahead he saw the hills end. It must be the location.

He hurried forward, around a sheer cliff where half a hill had disappeared, out onto the great leveled space . . . and stopped, shoulders sagging in defeat.

Before him marble steps led up to a portico of massive, broken columns. Beyond, where the palace should have stood, a huge pit opened into the depths, a pit that pulsed with red light and echoed with the bubbling of boiling rock far below.

There could be nothing there, he told himself. And yet there must be. Samarra had foretold that his entry into the Blasted Lands would bring at least the chance of Jhandar's destruction. Somewhere within that blighted region something must exist that could be used against the necromancer. He had to find it.

A slavering roar spun him around, an involuntary, "Crom!" wrenched from his lips.

Facing him was a creature twice the height of a man, its gangrenous flesh dripping phosphorescent slime. A single rubiate eye set in the middle of its head watched him with a horrifying glimmer of intelligence, but with hunger as well. And that gaping fanged maw, the curving needle claws that tipped its fingers, told what it chose to eat.

Even as the creature faced him, Conan acted. Waving his sword, he screamed as if about to attack. The beast reared back to take his charge, and Conan darted for the cliff. A being of such size could not be his equal at scaling sheer heights, he thought.

Thrusting his blade into its scabbard as he ran, he reached the cliff and climbed without slowing, fingers searching out crevices and holds with a

speed he had never matched before. Chances he
would have eschewed if men had pursued him he
now took as a matter of course, hooking his fingernails in cracks he could not even see, planting his
feet on stone that crumbled at his weight, yet
moving with such desperate quickness that he was
gone before its crumbling was complete. Catching
the top of the cliff, he heaved himself over, lay
with chest heaving.

A slime-covered, clawed hand slammed down a
handsbreadth from his head. Cursing, Conan
rolled to his feet, blade whispering into his grip.
Its eye above the rim of the cliff, the beast saw him
and roared, clawing with its free hand for him instead of securing its hold. Burnished steel blazed
an arc through the air, severing the hand that held
the ground. With a scream like all the fiends of the
pit the beast toppled back, and down, into the fetid
mists. The crash of its fall sent a shiver through
the cliff that Conan could feel through his boots.

The clawed hand, faintly glowing, still lay where
he had severed it. Glowing slime oozed from it like
blood. He was relieved, after the sendings in
Aghrapur, to see that it did not so much as twitch
by itself. With the tip of his sword he flipped it
into the vapors below.

Even through the clouded gloom Conan could
yet see the broken pillars of Jhandar's palace;
from his vantage point they were outlined in the
fiery glow from the pit. No use could he see in
returning there, however. His search must lead
elsewhere. He started down the steep slope that
backed the cliff, leaping to cross the fissures that
slashed and re-slashed the terrain, dodging among
boulders, crazed with a thousand lines like ill-

mended pottery, abruptly lost in fetid gray curtains of drifting mist then as suddenly revealed again.

Stone clattered against stone behind him, toward the top of the precipitous slope. Weighing the broadsword in his hand, Conan peered back, attempting in vain to pierce the sheets of fog. He *could* have missed seeing some small creature on the clifftop in the mists. A thud, as of a heavy body falling, drifted down to him. He could *not* have missed something large enough to. . . . Then the one-eyed beast was rushing at him out of the vapors, clawed hand and the stump of its severed wrist both raised to strike.

Conan leaped back. And found himself falling into a gaping fissure. Twisting like a great cat he caught the rock rim, slammed against it supported only by a forearm. Dislodged stone rattled into the depths of the broad crack, the sound dwindling away without striking bottom, as if the drop went on forever.

The beast was moving too fast to stop. With a roar of frustrated rage it leaped for the far side of the fissure, its lone red eye glaring at the big Cimmerian. Awkwardly Conan thrust up at the creature with his broadsword as it passed over him. Snarling, the beast curled into a ball to avoid the blade, hit heavily on the other side of the wide crack, and went rolling down the steep slope, its cries of fury ripping through the fog.

Hurriedly Conan pulled himself out of the fissure. Silence descended abruptly, but he took that for no sign of the beast's demise. Not now.

As if to confirm his dire suspicions came the sound of scrabbling claws and hungry panting.

The creature yet survived, and was climbing toward him.

Being above on the slope might give him slight advantage—perhaps—but the young Cimmerian had not come to this hellish place to slay monsters. He began to run down the length of the crevice, cursing under his breath at every stone that turned beneath his boot and clattered downhill. Sheer distance from where the thing had last seen him would be his safeguard. At least, it would be so long as the beast did not hear him and follow. Had he half the luck of those ill-begotten heroes of the thrice-accursed sagas, the creature would make bootless search of the hill while he completed his own quest.

Halting, he pricked his ears for sounds of the one-eyed beast . . . and heard it still directly below him, but nearer now. Black Erlik's Bowels and Bladder! He wished he had half a score of those feckless spinners of tales there with him, to see what trials men of flesh and bone faced when confronted with the monsters so easily despatched with words in a market square. He would have fed two or three of them to the beast, feet first.

An he was forced to face the creature—and he could see no other way—the time and the place were as any others. Did he continue to run, the facing would merely be at another place, perhaps when he had run himself to exhaustion. Mayhap it would be off balance for a moment, leaping across the fissure from down slope. If he attacked then. . . . At that moment he noticed that the fissure he had followed had dwindled to a handspan crack.

For a moment the Cimmerian was too angry

even to curse. For a simple lack of keeping his eyes
open he had placed himself in worse danger. The
great beast was no more than fifty paces straight
down the slope, with only the steepness to slow it
and naught between it and. . . . Straight down the
slope. He peered toward the climbing beast. Its
red eye was visible, glowing, as was the pale,
leprous phosphoresence of its body; and it was
making better going of the shattered hillside than
any human could have. It seemed to move with the
speed and tenacity of a leopard.

Conan knew he needed long headstart on the
creature if he was to escape it long enough to
carry out his search; still, the merest breath of a
chance had come to his brain, as fresh air in the
foulness about him.

He cast about hurriedly for what he needed, and
found it but ten paces away, a shadowy bulk near
as tall as he, but seeming squat for its thickness,
obscured by a curtain of fog that clung rather than
drifting. Quickly his eyes sought the beast. Some
forty paces below, the glowing mass edged sideways until it was once more directly below the
Cimmerian. Forty paces. Conan waited.

The slavering beast clawed its way nearer,
nearer. Thirty-five paces. Thirty. Conan could
hear its rasping pant now. Ravenous hunger was
in it as well, and in that sanguinary eye was something else, a pure desire to kill divorced from the
need for meat. The hairs on the back of his neck
stirred. Twenty-five paces. Twenty. Conan drifted
back, through the sheet of filthy gray mist behind
him. Screaming with rage, not to be denied, the
creature quickened its climb.

Knees bent, Conan set his broad back to the uphill side of the boulder he had chosen and heaved. Shrieks of primordial rage echoed over the hills. The Cimmerian's every thew strained, great muscles corded and knotted till they seemed carved from some more obdurate substance than the stone with which he fought. The boulder shifted a fingerwidth. The howls came closer. In moments the foul creature would be upon him. The sweat of effort at the limits of human ability rolled down Conan's face and chest. The great stone moved again. And then it was rolling free.

Conan spun in time to see the boulder strike the now narrow crack in the hillside, bound into the air, and catch the monstrous creature full in the chest. Even as the beast was borne backward down the slope, screaming and clawing at the massive stone as if it were a living enemy, Conan set off at a dead run, diagonally down the hill, leaping crevices with reckless disregard for the dangers of falling, racing toward the barrier.

He did not intend to leave the Inner Circle yet, but neither did he believe the boulder would slay the one-eyed beast. He would not believe that being *could* die until he had seen it dead. Or perhaps it already was; he had seen stranger things. But in the Outer Circle, the unseen things with claws had feared to approach the barrier. Could he reach those deadly wards before the one-eyed creature freed itself, it was possible the monstrous being would not search for him there.

Through curtains of noxious mist Conan ran like a ghostly panther, past pools of bubbling, steaming mud and geysers that sprayed boiling fountains into the night. The columns marking the

barrier appeared ahead in the sickly sallow moonlight.

In a silent rush the one-eyed beast hurtled from
the fog, lunging for Conan. Desperately the
Cimmerian threw himself aside; scythe-like claws
ripped across the front of his tunic, slashing it to
tatters. He rolled to his feet, broadsword at the
ready, facing the towering creature. Rumbling
growls sounded deep in the beast's throat as it
edged toward him. It had learned respect for the
steel that had taken its hand.

Blood trickled down Conan's chest from four
deep gashes, but that was not what concerned him
at the moment, nor even the fangs that hungered
for his flesh. Fumbling at his belt with his free
hand, he swallowed hard. The pouch was gone,
torn away by those dagger claws, and with it the
powder he needed to cross the barrier. With the
thought his eyes drifted toward the marking
columns . . . and there, at the base of a rough-
hewn monolith, lay the pouch and his hope of
escape.

Slowly, keeping the point of his sword directed
at the glowing beast, Conan began to edge sideways towards the crude pillar. The creature
hesitated, and a twisted intelligence shone in its
eye as it, too, saw the pouch. As if divining the importance of what lay within, the slime-covered giant
darted to stand over the small leather sack, almost
touching the deadly barrier. Its fanged mouth
twisted in what seemed almost a mocking smile.

Thus for the beast fearing the barrier, Conan
thought. An it could reason so, it would not leave
the pouch for him to find, even did he manage to

lead it away. It seemed that Erlik was enfolding his Cloak of Unending Night about him, yet a man was not meant to accept his own death meekly.

"Crom!" Conan roared, and attacked. "Crom and steel!"

Fangs bared in a snarl the creature dashed to meet him, but Conan did not mean to come to grips with the foul beast. At the last instant he dropped into a crouch, still moving, blade slashing across a belly of deathly argentine flesh covered with glowing slime, and ducked beneath slicing claws that struck only his cloak. For an instant Conan was snubbed short, then cloth ripped, and he was beyond the beast with the tatters of the garment dangling down his back.

Barely slowing, Conan bent to snatch his pouch from the ground, pivoted on one foot, and raced down the line of barrier stones. Stones grated close behind, and the Cimmerian whirled, broadsword striking at a clawed hand descending toward his head. Three cruel-tipped fingers fell, severed, but the mutilated hand slammed into Conan, driving him dazed to his knees.

Then he was enveloped in adamantine arms, being drawn toward the great flesh-rending teeth. Only Conan's sword arm was free of the unyielding grip, and with it he thrust his blade into that fanged mouth, the point knifing through flesh, grating on bone, bursting through the back of the beast's great head.

The creature snarled and snapped at the blade, trying with unabated fury to reach the Cimmerian, the stench of its breath flowing into Conan's nostrils. Like the iron bands of a torture device those huge arms tightened, till Conan thought his spine would snap. No longer could he feel his legs, or his trapped hand. He did not even know if he still held the pouch that contained his sole hope of leaving the Blasted Lands. All he could do was fight with his last measure of strength to keep that ravenous mouth from his throat.

Suddenly there was a greater worry than the beast in Conan's mind. Over the creature's shoulder he could see the marking pillars; its struggles were carrying them closer to that deadly shield. And closer. At least he would die with sword in hand, and not alone. Uncertainty flickered in the beast's blood-red eye as grim laughter burst from Conan's mouth. Contact with the barrier.

Pain ripped through the Cimmerian, pain such as he had never known. Skin flayed from muscle, muscle torn from bone, bone ground to powder and the whole thrown into molten metal, then the torturous cycle began again. And again. And. . . .

Conan found himself on the ground, on hands and knees, every muscle quivering with the effort of not falling flat on his face. Through blurred eyes he saw that he still clutched his pouch in a death-grip. He still had his means of escape from the Inner Circle, and in some fashion he had survived touching the barrier, but one thought dominated his swirling brain, the desperate need to regain his feet, to be ready to face the monster's next attack. His broadsword lay before him. Lurching forward, he grabbed the worn leather hilt, and almost let the blade fall. The leather was cracked and blistering hot.

Abruptly sound crashed in on him, crackling

and hissing like a thousand chained lightning bolts, and Conan realized that he had been deaf. Shakily he scrambled to his feet . . . and stood staring.

The beast lay across the barrier, twitching as scintillating arcs of power rose from one part of its body to strike another. Flames in a hundred hues lanced from the already blacking hulk.

A grin began on the Cimmerian's face, and died as he stared at the barrier. He was no longer within the Inner Circle. How he had survived crossing the barrier—perhaps the monstrous vitality of the beast had absorbed the greater part of the deadly force, partially shielding him—did not matter. What mattered was that he had but enough of the required powder to cross that boundary once. Did he enter again, he would never leave.

In silence he turned his back on the still-jerking body of the beast, on the Inner Circle, a dark light in his eyes that boded ill.

XXI

Akeba and the others were huddled around a tiny fire when Conan strode out of the Blasted Lands, wiping glittering black blood from his blade with the shredded remnants of his cloak. The Cimmerian announced his presence by tossing the bloody rag into the fire, where it flared and gave off thick, acrid smoke.

All three men leaped, and Sharak wrinkled his nose. "Phhaw! What Erlik-begotten stench is that?"

"We will return to the yurts," Conan said, slamming his sword home in its shagreen sheath, "but only briefly. I must get Samarra's help to reenter the Inner Circle."

"Then you found nothing," Akeba said thoughtfully. He eyed the dried blood on Conan's tattered tunic, the pouch crudely tied to his swordbelt, as he added, "Are you certain you want to go back, Cimmerian? What occurred in there?"

Tamur spoke. "No!" Everyone looked at him; he scrubbed at his mouth with the back of his hand before speaking further. "It is a taboo place. Do not speak of what happened within the barriers. It is taboo."

"Nonsense," Sharak snorted. "No harm can there be merely in the hearing. Speak on, Conan."

But the Cimmerian was of no mind to waste time in talk. The night was half gone. With a curt,

"Follow me," he started off into the night. The others kicked dirt over the fire and hurried after.

As soon as they arrived at Samarra's yurt, Conan motioned the rest to wait and ducked inside.

The interior was dark; not so much as a single lamp was lit, and the big charcoal fire was coal ash. Strange, Conan thought. Samarra, at least, would have remained awake to hear what he had found. Then the unnatural silence of the yurt struck him. There was a hollow emptiness that denied the presence of life. His broadsword eased into his hand almost of its own accord.

He started across the carpets, picking his way among the scattered cushions. Suddenly his foot struck something firmer than a cushion, yet yielding. With a sinking of his stomach, he knelt; his fingers felt along a woman's contours, the skin clammily cold.

"Conan! Look out!" Akeba shouted from the entrance.

Conan threw himself into a diving roll, striking something that bounced away with a clatter of brass, and came up in a wary crouch with his sword at the ready. Just as he picked out the shadow of what could have been a man, something hummed from the entrance and struck it. Stiffly the dim shape toppled to the ground with a thud.

"It's a man," Akeba said uncertainly. "At least, I *think* it's a man. But it did not fall as a man falls."

Conan felt around him for what he had knocked over. It was a lamp, with only half the oil spilled. Fumbling flint and steel from his pouch, he lit the wick. The lamp cast its light on the body he had stumbled over.

Samarra lay on her back, dead eyes staring up at the roof of the yurt. Blended determination and resignation were frozen on her features.

"She knew," Conan murmured. "She said if I entered the Blasted Lands many would die."

With a sigh he moved the light to the shape that had fallen so strangely. Akeba's arrow stood out from the neck of a yellow-skinned man in black robes, his almond eyes wide with disbelief. Conan prodded the body with his sword, and started in surprise. The corpse was as hard as stone.

"At least she took her murderer with her," Conan growled. "And avenged your Zorelle."

" 'Tis not he, though he is very like," Akeba said. "I will remember to my tomb the face of the man who killed my daughter, and this is not he."

Conan shifted the light again, back to Samarra. "I could have saved her," he said sadly, though he had no idea of how. "Had she told me . . . Yasbet!"

Leaping to his feet, he searched furiously through the other curtained compartments of the yurt. The structure was a charnel house. Slaves, male and female alike, lay in tangled heaps of cold flesh. None bore a wound, any more than did Samarra, but the face of each was twisted in horror. Nowhere did he find Yasbet.

When he returned to Akeba, Conan was sick to his stomach. *Many would die if he entered the Blasted Lands.* Samarra had said there were many branchings of the future. Could she not have found one to avoid this?

"Jhandar sent more than this one to follow us," he told the Turanian. "Yasbet is gone, and the others are dead. All of them."

Before Akeba could speak, Tamur stuck his

head into the yurt. "There are stirrings. . . ." His eyes lit on Samarra's body in the pool of lamp light. "Kaavan One-Father protect us! This is the cause! We will all be gelded, flayed alive, impaled—"

"What are you talking about?" Conan demanded. "The cause of what?"

"The yurts of the other shamans," Tamur replied excitedly. "Men are gathering there, even though none like to venture into the night this close to the Blasted Lands."

Akeba grunted. "They must have sensed the death of one of their own."

"But they'll not find us standing over the bodies," Conan said, pinching the lamp wick between his fingers. The dark seemed deeper once that small light was gone. He started for the door flap.

Outside, Sharak leaned on his staff and peered toward the distant torches that were beginning to move toward Samarra's yurt. The mutters of the men carrying those lights made a constant, angry hum. The old astrologer jumped when Conan touched his shoulder. "Do we return to the Blasted Lands, Conan, we must do it now. This lot will take it unkindly, our wandering their camp at night."

"Yasbet is gone," Conan told him quietly, "taken or slain. Samarra is dead." Sharak gasped. Conan turned away, and Sharak, after one quick glance at the approaching torches, fell silently in behind the others.

As four shadows they made they made their way between the dark yurts, out onto the plain, and hurried toward their camp, ignoring as best they could the rising tumult behind them. Then a great shout rose, a cry of rage from a hundred throats.

Akeba quickened his pace to come abreast of Conan. "They have found her," the Turanian said, "but may not think we slew her."

"We are strangers," Conan laughed mirthlessly. "What would your soldiers do if a princess of Aghrapur were murdered, and there were outlanders close to hand?"

The Turanian sucked air between his teeth. "Mitra send us time to get to our horses."

With no more words the four men broke into a run, Conan and Akeba covering the ground with distance-eating strides. Tamur ran awkwardly, but with surprising speed. Even Sharak kept up, wheezing and puffing, and finding breath to complain of his years.

"Awake!" Tamur cried as they ran into their dark camp. The fires had burned low. "To your horses!" Nomads rolled instantly from their blankets, booted and clothed, seized their weapons, and stared at him blankly. "We must flee!" Tamur shouted to them. "We stand outside the laws!" Leaping as if pricked, they darted for the horses. Tamur turned to Conan, shaking his head. "We shall not escape. We ride reedy coastal stock. Those who pursue will be astride war mounts. Our animals will drop before dawn, while theirs can maintain a steady pace all the way to the sea."

"The pack horses," Conan said. "Will they carry men?"

Tamur nodded. "But we have enough mounts for everyone."

"What if," Conan said slowly, "when our horses

are about to fall, we change to horses that, if tired
somewhat from running, have at least not carried
a man? And when those are ready to fall. . . ." He
looked at the others questioningly. He had heard
of this in a tavern, and tavern tales were not
always overly filled with truth. "We have several
extra mounts for each man. Even these war
mounts cannot outrun them all, can they?"

"It could work," Tamur breathed. "Kaavan One-
Father watch over us, it could work."

Akeba nodded. "I should have thought of that.
I've heard this is done on the southern frontier."

"But the trade goods," Sharak complained.
"You'll not abandon—"

"Will you die for them?" Conan cut him off, and
ran for the hobbled pack horses. The others
followed at his heels, the old astrologer last and
slowest.

The nomads wasted no time once Conan's idea
was explained to them, hastily fumbling in the
dark with bridles, finishing just as roaring horsemen burst from the among the Hyrkanian yurts.
Conan wasted but a single moment in thought of
the gold from their trading, and the greater part of
his own gold, hidden in a bale of tanned hides,
then he scrambled onto his mount with the others,
lashing it into a desperate gallop. Death rode on
their heels.

As they entered the tall, scrub-covered sand
dunes on the coast, four men rode double, and no
spare horses were left. The sweat-lathered mounts
formed a straggling line, but no man pressed his
horse for fear of the animal's collapse. In the sky
before them the sun hung low; the two-days'

journey had consumed less than one with the impetus of saving their lives.

Conan's shaggy mount staggered under him, but he could hear the crash of waves ahead. "How much lead do we have?" he asked Akeba.

"Perhaps two turns of the glass, perhaps less," the Turanian replied.

"They held their animals back, Cimmerian, when they saw they would not overtake us easily," Tamur added. His breath came in pants almost as heavy as those of his mount. He labored the beast with his quirt, but without real force. "Ours will not last much longer, but theirs will be near fresh when they come up on us."

"They'll come up on empty sand," Conan laughed, urging his shaggy horse to the top of a dune, "for we've reached the ship." Words and laughter trailed away as he stared at the beach beyond. The sand was empty, with only the cold remains of fires to show he had come to the right place. Far out on the water a shape could be seen, a hint of triangularity speaking of *Foam Dancer's* lateen sail.

"I never trusted that slime-spawn Muktar," Akeba muttered. "The horses are played out, Conan, and we're little better. This stretch of muddy sand is no fit place to die, if any place is fit, but 'tis time to think of taking a few enemies with us into the long night. What say you, Cimmerian?"

Conan, wrestling with his own thoughts, said nothing. So far he had come in his quest for a means to destroy Jhandar, and what had come of it? Samarra dead, and all her slaves. Yasbet taken by Jhandar's henchmen. Even in small matters the gods had turned their faces from him. The trade

goods for which he had spent his hundred pieces
of gold—and hard-earned gold it was, too, for the
slaying of a friend, even one ensorceled to
kill—were abandoned. Of the gold but two pieces
nestled in his pouch with flint, steel, Samarra's
pouch and a bit of dried meat. And now he had fallen
short by no more than half a turn of the glass.
Muktar had not even waited to discover that
Conan lacked the coin to pay for his return voyage.
Though, under the circumstances, a show of steel
would have disposed of that quibble.

"Are you listening?" Akeba demanded of him.
"Let us circle back on our trail to the start of the
dunes. We can surprise them, and with rest we
may give a good account of ourselves." Muttering
rose among the Hyrkanians.

Still Conan did not speak. Instead he chewed on
a thought. Yasbet taken by Jhandar's henchmen.
There was something of importance there, could
he but see it. A faint voice within him said that it
was urgent he did see it.

"Let us die as men," Tamur said, though his
tone was hesitant, "not struggling futilely, like
dungbeetles seized by ants." Some few of his
fellows murmured approval; the rest twitched
their reins fretfully and cast anxious backward
glances, but kept silent.

The Turanian's black eyes flicked the nomad
scornfully; Tamur looked away. "No one who calls
himself a man dies meekly," Akeba said.

"They are of our blood," Tamur muttered, and
the soldier snorted.

"Mitra's Mercies! This talk of blood has never
stayed one Hyrkanian's steel from another's
throat that I have seen. It'll not stay the hands of

those who follow us. Have you forgotten what they will do to those they take alive? Gelded. Flayed alive. Impaled. You told us so. And you hinted at worse, if there can *be* worse."

Tamur flinched, licking his lips and avoiding Akeba's gaze. Now he burst out, "We stand outside the law!" A mournful sigh breathed from the other nomads. Tamur rushed breathlessly on. "We are no longer shielded by the laws of our people. For us to slay even one of those sent by the shamans would be to foul and condemn our own spirits, to face an eternity of doom."

"But you didn't kill Samarra," Akeba protested. "Surely your god knows that. Conan, talk to this fool."

But the Cimmerian ignored all of them. The barest glimmerings of hope flickered in him.

"We will face the One-Father having broken no law," Tamur shouted.

"Erlik take your laws! You were willing to disobey the edict against revenging yourself on Jhandar." Akeba's thin mouth twisted in a sneer. "I think you are simply ready to surrender. You are all dogs! Craven women whining for an easy death!"

Tamur recoiled, hand going to the hilt of his yataghan. "Kaavan understands revenge. You Turanians, whose women have watered your blood for a thousand years with the seed of western weaklings, understand nothing. I will not teach you!"

Steel slid from scabbards, and was arrested half-drawn by Conan's abrupt, "The ship! We will use the ship."

Akeba stared at him. Some of the Hyrkanians

moved their horses back. Madmen were touched by the gods; slaying one, even in self-defense, was a sure path to ill luck.

Sharak, clinging tiredly to his mount with one hand and his staff with the other, peered ostentatiously after *Foam Dancer*. The vessel was but a mote, now. "Are we to become fish, then?" he asked.

"The galley," Conan said, his exasperation clear at their stupidity. "How much before us could Jhandar's henchmen have left the camp? And they had no reason to ride as we did, for no one was pursuing them. Their galley may still be waiting for them. We can rescue Yasbet and use it to cross the sea again."

"I'd not wager a copper on it," Akeba said. "Most likely the galley is already at sea."

"Are the odds better if you remain here?" Conan asked drily. Akeba looked doubtful. He ran an eye over the others; half the nomads still watched him warily. Sharak seemed lost in thought. "I'll not wait here meekly to be slaughtered," Conan announced. "You do what you will." Turning his horse to the south, he booted it into a semblance of a trot.

Before he had gone a hundred paces Sharak caught up to him, using his staff like a switch to chivy his shaggy mount along. "A fine adventure," the astrologer said, a fixed grin on his parchment face. "Do we take prisoners when we reach the galley? In the sagas heroes never take prisoners."

Akeba joined them in a gallop; his horse staggered as he reined back to their pace. "Money is one thing," the Turanian said. "My life I'm willing to wager on long odds."

Conan smiled without looking at either of them, a smile touched with grimness. More hooves pounded the sand behind him. He did not look around to see how many others had joined. One or all, it would be enough. It had to be. With cold eyes he led them south.

XXII

One horse sank to its knees, refusing to go on, as they passed the first headland, and another fell dead before they were long out of sight of the first. Thick scrub grew here in patches too large to ride around. There were no paths except those forced by the horses.

Conan grimaced as yet another man mounted double. Their pace was slower than walking. Keeping their strength was important if they were to face the galley's crew, or Jhandar's henchmen, but the horses were at the end of theirs. And time was important as well. They must reach the ship before Yasbet's captors did, or at least before they sailed, and before the pursuing Hyrkanians overtook them. The nomads would have little difficulty following their tracks down the coast.

Reaching a decision, he dismounted. The others stared as he removed his horse's crude rope bridle and began to walk. Sharak pressed his own mount forward and dropped off beside the big Cimmerian.

"Conan," Akeba called after him, "what—"

But Conan strode on; the rest could follow or not, as they chose. He would not spend precious moments in convincing them. With the old astrologer struggling to keep up he plunged ahead. Neither spoke. Breath now was to be saved for walking.

Where the horses had struggled to pass there
were spaces where a man might go more easily.
Akeba and the Hyrkanians were soon lost to sight,
had either chosen to look back. Neither did.

There was no smooth highway for them, though.
Even when the sandy ground was level, their boots
sank to the ankles, and rocks lay ready to turn
underfoot and throw the unwary into thornbushes
boasting black, finger-long spikes, that would rip
flesh like talons.

But then the ground was seldom level, except
for occasional stretches of muddy beach, pounded
by angry waves. For every beach there were a pair
of headlands to be descended on one side and
scaled on the other, with steep hills between, and
deep gullies between those. Increasingly the land
became almost vertical, up or down. One hundred
paces forward took five hundred steps to travel, or
one thousand. The horses would have been useless.

Of course, Conan reasoned, sweat rolling down
his face, grit in his hair and eyes and mouth, he
could move inland to the edge of the plain. But
then he would not know when he reached the
beach where the galley lay. He would not let
himself consider the possibility that it might no
longer be there. Too, on the plain they would leave
even clearer traces of his passage for their hunter,
and most of the time gained by traveling there
thus would be lost in struggling to the beaches
when they were sighted.

A crashing in the thick brush behind them
brought Conan's sword into his hand. Cursing,
Akeba stumbled into sight, his dark face coated
with sweat and dust.

"Two more horses died," the Turanian said without preamble, "and another went lame. Tamur is right behind me. He'll catch up if you wait. The others were arguing about whether to abandon the remaining horses when I left, but they'll follow as well, sooner or later."

"There is no time to wait." Resheathing his blade, Conan started off again.

Sharak, who had no breath for speaking, followed, and after a moment Akeba did as well.

Three men, the young Cimmerian thought, since Tamur would be joining them. Three and a half, an he counted Sharak; the old astrologer would be worth no more than half Akeba or Tamur in a fight, if that much. Mayhap some of the other nomads would catch up in time, but they could not be counted on. Three and a half, then.

As Tamur joined them, plucking thorns from his arm and muttering curses fit to curl a sailor's hair, fat raindrops splattered against the back of Conan's neck. The Cimmerian peered up in surprise at thick, angrily purple clouds. His eyes had been of necessity locked to the ground; he had not noticed their gathering.

Quickly the sprinkling became a deluge, a hail of heavy pounding drops. A wind rose, ripping down the coast, tearing at the twisted scrub growth, howling higher and higher till it rang in the ears and dirt hung in the air to mix with the rain, splashing the four men with rivulets of mud. Nearby, a thick-rooted thornbush, survivor of many storms, tore lose from the ground, tangled briefly in the branches around it, and was whipped away.

Tamur put his mouth close to Conan's ear and

shouted. "It is the Wrath of Kaavan! We must take shelter and pray!"

" 'Tis but a storm!" the Cimmerian shouted back. "You faced worse on *Foam Dancer*!"

"No! This is no ordinary storm! It is the Wrath of Kaavan!" The Hyrkanian's face was a frozen mask, fear warring plainly with his manhood. "It comes with no warning, and when it does, men die! Horses are lifted whole into the air, and yurts, with all in them, to be found smashed to the ground far distant, or never to be seen again! We must shelter for our lives!"

The wind was indeed rising, even yet, shaking the thickets till it seemed the scrub was trying to tear itself free and flee. Driven raindrops struck like pebbles flung from slings.

Akeba, half-supporting Sharak, raised his voice against the thundering wind and rain. "We must take shelter, Cimmerian! The old man is nearly done! He'll not last out this storm if we don't!"

Pushing away from the Turanian, Sharak held himself erect with his staff. His straggly white hair was plastered wetly to his skull. "If you are done, soldier, say so. I am not!"

Conan eyed the old man regretfully. Sharak was clinging to his staff as to a lifeline. The other two, for all they were younger and hardier, were not in greatly better condition. Akeba's black face was lined with weariness, and Tamur, his fur cap a sodden mass hanging about his ears, swayed when the wind struck him fully. Yet there was Yasbet.

"How many of your nomads followed, Tamur?" he asked finally. "Will they catch up if we wait?"

"All followed," Tamur replied, "but Hyrkanians

do not travel in the Wrath of Kaavan. It is death, Cimmerian."

"Jhandar's henchmen are not Hyrkanian," he shouted against the wind. "They will travel. The storm will hold the galley. We must reach it before the wind does and they put to sea. They, and Yasbet, will surely be aboard by then. If you will not go with me, then I go alone."

For a long moment there was no sound except the storm, then Akeba said, "Without that ship I may never get Jhandar."

Tamur's shoulders heaved in a sigh, silent in the storm. "Baalsham. Almost, with being declared outlaw, did I forget Baalsham. Kaavan understands revenge."

Sharak turned southward, stumping along leaning heavily on his staff. Conan and Akeba each grabbed one of the old man's arms to help him over the rough ground, and though he grumbled he did not attempt to pull free. Slowly they moved on.

Raging, the storm battered the coast. Stunted, wind-sculpted trees and great thornbushes swayed and leaned. Rain lashed them, and grit scoured through the air as if in a desert sandstorm. The wind that drove all before it drowned all sound in a demonic cacophony, till no man could hear the blood pounding in his own ears, or even his own thoughts.

It was because of that unceasing noise that Conan looked back often, watching for pursuit. Tamur might claim that no Hyrkanian would venture abroad in the Wrath of Kaavan, but it was the Cimmerian's experience that men did what they had to and let gods sort out the rights and

wrongs later. So it was that he saw his party had
grown by one in number, then by two more, and by
a fourth. Rain-soaked and wind-ravaged, the
grease washing from their lank hair and the filth
from their sheepskin coats, the rest of Tamur's
followers staggered out of the storm to join them,
faces wreathed in joyous relief at the sight of the
others. What had driven them to struggle through
the storm—desire for revenge on Jhandar, fear of
their pursuers, or terror of facing the Wrath of
Kaavan alone? Conan did not care. Their numbers
meant a better chance of rescuing Yasbet and
taking the galley. With a stony face that boded ill
for those he sought, the huge Cimmerian struggled
on into the storm.

It was while they were scaling the slope of a
thrusting headland, a straggling file of men
clinging with their fingernails against being
hurled into the sea, that the wind and rain
abruptly died. Above the dark clouds roiled, and
waves still crashed against cliff and beach, but
comparative silence filled the unnaturally still air.

" 'Tis done," Conan called to those below, "and
we've survived. Not even the wrath of a god can
stop us."

But for all his exuberant air, he began to climb
faster. With the storm done the galley could sail.
Tamur cried out something, but Conan climbed
even faster. Scrambling atop the headland, he
darted across, and almost let out a shout of joy.
Below a steep drop was a length of beach, and
drawn up on it was the galley.

Immediately he dropped to his belly, to avoid
watching eyes from below, and wriggled to the
edge of the drop. The vessel's twin masts were dis-

mounted and firmly lashed on frames running fore and aft. No doubt they had had time to do little more before the storm broke on them. Two lines inland to anchors in the dunes, to hold the ship against the action of the waves, and the galley had been winched well up the beach, yet those waves had climbed the sand as well, and still clawed at the vessel's sides. Charred planks at the stern, and the blackened stumps of railing, spoke of their first meeting.

As each of the others reached the top of the headland they threw themselves to the ground beside Conan, until a line of men stretched along the rim, peering at the ship below.

"May I roast in Zandru's Hells, Cimmerian," Akeba breathed, "but I did not think we'd do it. The end of the storm and the ship, just as you said."

"The Wrath of Kaavan is not spent," Tamur said. "That is what I was trying to tell you."

Conan rolled onto one elbow, wondering if the nomad's wits had been pounded loose by the storm. "There is no rain, no wind. Where then is the storm?"

Tamur shook his head wearily. "You do not understand, outlander. This is called Kaavan's Mercy, a time to pray for the dead, and for your life. Soon the rain will come again, as suddenly as it left, and the wind will blow, but this time it will come from the other direction. The shamans say—"

"Erlik take your shamans," Akeba muttered. The nomads stirred, but were too tired to do more than curse. "If he speaks the truth, Cimmerian, we're finished. Without rest, a troupe of dancing girls could defeat us, but how can we rest? If we don't take that ship before this accursed Wrath of Kaavan returns. . . ." He slumped, chin on his arms, peering at the galley.

"We rest," Conan said. Drawing back from the edge, Conan crawled to Sharak. The aged astrologer lay like a sack of sodden rags, but he levered himself onto his back when Conan stopped beside him. "Lie easy," the Cimmerian told him. "We'll stay here a time."

"Not on my account," Sharak rasped. He would have gotten to his feet had Conan not pressed him back. "This adventuring is a wet business, but my courage has not washed away. The girl, Conan. We must see to her. And to Jhandar."

"We will, Sharak."

The old man subsided, and Conan turned to face Akeba and Tamur, who had followed him from the rim. The other nomads watched from where they lay.

"What is this talk of waiting?" the Turanian demanded. "Seizing that galley is our only hope."

"So it is," Conan agreed, "but not until the storm comes again."

Tamur gasped. "Attack in the face of the Wrath of Kaavan! Madness!"

"The storm will cover our approach," Conan explained patiently. "We must take the crew by surprise if we are to capture them."

"Capture them?" Tamur said incredulously. "They have served Baalsham. We will cut their throats."

"Can you sail a ship?" Conan asked.

"Ships! I am a Hyrkanian. What care I for. . ." A poleaxed expression spread over the nomad's face, and he sank into barely audible curses.

In quick words Conan outlined his plan. "Tell the others," he finished, and left them squatting there.

Crawling back to the rim, he lowered himself full-length on the hard, wet ground, where he could watch the ship. The vessel could not sail until the storm had passed. With the patience of a great cat watching a herd of antelope draw closer, he waited.

The rain returned first, a pelting of large drops that grew to a roaring downpour, and the wind followed close behind. From the south it screamed, as Tamur had predicted, raging with such fury that in moments it was hard to believe it had ever diminished.

Wordlessly, for words were no longer possible, Conan led them down from the height, each man gripping the belt of the man ahead, stumbling over uneven ground, struggling against the wind with grim purposefulness. He did not draw his sword; this would be a matter for bare hands. Unhesitatingly Conan made his way across the sand, through blinding rain. Abruptly his outstretched hand touched wood. The side of the ship. A rope lashing in the wind struck his arm; he seized the line before it could whip away from him, and climbed, drawing himself up hand over hand. As he scrambled over the rail onto the forepart of the galley he felt the rope quiver. Akeba was starting up.

Quickly Conan's eyes searched the deck. Through the solid curtain of rain washing across the vessel, he could see naught but dim shapes, and none looked to be a man, yet it was his fear that even in the height of the storm a watch was kept.

Akeba thumped to the deck beside him, and Conan started aft with the Turanian close behind. He knew the rest would follow. They had nowhere else to go.

A hatch covered the companionway leading down into the vessel. Conan exchanged a glance with Akeba, hunched against the driving rain. The Turanian nodded. With a heave of his arm Conan threw the hatchcover back and leaped, roaring, down the ladder.

There were four men, obviously ship's officers, in the snug, lantern-lit cabin, swilling wine. Goblets crashed to the deck as Conan landed in their midst. Men leaped to their feet; hands went to sword hilts. But Conan had landed moving. His fist smashed behind an ear, sending its owner to the deck atop his goblet. A nose crunched beneath a backhand blow of the other fist, and his boot caught a third man in the belly while he still attempted to come fully erect.

Now his sword came out, its point stopping a fingerbreadth from the beaked nose of the fourth man. The emerald at his ear and the thick gold chain about his neck named him captain of the vessel as surely as their twin queues named all four sailors of the Vilayet. The slab-cheeked captain froze with his blade half drawn.

"I do not need all of you," Conan snarled. " 'Tis your choice."

Hesitantly licking his lips, the captain surveyed his fellows. Two did not stir, while the third was attempting to heave his guts up on the deck. "You'll not get away with this," he said shakily.

"My crew will hang your hearts in the rigging."
But he slowly and carefully moved his hand from
his weapon.

"Why you needed me," Akeba grumbled from a
seat on the next-to-bottom rung of the ladder, "I
don't see at all."

"There might have been five," Conan replied
with a smile that made the captain shiver. "Get
Sharak, Akeba. It's warm in here. And see how the
others are doing." With a sigh the soldier clattered
back up the ladder into the storm. Conan turned
his full attention on the captain. "When are those
who hired you returning?"

"I'm a trader here on my own—" Conan's blade
touched the captain's upper lip; the man went
cross-eyed staring at it. He swallowed, and tried to
move his head back, but Conan kept a light
pressure with the edged steel. "They didn't tell
me," the sailor said hastily. "They said I was to
wait until they returned, however long it might be.
I was of no mind to argue." His face paled, and he
clamped his lips tight, as if afraid to say more.

While Conan wondered why the galley's passengers had affected the captain so, Akeba and
Tamur scrambled down the ladder, drawing the
hatch shut on the storm behind them. The
Turanian half-carried Sharak, whom he settled on
a bench, filling a goblet of wine for him. The
astrologer mumbled thanks and buried his face in
the drink. Tamur remained near the ladder,
wiping his dagger on his sheepskin coat.

Conan's eyes lit on that dagger, and he had to
bite his tongue to keep from cursing. Putting a
hand on the captain's chest, he casually pushed
the man back down in his seat. "I told you we need

these sailors, Tamur. How many did you kill?"

"Two, Cimmerian," the nomad protested, spreading his hands. "Two only. And one carved a trifle. But they resisted. My people watch the rest." A full dozen remain."

"Fists and hilts, I said," Conan snarled. He had to turn away lest he say too much. "How do you feel, Sharak?"

"Much refreshed," the astrologer said, and he did seem to be sitting straighter, though he, like all of them, dripped pools of water. "Yasbet is not here?"

Conan shook his head. "But we shall be waiting when she is brought."

"Then for Jhandar," Sharak said, and Conan echoed, "Then for Jhandar."

"They resisted," Tamur said again, in injured tones. "There are enough left to do what they must." No one spoke, or even looked at him. After a moment he went on. "I went down to the rowing benches, Conan, to see if any of them were hiding among the slaves, and who do you think I found? That fellow from the other ship. What is he called? Bayan. That is it. Chained to a bench with the rest." Throwing back his head, the nomad laughed as if it were the funniest story he had ever heard.

Conan's brow knitted in a frown. Bayan here? And in chains? "Bring him here, Tamur," he snapped. "Now!" His tone was such that the Hyrkanian jumped for the ladder immediately. "Tie these others, Akeba," Conan went on, "so we do not have to worry about them." With his sword he motioned the captain to lie down on the deck; fuming, the hook-nosed seaman complied.

By the time the four ship's officers, two still un-

conscious, were bound hand and foot, Tamur had
returned with Bayan. Other than chains, the wiry
sailor from *Foam Dancer* wore only welts and a
filthy twist of rag. He stood head down, shivering
wetly from his passage through the storm,
watching Conan from the corner of his eye.

The big Cimmerian straddled a bench, holding
his sword before him so that ripples of lantern
light ran along the blade. "How came you here,
Bayan?"

"I wandered from the ship," Bayan muttered,
"and these scum captured me. There's a code
among sailors, but they chained me to an oar," he
raised his head long enough to spit at the tied
figure of the captain, "and whipped me when I
protested."

"What happened at *Foam Dancer*? You didn't
just wander away." The wiry man shifted his feet
with a clank of iron links, but said nothing. "You'll
talk if I have to let Akeba heat his irons for you."
The Turanian blinked, then grimaced fiercely;
Bayan wet his lips. "And you'll tell the truth,"
Conan went on. "The old man is a soothsayer. He
can tell when you lie." He lifted his sword as if
studying the edge. "For the first lie, a hand. Then a
foot. Then. . . . How many lies can you stand?
Three? Four? Of a certainty no more."

Bayan met that glacial blue gaze; then words
tumbled out of him as fast as he could force them.
"A man came to the ship, a man with yellow skin
and eyes to freeze your heart in your chest. Had
your . . . the woman with him. Offered a hundred
pieces of gold for fast passage back to Aghrapur.
Said this ship was damaged, and he knew *Foam
Dancer* was faster. Didn't even bother to deny

trying to sink us. Muktar was tired of waiting for you, and when this one appeared with the woman, well, it was plain you were dead, or it seemed plain, and it looked easy enough to take the woman and the gold, and—"

"Slow down!" Conan commanded sharply. "Yasbet is unharmed?"

Bayan swallowed hard. "I . . . I know not. Before Mitra and Dagon I swear that I raised no hand against her. She was alive when I left. Muktar gave a signal, you see, and Tewfik and Marantes and I went at the stranger with our daggers, but he killed them before a man could blink. He just touched them, and they were dead. And then, then he demanded Muktar slit my throat." He made a sound, half laughter, half weeping. "Evidence of future good faith, he called it. And that fat spawn of a diseased goat was going to do it! I saw it on his face, and I ran. I hope he's drowned in this accursed storm. I pray he and *Foam Dancer* are both at the bottom of the sea."

"An ill-chosen prayer," Conan said between clenched teeth. "Yasbet is on that vessel." With a despairing wail Bayan sank groveling to his knees. "Put him back where he was," Conan spat. Tamur jerked the wiry seaman to his feet; the Cimmerian watched them go. "Is this galley too damaged to sail?" he demanded of the captain.

The hook-nosed man had lain with his mouth open, listening while Bayan talked. Now he snorted. "Only a dirt-eater would think so. Once this storm is gone, give me half a day for repairs and I'll sail her anywhere on the Vilayet, in any weather."

"The repairs you need, you'll make at sea,"

Conan said levelly. "And we sail as soon as the storm abates enough for us to get off this beach without being smashed to splinters." The captain opened his mouth, and Conan laid his blade against the seaman's throat. "Or mayhap one of these other three would like to be captain."

The captain's eyes bulged, and his mouth worked. Finally he said, "I'll do it. 'Tis likely we'll all of us drown, but I'll do it."

Conan nodded. He had expected no other decision. Yasbet was being carried closer to Jhandar by the moment. The storm drumming against the hull seemed to echo the sorcerer's name. Jhandar. This time they would meet face to face, he and Jhandar, and one of them would die. One or both. Jhandar.

XXIII

Jhandar, lounging on cushions of multicolored silk spread beside a fountain within a walled garden, watched Davinia exclaiming over his latest gifts to her, yet his thoughts were elsewhere. Three days more and, as matters stood, all his plans would come to naught. Could the wench not sense the worry in him?

"They are beautiful," Davinia said, stretching arms encircled by emerald bracelets above her head. Another time he would have felt sweat popping out on his forehead. Her brief, golden silks left the inner slopes of her rounded breasts bare, and her girdle, two fingerwidths of sapphires and garnets hung with the bright feathers of rare tropic birds, sat low on the swelling of her hips. Sulty eyes caressed him. "I will have to think of a way to show my gratitude," she purred.

He acknowledged her only with a casual wave of his hand. In three days Yildiz, that fat fool, would meet with his advisors to decide where to use the army he had built. Of the Seventeen Attendants, eight would speak for empire, for war with Zamora. Only eight, and Jhandar knew that Yildiz merely counted the number of those who supported or opposed, rather than actually weighing the advice given. Jhandar needed one more to speak for war. One of the nine other. Who could have

believed the nine lived lives which, if not completely blameless, still gave him no lever to use
against them? One more he needed, yet all the nine
would speak for peace, for reducing the numbers
of the army. Short of gaining Yildiz's own ear, he
had done all that could be done, yet three days
would see a year's work undone.

It would take even longer to repair matters. He
must first arrange the assassination of an
Attendant, perhaps more than one if his efforts to
guide the selection of the new Attendant failed.
Then it would take time to build the army again. If
things were otherwise, three days could see the be-
ginnings of an empire that would be his in all but
name. Kings would journey to him, kneel at his
feet to hear his commands. Instead, he would have
to begin again, wait even longer for that he had
awaited so long.

And that wait added another risk. What had the
man Conan sought in Hyrkania? What had he
found that might be used against the Power? Why
did Che Fan not return with the barbarian's head
in a basket?

"You will let me have them, Jhandar?"

"Of course," he said absently, then pulled
himself from his grim ruminations. "Have what?"

"The slaves." There was petulance in Davinia's
voice, a thing he had noticed more often of late.
"Haven't you been listening?"

"Certainly I've been listening. But tell me about
these slaves again."

"Four of them," she said, moving to stand
straddle-legged beside him. Now he could feel
sweat on his face. Sunlight surrounded her with a
nimbus, a woman of golden silk, glowing hot.

"Well-muscled young men, of course," she went on. "Two of blackest hue, and two as pale as snow. The one pair I will dress in pearls and rubies, the other in onyx and emeralds. They will be as a frame for me. To make me more beautiful for you," she added hastily.

"What need have you for slave boys?" he growled. "You have slaves in plenty to do your bidding. And that old hag, Renda, to whom you spend so much time whispering."

"Why, to bear my palanquin," she laughed, tinkling musical notes. Fluidly she sank to her knees, bending till her breasts pressed against his chest. Her lips brushed the line of his jaw. "Surely my Great Lord would not deny my bearers. My Great Lord, who it is my greatest pleasure to serve. In every way."

"I can deny you nothing," he said thickly. "You may have the slaves."

In her eyes he caught a fleeting glimpse of greed satisfied, and the moment soured for him. She would leave him did she ever find one who could give her more. He meant to be sure there could never be such a one, but still. . . . He could bind her to him with the golden bowl and her heart's blood. None who saw or talked with her would ever know she did not in truth live. But he would know.

Someone cleared his throat diffidently. Scowling, Jhandar sat up. Zephran stood on the marble path, bowing deeply over folded hands, eyes carefully averted from Davinia.

"What is it?" Jhandar demanded angrily.

"Suitai is returned, Great Lord," his shaven-headed myrmidion replied.

Instantly Jhandar's anger was gone, along with his thoughts of Davinia. Careless of his dignity, he scrambled to his feet. "Lead," he commanded. Dimly he noted that Davinia followed as well, but matters not of the flesh dominated his mind once more.

Suitai waited in Jhandar's private audience chamber, its bronze lion lamps unlit at this hour. A large sack lay on the mosaicked floor at the Khitan's feet.

"Where is Che Fan?" Jhandar demanded as he entered.

"Perished, Great Lord," Suitai replied, and Jhandar hesitated in his stride.

Despite his knowledge to the contrary, Jhandar had begun to think in some corners of his mind that the two assassins were indestructible. It was difficult to imagine what could slay one of them.

"How?" he said shortly.

"The barbarian enlisted the aid of a Hyrkanian witch-woman, Great Lord. She, also, died."

That smile meant that Suitai had been her killer, Jhandar thought briefly, without interest. "And the barbarian?"

"Conan is dead as well, Great Lord."

Jhandar nodded slowly, feeling a strange relief. This Conan had been but a straw in the wind after all, catching the eye as it flashed by, yet unimportant. Suitai's smile had faded at the mention of the barbarian, no doubt because Che Fan had actually slain the fellow. At times he thought that Suitai's thirst for blood would eventually prove a liability. Now he had no time for such petty worries.

"The crew of the galley was disposed of as I

commanded, Suitai? I wish no links between myself and Hyrkania." Not until he was able to control that region the shamans had blasted, thus containing whatever might be of danger to him within. Not until his power was secure in Turan.

The tall Khitan hesitated. "The galley was damaged, Great Lord, and could not put to sea. I left its crew waiting for me. Without doubt the coastal tribes have attended to them by now. Instead I hired the vessel the barbarian used, and came ashore well north of the city."

"And the crew of this ship?"

"Dead, Great Lord. I slew them, and guided the ship to the beach myself." An unreadable expression flickered across the assassin's normally impassive face, and Jhandar eyed him sharply. Suitai shifted uneasily beneath that gaze, then went on slowly. "The captain, Great Lord, a fat man called Muktar, leaped into the sea, surely to drown. I have no doubt of it."

"You have no doubt of a great many things, Suitai." Jhandar's voice was silky, yet dripped venom like a scorpion's tail.

Sweat appeared on Suitai's brow. The mage had a deadly lack of patience with those who did not perform exactly as he commanded. Hurriedly the Khitan bent to the large sack at his feet.

"I brought you this gift, Great Lord." The lashings of the sack came loose, and he spilled a girl out onto the mosaicked floor, wrists bound to elbows behind her back, legs doubled tightly against her breasts, the thin cords that held her cutting deeply into her naked flesh. She grunted angrily into her gag as she tumbled onto the floor, and attempted to fight her bonds, but only her toes and fingers wriggled. "The girl the barbarian stole from the compound, Great Lord," Suitai announced with satisfaction.

Jhandar snorted. "Don't think to make up for your shortcomings. What is one girl more or less to—"

"Why, it's Esmira," Davinia broke in.

The necromancer scowled irritably. He had forgotten that she had followed him. "That's not her name. She is called. . . ." It took a moment, though he did remember marking the wench for his bed, long ago it seemed. ". . .Yasbet. That's it. Now return to the garden, Davinia. I have matters to discuss here that do not concern you."

Instead the lithe blonde squatted on her heels by the bound girl, using both hands to twist the struggling wench's gagged face around for a better look. "I tell you this is the Princess Esmira, Prince Roshmanli's daughter."

Jhandar's mouth was suddenly dry. "Are you certain? The rumors say the princess if cloistered."

She gave him a withering look that would have elicited instant and painful punishment for anyone else. From her, at this moment, he ignored it. The prince was Yildiz's closest advisor among the Attendants, of the nine, a man who seduced no woman with a husband and gambled only with his own gold. Yet it was said his daughter was his weakness, that he would do anything to shelter her from the world. For the safety of his Esmira, would Roshmanli send Turan to war? He had had men slain for casting their eyes upon her. If handled carefully, it could be done.

Then his eyes fell on Davinia, smiling smugly as

he examined the bound girl, and a new thought came to him.

He pulled the blonde to her feet. "You say you want only to serve me. Do you speak the truth?"

"To you," she replied slowly, "I speak only truth."

"Then this night there will be a ceremony. In that ceremony you will plunge a dagger into the heart of this girl." He gazed deeply into her eyes, searching for hesitation, for vacillation. There was none.

"As my Great Lord commands me," Davinia said smoothly.

Jhandar felt the urge to throw back his head and laugh wildly. She had taken the first step. Once she had wielded the knife, she would be bound to him more firmly than with iron chains. And by the same stroke he would gain the ninth voice among the King's Attendants. All of his dreams were taking shape. Empire and the woman. He would have it all.

XXIV

Dark seas rolled beneath the galley's ram, phosphorescence dancing on her bow wave, as the measured sweep of three score oars drew it on. Ahead in the night the darker mass of the Turanian coast was marked by white-breaking waves glinting beneath the pale, cloud-chased moon.

Echoes of those crashing breakers rolled across the waters to Conan. He stood in the stern of the galley, where he could keep close watch on both captain and steersman. Already they had attempted to take the ship other than as he directed—perhaps into the harbor at Aghrapur, so that he and the rest could be seized as pirates— and only the scanty knowledge he had gained with the smugglers had thus far thwarted them. The rest of the vessel's crew, sullen and disarmed, worked under the watchful eyes of Akeba, Tamur, and the nomads. Sharak clung to the lines that supported the foremast, and gazed on the heavens, seeking the configurations that would tell their fates that night.

Conan cared not what the stars foretold. Their destinies would be as they would be, for he would not alter what he intended by so much as a hair. "There," he said, pointing ahead. "Beach there."

"There's nothing there," the captain protested.

"There," Conan repeated. " 'Tis close enough to where we're going. I'd think you would be glad to see our backs, wherever we wanted to be put ashore."

Grumbling, the slab-cheeked captain spoke to his steersman, and the galley shifted a point to larboard, toward the stretch of land at which the big Cimmerian had pointed.

With scanty information had Conan made his choice. The distant glow of lamps from Aghrapur to the south. A glimpse at the stars. Instinct. Perhaps, he thought, that last had played the most important part. He *knew* that on that shore stood the compound of the Cult of Doom, Yasbet's place of imprisonment, and Jhandar, the man he must kill even if he died himself.

Sand grated beneath the galley's keel. The vessel lurched, heeled, was driven further forward by the motion of long sweeps. Finally motion ceased; the deck tilted only slightly.

"It's done," the hook-nosed captain announced, anger warring with satisfaction on his face. "You can leave my vessel, now, and I'll give burnt offerings to Dagon when you're gone."

"Akeba!" Conan called. On receiving an answering hail he turned back to the captain. "I advise you to go south along the coast, you and your crew. I do not know what will happen here this night, but I fear powers will be unbound. One place I have seen where such bonds were cut; there nightmares walked, and some would count death a blessing."

"Sorcery?" The word was a hiss of indrawn breath in the captain's mouth, changing to shaky, blustering laughter. "An sorceries are to be loosed, I have no fears of being caught in them. I will be clear of the beach before you, and I will go

south as fast as whips can drive my oar-sl—"
Hatch covers crashing open amidships cut him
off, and the clatter of men scrambling on deck,
whip-scarred, half-naked men falling over themselves in their eagerness to dash to the rail and
drop to the surf below. The hook-nosed man's eyes
bulged as he stared at them. "You've loosed the
oar slaves! You fool! What—" He spun back to
Conan, and found himself facing the Cimmerian's
blade.

"Three score oars," Conan said quietly, "and
two men chained to each. I have no love for chains
on men, for I've worn them around my own neck.
Normally I do not concern myself with freeing
slaves. I cannot strike off all the chains in the
world, or in Turan, or even in a single city, and if I
could, men would find ways to put them back
again before they had a chance to grow dusty.
Still, the world may end this night, and the men
who have brought me to my fate deserve their
freedom, as they and all the rest of us may be dead
before dawn. You had best get over the side,
captain. Your own life may depend on how fast
you can leave this place."

The hook-nosed captain glared at him, face
growing purple. "Steal my slaves, then order me
off my own vessel? Rambis!" He bit it off as he
stared at the vacant spot by the steering oar.
Conan had seen the man slip quietly over the
railing as he spoke.

Discovery of the defection took what was left of
the captain's backbone. With a strangled yelp he
leaped into the sea.

Sheathing his sword, Conan turned to join his
companions, and found himself facing some two

dozen filthy galley slaves, gathered in a different knot amidships. Akeba and the Hyrkanians watched them warily.

A tall man with a long, tangled black beard and the scars of many floggings stepped forward, ducking his head. "Your pardon, lord. I am called Akman. It is you who has freed us? We would follow you."

"I'm no lord," Conan said. "Be off with you while you have time, and be grateful you do not follow me. I draw my sword against a powerful sorcerer, and there is dying to be done this night." A handful of the former slaves melted into the darkness, splashes sounding their departure.

"Still there are those of us who would follow you, lord," Akman said. "For one who has lived as a dead man, to die as a free man is a greater boon than could be expected from the gods."

"Stop calling me lord," Conan growled. Akman bowed again, and the other rowers behind him. Shaking his head, Conan sighed. "Find weapons, then, and make peace with your gods. Akeba! Tamur! Sharak!"

Without waiting to see what the freed slaves would do, the big Cimmerian put a hand to the railing and vaulted into waist-deep seas that broke against his broad back and sent foam over his shoulders. The named men followed as he waded to shore, a stretch of driftwood-covered sand where moon-shadows stirred.

"They'll be more hindrance than help, those slaves," Sharak grumbled, attempting to wring seawater from his robes without dropping his staff. "This is a matter for fighting men."

"And you are the stoutest of them all," Akeba

laughed, clapping the old astrologer on the shoulder and almost knocking him down. His laughter sounded wild and grim, the laughter of a man who would laugh in the face of the dark gods and was doing so now. "And you, Cimmerian. Why so somber? Even if we die we will drag Jhandar before Erlik's Black Throne behind us."

"And if Jhandar looses the magicks that he did when he was defeated before?" Conan said. "There are no shamans to contain them here."

They stared at him, Akeba's false mirth fading. Sharak held a corner of his robes in two hands, his dampness forgotten, and Conan thought he heard Tamur mutter a prayer.

Then the men from the galley were clambering up the beach, the half score who had not succumbed to fear or good sense, led by Akman with a boarding pike in his calloused hands. The Hyrkanian nomads came too, cursing at the wet as they waded through the surf. A strange army, the Cimmerian thought, with which to save the world.

He turned from the sea. They followed, a file of desperate men snaking into the Turanian night.

"Must I actually put a knife in her heart?"

Davinia's question jangled in Jhandar's mind, which had been almost settled for his period of meditation. "Do you regret your decision?" he demanded. In his thoughts, he commanded her: have no regrets. Murder a princess in sorcerous rites. Be bound to me by ties stronger than iron.

"No regrets, my Great Lord," she said slowly, toying with the feathers of her girdle. When she lifted her gaze to his her sapphire eyes were clear and untroubled. "She has lived a useless life. At least her death will be to some purpose."

Despite himself he could not stop the testing. "And if I said there was no purpose? Just her death?" Her frown almost stopped his heart.

"No purpose? I do not like getting blood on my hands." She tossed her blonde mane petulantly. "The feel of it will not wash away for days. I will not do it if there is no purpose."

"There is a purpose," he said hastily, "which I cannot tell you until the proper time." And to forestall questions he hurried from the room.

His nerves burned with how close he had come to dissuading her. Almost, he thought, there would be no joy in achieving all his ambitions without her. Some rational corner of his mind told him the thought was lust-soaked madness. The fruition of his plans would hold her to him, for where would she then find one of greater power or wealth? With the taking of Yasbet—if she chose to call herself so, so he would think of her—all would be in place. His power in Turan would be complete. But Davinia. . . .

He was still struggling with himself when he settled in the simple chamber, before the Pool of the Ultimate. That would not do. He must be empty of emotion for the Power to fill him. Carefully he focused on his dreams. War and turmoil would fill the nations, disorder hastened by his ever-growing band of the Chosen. Only he would be able to call a halt to it. Kings would kneel to him. Slowly the pool began to glow.

From the branches of the tree, Conan studied the compound of the Cult of Doom. Ivory domes gleamed in the dappled moonlight, and purple spires thrust into the sky, but no hint of light showed within those high marble walls, and no one stirred. The Cimmerian climbed back down to the ground, to the men waiting there.

"Remember," he said, addressing himself mainly to the former galley slaves, "any man with a weapon must be slain, for they will not surrender." The Hyrkanians nodded somberly; they knew this well.

"But the black-robed one with the yellow skin is mine," Akeba reminded them. Time and again on the short march he had reiterated his right to vengeance for his daughter.

"The black-robe is yours," Akman said nervously. "I but wish you could take the demons as well."

Sharak shook his staff, gripping it with both hands as if it were a lifeline. "I will handle the demons," he said. "Bring them to me." A wind from the sea moaned in the treetops as if in answer, and he subsided into mutters.

"Let us be on with it," Tamur said, fidgeting—whether with eagerness or nervousness, Conan could not tell.

"Stay together," the Cimmerian said by way of a last instruction. "Those who become separated will be easy prey." With that he led them down to the towering white wall.

Grapnels taken from the galley swung into the air, clattered atop the wall and took hold. Men swarmed up ropes like ants and dropped within.

Once inside the compound Conan barely noticed the men following him, weapons in hand, falling back on either side so that he was the point of an arrow. His own blade came into his hand. Jhandar. Ignoring other buildings, Conan strode

toward the largest structure of the compound,
an alabaster palace of golden onion-domes and
columned porticos and towers of porphyry.
Jhandar would be there in his palace. Jhandar and
Yasbet, if she still lived. But first Jhandar, for
there could be no true safety for Yasbet until the
necromancer was dead.

Suddenly there was a saffron-robed man before
him, staring in astonishment at the intruders.
Producing a dagger, he screamed, "In the name of
Holy Chaos, die!"

A fool to waste time with shouts, Conan thought,
wrenching his blade free so the man's body could
fall. And in Crom's name, what god was this
Chaos?

But the noise produced another shaven-headed
man, this with a spear that he thrust at Conan,
sounding the same cry. The Cimmerian grasped
the shaft to guide the point clear of his body; the
point of his broadsword ended the strange shout
in a gurgle of blood.

Then hundreds of saffron-robed men and
women were rushing into the open. At first they
seemed only curious, then those nearest Conan
saw the bodies and screamed. In an instant panic
seized them by the throat, and they became a
boiling mass, seeking only escape, yet almost over-
whelming those they feared in a tide of numbers.

Forgetting his own instructions to stay together,
Conan began to force his way through the pack of
struggling flesh, toward the palace. Jhandar, was
the only thought in his head. Jhandar.

"Great Lord, the compound is under attack."
Jhandar stirred fretfully in his communion with

the Power. It took a moment for him to pull his eyes from the glowing pool and focus them on Suitai, standing ill at ease in the unnatural glow that filled the chamber.

"What? Why are you disturbing me here, Suitai? You know it is forbidden."

"Yes, Great Lord. But the attack. . . ."

That time the word got through to Jhandar. "Attack? The army?" Had disaster come on him yet again?

"No, Great Lord. I know not who they are, or how many. The entire compound is in an uproar. It is impossible to count their numbers. I slew one; he was filthy and half-naked, and bore the welts of a lash."

"A slave?" Jhandar asked querulously. It was hard to think, with his mind attuned to the communion and that communion not fully completed. "Take the Chosen and dispose of these interlopers, whoever they are. Then restore order to the compound."

"All of the Chosen, Great Lord?"

"Yes, all of them," the necromancer replied irritably. Could the man not do as he was told? He must settle his mind, complete his absorption of the Power.

"Then you will delay the ceremony, Great Lord?"

Jhandar blinked, found his gaze drifting to the Pool of the Ultimate, and jerked it back. "Delay? Of course not. Think you I need those fools' rapturous gazes to perform the rite?" Desperately he fought to stop his head spinning, to think clearly. "Take the Chosen as I commanded you. I will myself bring the girl to the Chamber of Sacrifice and do what is necessary. Go!"

Bowing, the black-robed Khitan sped away, glad to be gone from the presence of that which was bound in that room.

Jhandar shook his head and peered into the pool. Glowing mists filled the limits of the wards, an unearthly dome that seemed to draw him into its depths. Angrily he pushed that feeling aside, though he could not rid himself of it. He was tired, that was all. There was no need to complete the communion, he decided. Disturbed as he was, completion might take until dawn, and he had no time to wait. The girl must be his tonight. As it was the Power flowed along his bones, coursed in his veins. He would perform the rite now.

Gathering his robes about him, he left to fetch Yasbet and Davinia to the Chamber of Sacrifice.

XXV

Warily, sword at the ready, Conan moved along one wall of a palace corridor, with no eye for rich tapestries or ancient vases of rare Khitan porcelain. Akeba stalked along the other, tulwar in hand. As a pair of wolfhounds they hunted.

The Cimmerian did not know where the others were. From time to time the clash of steel and the cries of dying men sounded from outside, or echoed down the halls from other parts of the palace. Who won and who died he could not tell, and at that moment he did not care. He sought Jhandar, and instinct told him he drew closer with every step.

Silent as death three saffron-robed men hurtled from a side corridor, scimitars slashing.

Conan caught a blade on his broadsword, sweeping it toward the wall and up. As his own blade came parallel to the floor he slipped it off the other in a slashing blow that half-severed his opponent's head. Flashing swiftly on, his sword axed into the second man's head a heartbeat before Akeba's steel buried itself in the man's ribs. Twice-slain, the body fell atop that of he who had faced the Turanian at the first attack.

"You work well," Akeba grunted, wiping his blade on a corpse's robe. "You should think of the army if we live to leave this. . . ." His words trailed off as both men became aware of a new presence in the corridor. The black-robed Khitan assassin.

Unhurriedly he moved toward them, with the casual confidence of a great beast that knows its kill is assured. His hands were empty of weapons, but Conan remembered well the dead in Samarra's yurt, with no wound on any but looks of horror on every face, and Zorelle, dead from a touch.

Conan firmed his grip on the worn leather hilt of his broadsword, but as he stepped forward Akeba laid a hand on his arm. The soldier's voice was as cold as frozen iron. "He is mine. By right of blood, he is mine."

Reluctantly Conan gave way, and the Turanian moved forward alone. Of necessity the big Cimmerian waited to watch his friend do battle. Jhandar was still uppermost in his mind, but the way to him led deeper into the palace, past the murderously maneuvering pair before him.

The Khitan smiled; his hand struck like a serpent, and, like a mongoose, Akeba was not there. The assassin flowed from the path of the soldier's flashing steel, yet the smile was gone from his face. Like malefic dancers the two men moved, lightning blade against fatal touch, each aware of the other's deadliness, each intent on slaying. Abruptly the Khitan deciphered the pattern of Akeba's moves; the malevolent hand darted for the soldier's throat. Desperately Akeba blocked the blow, and it struck instead his sword arm. Crying out, the Turanian staggered back, tulwar falling, arm dangling, clawing with his good hand for his dagger. The assassin paused to laugh before closing for the kill.

"Crom!" Conan roared, and leapt.

Only the Khitan's unnatural suppleness saved him from the blade that struck where he had been. Smiling again, he motioned the Cimmerian to come to him, if he dared.

"I promised to let you kill him," Conan said to Akeba, without taking his eyes from the black-robed man, "not the other way around."

The Turanian barked a painful laugh. He clutched his dagger in one hand, but the other twitched helplessly at his side and only the tapestry-covered wall kept him from falling. "As you've interfered," he said between clenched teeth, "then you must kill him for me, Cimmerian."

"Yes," the assassin hissed. "Kill me, barbarian."

Without warning, Conan lunged, blade thrusting for the black-robed one's belly, but the killer seemed to glide backwards, stopping just beyond the sword's point.

"You must do better, barbar. Che Fan was wrong. You are just another man. I do not think you truly entered the Blasted Lands, but even if you did, you survived only by luck. I, Suitai, will put an end to you here. Come to me and find your death."

As the tall man spoke Conan moved slowly forward, sliding his feet along the marble floor so that he was at no time unbalanced. His sword he held low before him, point flickering from side to side like the tongue of a viper, light from the burnished brass lamps on the walls glittering along the steel, and though the Khitan spoke confidently, he kept an eye on that blade.

Abruptly, as the assassin finished his speech, Conan tossed his sword from right hand to left, and Suitai's gaze followed involuntarily. In that instant the Cimmerian jerked a tapestry from the wall to envelop the other man. Even as the hanging tangled about the Khitan's head and chest Conan lunged after, steel ripping through cloth and flesh, grating on bone.

Slowly the assassin heaved aside the portion of the tapestry that covered his head. With glazing eyes he stared in disbelief at the blade standing out from his chest, the dark blood that spread to stain his robes.

"Not my death," Conan told him. "Yours."

The Khitan tried to speak, but blood welled from his mouth, and he toppled, dead as he struck the marble floor. Conan tugged his blade free, cleaning it on the tapestry as he might had it been thrust into offal.

"I give you thanks, my friend," Akeba said, pushing unsteadily away from the wall. His face gleamed with the sweat of pain, and his arm still dangled at his side, but he managed to stand erect as he looked on the corpse of his daughter's murderer. "But now you have hunting of your own to do."

"Jhandar," Conan said, and without another word he was moving forward again.

Like a great hunting cat he strode through halls lit by glittering brass lamps, but bare of life. The gods smiled on those who did not meet him in those passages, for he would not now have slowed to see if they bore weapons or not. His blood burned for Jhandar's death. Any who hindered or slowed him now would perish in a pool of their own blood.

Then great bronze doors stood before him,

doors scribed with a pattern that seemed to have
no pattern, that rejected the eye's attempt to focus
on it. Setting hands against those massive metal
slabs, muscles cording with strain, he forced the
portals open. Sword at the ready, he went
through.

In an instant the horror of that great circular
chamber engraved itself on his brain. Yasbet lay
chained and gagged on a black altar, to one side of
her Davinia, knife upraised to plunge into the
bound girl's heart, to the other Jhandar, an arcane
chant rising from his mouth to pierce the air. Over
the entire blood-chilling tableau a shimmering
silvery-azure dome was forming.

"No!" Conan shouted.

Yet even as he dashed forward he knew he
would not reach them before that knife had done
its terrible work. He fumbled for his dagger.
Davinia froze at his cry. Jhandar's incantation
died as he spun to confront the man who had
dared interrupt the rite; the glow disappeared as
his words ceased. Desperately Conan hurled his
dagger—toward Davinia, for she still held her
gleaming blade poised above Yasbet—but Jhandar
turning, moved between them. The mage
screamed as the needle-sharp steel sliced into his
arm.

Clutching his wound, blood dripping between
his fingers, Jhandar turned a frightful glare on
Conan. "By the blood and earth and Powers of
Chaos I summon you," he intoned. "Destroy this
barbarian?" Davinia shrank back, as if she would
have fled had she dared.

The floor trembled, and Conan skidded to a halt
as chunks of marble erupted almost beneath his

feet. Leather-skinned and fanged, a sending such as those he had faced before clawed its way clear of dirt and stone. With a wild roar, the Cimmerian brought his blade down with all his might in an overhead blow, slicing through the demoniac skull to the shoulders. Yet, unbleeding and undying, it struggled to reach him, and he must needs chop and chop again, hacking the monstrous thing apart. Even then its fragments twitched in unabated fury. More creatures tore through stone between him and the altar, and still more to either side of him, snarling in bloodlust. As a man might reap hay Conan worked his sword, steel rising and falling tirelessly. Severed limbs and heads and chunks of obscene flesh littered the floor, yet there were more, always more, ripping passage from the bowels of the earth. Cut off from Yasbet and the altar, it was but a matter of time before he was overwhelmed by sheer numbers.

A smile, pained, yet tinged with satisfaction at the Cimmerian's coming doom, appeared on Jhandar's face. "So Suitai lied," he rasped. "I will settle with him for it. But now, barbar, pause a moment in your exertions, if you can, to watch the fate of this woman, Esmira. Davinia! Attend the rite as I commanded you, woman!"

Terror twisting her face, Davinia raised the silver-bladed dagger once more. Her eyes bulged when they strayed to the deformed creatures battling Conan, but her hand was steady. Jhandar began again his invocation of the Power.

Raging, Conan tried to clear a path to the altar with his sword, but for each diabolic attacker he hewed to the floor, it seemed that two more appeared.

There was a commotion behind the Cimmerian, and a saffron-robed man staggered into his view, blood streaming down his face, weakly attempting to lift his sword. After him followed Sharak. Conan was so amazed that he hesitated with sword raised, staring. In that momentary respite the creatures tightened their circle about him, and he was forced to redouble his efforts to stop their advance.

Sharak's staff cracked down on his opponent's head; blood splattered from that shaven skull, and its owner fell, his sword sliding across the floor to stop against the altar. Irritably Jhandar looked over his shoulder, but did not stop his chant.

Conan lopped off a fang-mouthed head and kicked the headless body, now clawing blindly, into the path of another creature. His sword took an arm, then a leg, sliced away half of a skull, but he knew his sands had almost run out. There were just too many.

Abruptly Sharak was capering beside him, waving his staff wildly.

"Be gone from here," Conan shouted. "You are too old to—"

Sharak's staff thumped a leathery skull, and the creature screamed. At the altar Jhandar jerked as if he had felt the blow. Even the other beings froze as sparks ran along the struck creature's blue-gray skin. With a clap, as of thunder, it was gone, leaving only oily, black smoke that drifted upward.

"I told you it had power!" the old astrologer cried wildly. He struck out again; more greasy smoke rose toward the vaulted ceiling.

Now those hell-born backed warily from Conan

and Sharak, rolling fearsome red eyes at Jhandar. For that moment at least, the way to the altar was clear, and Conan dashed for the black stone.

For but a heartbeat Jhandar faced that charge, then howled, "There are Powers you have not seen in your nightmares! Now face them!" and darted across the floor and down a small arched passage. With his departure the creatures, yet whole, seemingly freed of his command, vanished also.

Indecision racked Conan. For all he had sworn the necromancer would be dealt with first, Yasbet lay chained before him, with Davinia. . . .

As his gaze fell on her, the lithesome blonde backed away, wetting her lips nervously. "I heard you had sailed away, Conan," she said, then quickly abandoned that line as his face did not soften. "I was forced, Conan. Jhandar is a sorcerer, and forced me to this." She held the dagger low in the thumb-and-forefinger grip of one who knew how to gut a man, but she did not move toward Conan.

One eye on Davinia, Conan stepped up to the altar. Yasbet writhed in her chains. Four times his blade rang against her bonds, and steel conquered iron.

Ripping the gag from her mouth, Yasbet scrambled from the altar and plucked the dead Cult member's sword from the floor. Her hair lay wildly on her shoulders and breasts; she looked a naked goddess of battles. "I will deal with this. . . ." Words failed her as she glared at Davinia.

"Fool wench," Conan snapped. "I did not free you to see you stabbed!"

" 'Tis a Cimmerian fool I see," Sharak called. He

still leaped about like a puppeteer's stick figure, disposing with his staff of the portions of creatures that littered the chamber floor. "The necromancer must be slain, or all this is for naught!"

The old man spoke true, Conan knew. With a last look at Yasbet, closing grimly in on a snarling Davinia, he turned into the small passage Jhandar had taken.

It was not long, that narrow corridor. Almost immediately he saw a glow ahead, the same silver blue that had shone about the altar, yet a thousand times brighter. Quickening his pace, he burst into a small, unadorned chamber. In its center, surrounded by plain columns, a huge bubble of roiling mist burned and pulsed. Barely, through the brightness, Conan could make out Jhandar beyond the pool, arms outspread, his voice echoing like a bronze bell in words beyond understanding. Yet it was the brilliantly shining mass that held his eye, and hammered at him as it did. From those pulsating mists radiated, neither good nor evil, but the antithesis of being, beating at his mind, threatening to shatter all that was in him into a thousand fragments.

Pale images, washed out by the blinding glow, moved at the edge of his vision, then resolved themselves into two of the leather-skinned beings from the grave, sidling toward him along the wall as if they feared that shining. He knew that he must deal with the creatures and reach Jhandar, reach him quickly, before he completed whatever sorceries he was embarked upon, yet within the Cimmerian there was struggle. Never had he given in while he had strength or means to resist, but a

thought strange to him now crept into his mind.
Surrender. The mist was overpowering. Then, as if
the words were a spark, rage flared in him. As a
boy in the icy mountains of Cimmeria he had seen
men, caught in an avalanche, hacking at towering
waves of snow and dirt as they were swept away,
refusing to accept the thing that killed them. He
would not surrender. *He—would—not—surrender!*

A wordless scream of primal rage burst from
Conan's throat. He spun, swinging his sword like
an axe. Head and trunk of the foremost creature
toppled, sliced cleanly from its hips and legs.
Jhandar, rang in the Cimmerian's brain, and he
was moving even as his steel broke free of that unnatural flesh.

But such a creature could not be slain like a
mortal. The upper portion twisted as it fell, seized
Conan about the legs, and together they crashed to
the stone floor. Jagged teeth slashed Conan's
thigh, yet in the beserker rage that gripped him he
was as much beast as that he fought. His fisted hilt
smashed into the creature's skull, again and again,
till he pounded naught but slimy pulp. Yet those
mindless arms gripped him still.

And Jhandar's chant continued unabated, as if
he were too enmeshed in the Power to even be
aware of another's presence.

Claws clattering on marble warned the Cimmerian that the second creature drew near.
Wildly, half-blinded by the ever-brightening glow,
Conan struck out. His blade caught but an ankle,
yet the thing stumbled, flailed for balance . . . and
fell shrieking against the shining dome. Lightnings
arced and crackled, and the creature was gone.

The way to Jhandar was open. Grim determination limning his icy eyes, Conan crawled.
Animal fury burned in his brain. Now the sorcerer
would die, if he had to rip out his throat with
bared teeth. Yet in a small, sane corner of his mind
there was despair. Jhandar's ringing incantation
was rising to a crescendo. The necromancer's foul
work would be done before Conan reached him.
Powers of darkness would be loosed on the land.

Something about the way the last beast had disappeared tugged at him. It reminded him of . . .
what? The barrier to the Blasted Lands. Feverish-
ly he dug into his pouch—it had to be there!—and
drew out the small leather bag of powder Samarra
had given him. Almost did he laugh. If nightmares
were loosed to walk, still this time Jhandar would
not escape. Undoing the rawhide strings that held
the bag closed, he carefully tossed it ahead of him,
toward the oblivious, chanting sorcerer. On the
very edge of the burning dome the bag fell, open,
contents spilling broadly. It had to be enough.

"Your vengeance, Samarra," Conan murmured,
and slowly, coldly, spoke the words the shamaness
had taught him. As the last syllable was pro-
nounced, a shimmer sprang into being above the
powder.

Jhandar's words of incantation faltered. For a
brief moment he stared at the shimmer. Then he
screamed. "No! Not yet! Not till I am gone!"

Through that shimmer, that weakened area of
the wards that held the Pool of the Ultimate,
flowed *something*. The mind could not encompass
it, the eye refused to see it. Silver flecks danced in
air that was too azure. No more did it seem, yet an

ever-deepening channel was etched into the
marble floor as it came from the pool. It touched
pillars about the circumference of the pool;
abruptly half pillars dangled in the air. The ceiling
creaked. It washed against a wall, and stones
ceased to exist. The wall and part of the ceiling
above collapsed. The rubble fell into that
inexorable tide of nonexistence, and was not.

Some measure of sanity returned to Conan in
the face of that horror. Part of *it* moved toward
him, now. Desperately he sliced with his broadsword at the undying arms that gripped his legs.

Jhandar turned to run, but as he ran the fringes
of that flowing *thing* touched him. Only the
fringes, the outer mists, yet full-throated he
screamed, like a woman put to torture or a soul
damned. Saffron robes melted like dew, and on his
legs flesh disappeared at every touch of that mist.
Bone gleamed whitely, and he fell shrieking to
match the cries of all the victims he had ever laid
on his black altar.

With a groan the far end of the chamber collapsed into vapor, though with less sound than
Jhandar's screams. Conan redoubled his efforts,
hacking at the tough flesh. The last sinew was
severed; the unnatural grip was gone.

As the Cimmerian rolled to his feet and dove for
the entrance passage, the invisible silver-flecked
tide washed over the spot where he had been. Ignoring his gashed thigh, Conan ran, the sounds of
Jhandar shrieking to the gods for mercy echoing
in his ears.

When the Cimmerian reached the altar chamber, Sharak was peering down the passage. From a

safe distance. "What was that screaming?" the
astrologer asked, then added thoughtfully, "It's
stopped."

"Jhandar's dead," Conan said, looking for Yasbet. He found her slicing the dead cult member's
robes into some sort of garment, using the very
dagger Davinia had intended for her heart. The
blonde knelt fearfully nearby, bruised but un-
bloodied, gagged with the remnants of her own
golden silks. A strip of the same material bound
her hands; another circled her neck as a leash,
with the end firmly in Yasbet's grasp.

Suddenly the earth moved. The floor heaved,
twisted, and sagged toward the chamber from
which Conan had fled.

"It's eating its way into the bowels of the earth,"
he muttered.

Sharak eyed him quizzically. "It? What? Nothing could—"

Again the ground danced, but this time it did not
stop. Lamps crashed from the ceiling, splattering
patches of burning oil. Dust rose, beaten into the
air by the quivering of the floor, a floor that was
tilting more with every heartbeat.

"No time," Conan shouted, grabbing Yasbet's
hand. "Run!" And he suited his actions to his
words, drawing Yasbet behind him, and perforce
Davinia, for the dark-eyed woman would not
loosen her grip on the blonde's leash. With surprising swiftness Sharak followed.

Down crumbling halls they ran, past flame-filled
rooms, priceless rugs and rare tapestries the fuel.
Dust filled the air, and shards of stone from
collapsing ceilings.

Then they were outside, into the night, but there

was no safety. The rumblings of the ground filled the air as if Erlik himself walked the face of the earth, making it tremble beneath his footsteps. Great trees toppled like weeds, and tall spires fell thunderously in ruin.

Here there were people, hundreds of them, fleeing in all directions, fur-capped Hyrkanians mixed with saffron-robed cult members. But safety did not always come with flight. Ahead of him, Conan saw a rift open in the earth beneath the very feet of four running men, three with shaven heads, one in a bulky sheepskin coat. When the Cimmerian reached the spot the ground had closed again, sealing all four in a common tomb.

Other fissures were opening as well, great crevasses that did not close. A tower tilted slowly, shaking with the earth, and slid whole into a great chasm that widened and lengthened even as Conan looked.

At the wall there was no need to climb. Great lengths of it had fallen into rubble. Over those piled stones they scrambled. Conan would not let them slow. Memories of the Blasted Lands drove him on, away from the compound, into the forest surrounding, further and further, till even his great muscles quivered with effort and he half-carried and half-dragged Yasbet and Davinia.

With shocking abruptness the land was still. Dead silence hung in the air. A new sound began, a hissing roar, building.

Hanging onto a tree, Sharak looked a question at Conan.

"The sea," Conan panted. The women stirred tiredly in his encircling grasp. "The fissures have reached the sea."

Behind them the sable sky turned crimson. With a roar, fiery magma erupted, scarlet fountains mixed with roaring geysers of steam as the sea sought the bowels of the earth. The air stirred, became a zephyr, a gale, a whirlwind rushing in to battle with the ultimate void.

Conan tried to hold the women against the force of that wind, but the strength of it grew seemingly without end. One moment he was standing, the next he was down, his hold on the women gone, clutching the ground lest he be sucked back toward the holocaust. Dirt, leaves, branches, even stones, filled the air in a hail.

"Hold on!" he tried to shout to them, but the fury of the wind drove the words back in his teeth.

Then the earth began to heave again. The Cimmerian had only an instant to see a broken branch flying toward him, and then his head seemed to explode into blackness.

Epilogue

Conan woke to daylight. The flat coastal forest had become rolling hills, covered with a tangle of uprooted trees. Yasbet. Scrambling to his feet, he began to pick his way among trees tossed like jackstraws, calling her name without reply. Then, as he topped a hill, he fell silent in amazement.

The hills were not the only change that had been wrought upon the land. A bay now cut into the land, its surface covered thickly with dead fish. Wisps of steam rolled up from that water, and he was ready to wager that despite all of the sea to cool it the waters in that bay would remain hot for all time.

"The compound stood there," a hoarse voice said, and Sharak limped up to stand beside him. Somehow, he saw, the astrologer had kept his staff through all that had occurred. Now he leaned on it tiredly, his robes torn and his face muddy.

"I do not think fishermen will often cast their nets in those waters," Conan replied. Sharak made a sign against evil. "Have you seen Yasbet?"

The astrologer shook his head. "I have seen many, mainly cult members leaving this place as fast as they can. I have seen Tamur and half a dozen of the Hyrkanians, wanting only to be gone from Turan, yet unsure of their welcome at home. I wager we'll find them in a tavern in Aghrapur. I saw Akman, hurrying west." His voice saddened. "Yasbet, I fear, did not survive."

"I did, too, you old fool," the girl's voice called.

A broad smile appeared on Conan's face as he watched her clamber up the hill, still leading Davinia on her leash, and Akeba following close behind. All three were streaked with mud, a condition the Cimmerian realized for the first time that he shared.

"I lost my sword," she announced when she reached them. A narrow length of saffron was her only garment, affording her little more covering than the tavern girls of Aghrapur, but if anything her costume seemed to add to her jauntiness. "But I'll get another one. You owe me more lessons, Conan." Her smile became mischievious. "In the sword, and other things."

Akeba coughed to hide a grin; Sharak openly leered.

"You'll get your lessons," Conan said. "But why are you still pulling Davinia about? Set her free, or kill her, if that's your wish. You have the right, for she would have killed you."

The blonde's knees buckled. She crouched weeping at Yasbet's feet, her beauty hidden by layers of filth.

"I'll do neither," Yasbet said, after studying the cringing woman. "I'll sell her to a brothel. 'Tis all she's fit for, and a fitting place for her." Davinia moaned into her gag; the horror in her eyes indicated she might rather be slain. "And thus," Yasbet added, "will I get the wherewithal for my sword."

"I am as glad as any to see the rest of you,"

Akeba said, "but I would as soon be gone from this place."

"Yes," Sharak said excitedly. "I must return to Aghrapur. With the powers of my staff proven, I can double, no, triple my fees. You will attest to it, will you not, Akeba?"

"Attest to what?" the soldier demanded. "Are you making claims about that stick again?"

Offering a helping hand to Yasbet, Conan started down the hill, away from the bay, toward Aghrapur. "Jhandar called you by another name than Yasbet," he said as she scrambled after him. "What was it?"

"You must have misheard," she told him blandly. "Yasbet is all the name I have." Davinia pressed forward, making urgent sounds at Conan through her gag. Yasbet glared over her shoulder. "Do you want a sound switching before you're sold?" Eyes wide with shock, the blonde fell silent, and thereafter would not even meet the Cimmerian's gaze.

Conan nodded to himself. Clearly Yasbet was lying, but some said that was a woman's right. He would not press her on it.

Snatches of conversation drifted foward from the two men behind.

"If Conan saw it, let him attest to it. I saw nothing."

"But you are a sergeant, an official as it were. Can you not see how much better your word would be? I'm certain Conan will tell you what he saw."

The smile Conan had worn since seeing Yasbet alive widened even further. For all the days before, there was much to be said for this day. He was alive, with a little gold—he checked his pouch to see if the two coins still rested there; they did—good friends, and a pretty woman. What more could any man ask for? What more?

CONAN

- [ ] 54238-X CONAN THE DESTROYER $2.95
  54239-8 Canada $3.50

- [ ] 54228-2 CONAN THE DEFENDER $2.95
  54229-0 Canada $3.50

- [ ] 54225-8 CONAN THE INVINCIBLE $2.95
  54226-6 Canada $3.50

- [ ] 54236-3 CONAN THE MAGNIFICENT $2.95
  54237-1 Canada $3.50

- [ ] 54231-2 CONAN THE UNCONQUERED $2.95
  54232-0 Canada $3.50

- [ ] 54246-0 CONAN THE VICTORIOUS $2.95
  54247-9 Canada $3.50

- [ ] 54248-7 CONAN THE FEARLESS (trade) $6.95
  54249-5 Canada $7.95

- [ ] 54242-8 CONAN THE TRIUMPHANT $2.95
  54243-6 Canada $3.50

- [ ] 54244-4 CONAN THE VALOROUS (trade) $6.95
  54245-2 Canada $7.95

Buy them at your local bookstore or use this handy coupon:
Clip and mail this page with your order

TOR BOOKS—Reader Service Dept.
49 W. 24 Street, 9th Floor, New York, NY 10010

Please send me the book(s) I have checked above. I am enclosing
$_____ (please add $1.00 to cover postage and handling).
Send check or money order only—no cash or C.O.D.'s.

Mr./Mrs./Miss _____
Address _____
City _____ State/Zip _____
Please allow six weeks for delivery. Prices subject to change without
notice.

For the millions of people who have read the books, enjoyed the comics and the magazines, and thrilled to the movies, there is now —

THE CONAN

FAN CLUB

S.Q. Productions Inc., a long time publisher of science fiction and fantasy related items and books is announcing the formation of an official Conan Fan Club. When you join, you'll receive the following: 6 full color photos from the Conan films, a finely detailed sew-on embroidered patch featuring the Conan logo, a full color membership card and bookmark, and a set of official Conan Fan Club stationary.

Also included in the fan kit will be the first of 4 quarterly newsletters. **"The Hyborian Report"** will focus on many subjects of interest to the Conan fans, including interviews with Conan writers and film stars. And there'll be behind-the-scenes information about the latest Conan movies and related projects, as well as reports on other R.E. Howard characters like Red Sonja and King Kull. Fans will also be able to show off their talents on our annual costume and art contests. **"The Hyborian Report"** will be the one-stop information source for the very latest about Conan.

Another aspect of the club that fans will find invaluable is the **Conan Merchandise Guide,** which will detail the hundreds of items that have been produced, both in America **and** Europe. And as a member of the club, you'll receive notices of **new** Conan products, many created just for the club! Portfolios, posters, art books, weapon replicas (cast from the **same** molds as those used for the movie weapons) and much, much more! And with your kit, you'll get coupons worth $9.00 towards the purchase of items offered for sale.

Above all, The Conan Fan Club is going to be listening to the fans, the people who have made this barbarian the most famous in the world. Their suggestions, ideas, and feedback is what will make the club really work. The annual membership is only **$10.00.** Make all checks and money orders payable to: **CONAN FAN CLUB
PO Box 4569
Toms River, NJ 08754**

Response to this offer will be tremendous, so please allow 10-12 weeks for delivery.